THE FORSAKEN KING

Forsaken Book 1

PENELOPE BARSETTI

Hartwick Publishing

Hartwick Publishing

The Forsaken King

Copyright © 2021 by Penelope Barsetti

All rights reserved.

Contents

Prologue

THE WINTER WINDS ROLLED OVER THE HILLS AND DIRECTLY into the castle. It blew like a whistle, a scratch against the ears that tore the eardrums. The doors shuddered back and forth as they flapped in the wind, and glass crystals sprinkled across the snow on the stone floor. It shone like diamonds.

It would have been beautiful if it weren't for all the blood.

Impaled right on the throne, a sword shoved into his open mouth to pin him in place. His blood had soaked into the cushion, and once that became saturated, it dripped to the floor, the snow, the rug.

Everywhere.

It was time to look away. But he couldn't.

Hurried footsteps ran down the hallway. The boy rounded the corner, dressed in breeches and a tunic because there was no time for armor. "We have to go." He was careful not to look at the scene, as if he already knew what was there.

He remained, his wet, angry tears unable to stop, to close it off.

Then a woman's scream pierced the castle.

It broke the trance, and he was finally able to pull his gaze away from the fallen king. "Mother."

He winced when he recognized the sound. "They have her."

The scream sounded again…and he knew exactly what was transpiring.

The sword hung by his side, and he breathed a few heavy breaths as they shared a look. "She'd want us to run."

His jaw clenched when he heard the scream again, when he imagined what was happening to her that very moment. "No." He pulled his sword from his scabbard and moved into the hallway. "Come on, Ian."

Ian followed behind him. "They killed all the guards. We don't have a chance—"

He turned on the spot. "Then leave. Father is gone. So now, I'm king. I will defend my castle—and I will defend my family."

Ian's eyes shifted back and forth as he looked into his brother's eyes. "I admire your courage, but our training has barely begun. We have no chance against these guys—"

"Then I'll die."

"I think watching her son die is worse than what's happening to her right now."

His heart beat slowly like the drum in a ballad, but everything else about him was tense. The way he gripped the hilt of his sword. The way his face tightened with the jaw-breaking tension. The way his body craved blood like it was a mouthwatering feast. "Then go, Ian." He pulled him into his chest for a quick embrace. "Continue the family name—and avenge us." He released his hold and turned with his eyes closed, so he wouldn't have to look at him, wouldn't have to see his brother for the last time.

He rounded the corner at a run, following the screams, jumping over the bodies of the dead guards that had been slain in the middle of the night. His boot nearly slipped on a pool of blood, but he righted himself before the fall and kept going.

The screams grew louder.

The bedchamber door was open, the light from the gas lanterns casting a dim glow on the wall and into the corners.

Facedown, she was pressed into the bed, her gown shoved up around her waist. One guard had her hands pinned on one side of the bed—and a monster had her at the waist on the other side.

She tried to fight, tried to throw her hips up, but it was no use.

His dark hair was in loose curls, and a strand fell in

front of his forehead, on top of the shine from his sweat. His breeches were tugged down, and the bottom of his tunic covered his desperate cock. "What a pleasure, Your Highness."

He burst into the room and went for the guard that had her by the hands. The blade went deep into his back, and he twisted, severed his spine so he'd never walk again even if he survived.

The guard spat out a cough of blood directly onto his mother before he collapsed.

"Run!"

The chaos was enough to distract the pant-less asshole at the edge of the bed, and she threw her body hard and slammed her fists into his chest.

He stumbled back, tripping over his own pants, and fell backward. "Agh!"

A dagger had fallen to the floor, and she was quick to snatch it before she sprinted around the bed and grabbed her son's hand with an iron grip. It was the same way she'd grasped him his entire life, pulling him out of the path of a guest at the ball, guiding him away from the cart headed right his way, tugging him out of his room so he could see the hawk in the sky through the window.

He squeezed her back.

A voice shook the walls of the castle. "*Get them!*"

She quickened her pace, running down one hallway then the next, trying to get to the outside as quickly as possible. Every window they passed was frosted in the corners, the white snow visible in the darkness.

Left and right they went until she spotted the guards at the end of the hallway.

She yanked him into an open room and up along the wall.

With their backs flush against the wall and their breaths heavy, they listened to the footsteps grow louder from the heavy boots of the men who had infiltrated the castle as they all slept.

She was still, her eyes turned to the open door, her hand on her son's.

The guards took a quick peek inside then kept going.

He felt a small reprieve, but he knew that wouldn't last.

"Where's your brother?" she whispered.

"He left."

"Good. You should have done the same."

"Mother—"

"When you have your own children someday, you will understand." Instead of panic and fear, there was only confidence. Their world had crumbled down around them, but her hand remained steady.

"Dad's dead."

There was a slight twinge in her eyes, but it didn't last long. "I know. He would have come for me, otherwise…"

"Who are they?"

"I don't know." She turned to the door again. "Come on, let's go." She still had his hand as she turned into the hallway and kept going. They were deep in the castle, moving to the rear where the servants' quarters were located.

She turned right—then halted.

"Found the bitch!"

They darted the other way, sprinting down the hallway.

He tore his hand away from hers to keep up. "Mother, where are we going—"

Two men dressed in all black emerged into their path, grinning like this was nothing but a pleasure.

Her dagger went straight into the neck of one, hitting the artery as if she could see it through the skin.

He stabbed the other in the stomach, taking advantage of their smugness to spill his innards out of his body.

Now the shouts were all over the castle as they homed in on where they were. The door that was supposed to take them to safety was barred by a mass of furniture, the dining table in the hall, along with all the chairs.

"Quick!" She started to tug things away.

He climbed on the table and slammed his sword into one of the windows. It shattered and wind immediately swept through the castle.

"That's my boy."

He wiped the glass away with his gloved hand so he could grip the sill. It was a two-story drop, but he threw himself over the ledge, let go, and crashed into the ground. The snow blanketed his fall, but not by much. "Come on!"

His mother didn't hesitate before she threw herself over, her long hair dragging behind her like wings, and then she landed in the spot directly next to him. Without a groan of complaint, she got up and tugged him to his feet. "Run."

They didn't get far, crashing right into the man from the foot of the bed.

He grabbed her by the neck and threw her down in the snow.

His sword flashed, but it never met his mark as he was yanked from behind. His body crashed back into the ground, and his sword went flying, disappearing into the snow. A heavy boot pushed into his chest, shoving him deeper into the powder so it started to fall into his face.

"Not my son!"

He couldn't see more than the guard on top of him, but he could hear his mother's fight, hear her scream, and that made him scream in return.

The guard shoved his boot right into his chest, and he gave a moan as the crack sounded in his ears.

"Get off him!"

"Come on, Your Highness." The man must have hit her, because she suddenly went quiet. "We have plans this evening. Get the boy."

The pain was so raw, he could barely breathe. His eyes smarted from both the injury and the freezing cold. He was tugged to his feet, his body still limp from the crushing of his chest.

Both semiconscious, they were dragged back to the castle, back down the hallways where he used to chase his brother, where he used to play hide-and-seek with the friendly guards. The place felt like home in every season, but now it felt like a place he'd never been before.

They wound up in the same bedchamber, and he was tied down to one of the chairs. Ropes too thick for his small wrists bound him absolutely still. He couldn't even tug; there was no leverage whatsoever. His ankles were bound together and secured to the chair as well, so the only mobility he had was the turn of his head.

His mother was thrown onto the bed again, her gown pushed up once more and her knickers down.

The man with the cruel eyes gave the biggest smile as he popped off the buttons of his breeches and got them down around his thighs. This time, he removed his tunic, showing himself fully on display.

This time, her wrists were tied to the bed so she couldn't go anywhere.

He tried to fight, tried to jerk the chair over, to do something. But it was futile.

A blade suddenly appeared in his face, the steel right against the bridge of his nose.

"Tonight, you become a man." The man secured her ankles with the rope then crawled on top of her, where she continued to try to buck against him. "You're going to watch me turn your mother into a whore."

She launched her body backward, trying to throw him off. "You're barbaric!"

He shoved her back with a simple push of his hand. "And if you don't, if you blink, my friend here will carve out your eyelids."

The sword was tapped against his nose for good measure.

"Understand me, boy?"

All he could do was shake. All he could do was breathe. All he could do was suffer the agonizing torture and do nothing about it. "Why are you doing this?"

The man gave a chuckle as he positioned himself up against her. "If you had the chance to grow to manhood, you'd understand. You'd understand perfectly." He started to push inside her, and she tried to fight.

He clamped his eyes shut on instinct.

The knife cut his cheek. "What did Faron say?"

His eyes opened once more, and now they were wet with angry tears.

Faron started to move, pounding his mother's limp body into the bed, doing his best to make her scream, make her cry, make her beg for mercy.

But she didn't.

All he could do was sit there, tears pouring down his face, utterly helpless to do a damn thing.

———

IN THE BLIZZARD, they marched through piles of snow, right against the wind. Visibility was poor, and anything beyond a few feet was just a haze of gray. Their hair whipped behind them, and the dry air made their eyes tear.

With his wrists pinned behind him by the guard, he marched forward, shoved every few feet. He turned to his mother. He couldn't whisper because the wind was too loud, so he had to shout. "Mother…are you okay?"

She must not have heard him because she didn't say anything back.

Their march came to a halt, and they were both pushed forward.

He turned into the blizzard to see whatever they could, but then he realized where they were.

At the cliff.

Her arms immediately encircled him, protecting him from the cold, protecting him from everything that was out of her control. "Not my son…he's just a boy."

"*Sons.*" Faron grinned then gestured to one of his men.

Out of the blizzard, Ian was escorted by a guard, and he was forced forward too.

She dove for him, wrapping him in her arms and pulling him close. "Have mercy. Spare my sons." For the first time that night, she cried, clutching them both to her chest. "Please…I beg you."

Faron's grin remained plastered on his face with no effort whatsoever. It was natural. Simple. As easy as breathing. He stepped forward, his hair blown back by the wind, and despite the pressure on his eyes, he didn't squint. He wanted to enjoy this as much as possible, savor every second. "Tell me, where was your mercy?"

She clutched both boys to her chest, the tears leaving her cheeks the second they fell, carried on the wind.

He raised his voice and came closer. "Where was your mercy when we begged for asylum? It was nowhere, *Your Highness*." He rushed them now, his body commanding the piles of snow, and shoved her hard.

She threw the boys aside and shoved him back. "No!"

He punched her in the face then grabbed her by the hair. "You first."

"No!" She clawed at his face, carving rivers of blood that made him scream.

He punched her again—and again.

Her head dropped back, and her eyes glazed over.

When her body was limp as a fish, he pushed her.

And she fell.

Ian was the first to attack. "Ah!" He went for Faron's knees to trip him off his feet.

The other men in black rushed in, and the fight was over in seconds. Both boys were forced to their knees right at the cliff, the wind howling with a gust of snow crystals that sliced the skin.

Ian was kicked first—a boot to the back.

He toppled over and disappeared into the blizzard. His scream was swallowed by the air, taken somewhere far away in a matter of seconds.

The son that remained looked at the last place he had seen his brother, his small body disappearing into the gray clouds that obscured the bottom. With all his family gone, there was nothing to fight for anymore. A wave of calm settled over him, his body providing the cushion to make this transition easier.

The boot hit his back.

And then he was gone.

ONE

Ivory

────────────

THE SUMMER BREEZE GENTLY FLUTTERED MY WHITE curtains, a little raise there, a flick of movement here. The city sloped downward from where my bedroom was perched on the rise, cobblestone streets leading to little shops and inns. The church was the tallest building, the crown jewel on the very top of the domed roof.

My textbooks were scattered on the bed, my potions on the shelves against the wall. I tugged my boots over my breeches and put on a white linen tunic, something light to make the heat more bearable.

A knock sounded on my bedchamber door.

"Coming!" I grabbed my bag and stuffed it with all my supplies before I hustled out of the room.

I walked by the guard with a quick wave and hurried down the long hallway toward the grand staircase. My boots tapped against the stones beneath my feet in the breaks between the red rugs, and I passed the paintings of people long dead on the walls. When I rounded the corner, I gripped the gold banister and made my way down.

When I was little, I used to try to slide down the banister, and my mom would lose her shit.

I almost did it now…but I felt something.

A stare. One that lingered longer than it should. A kind that felt pressed right against my skin. Foreign as if it was from a stranger, but packed with enough intensity that it felt intimate…really intimate.

My gaze lifted and scanned the great hall as I continued my descent.

It took just a second to zero in on the location, to find exactly where it was coming from.

A guard stood next to the double doors, dressed in the uniform of the king. Black steel with the king's crest in the center of the breastplate. Black breeches with a sword at his side, a bow upon his back. The helmet concealed his forehead and everything below his eyes. Only his eyes were visible.

Bright blue. Striking. Deadly.

When I reached the bottom stair, I stilled as if I were under attack.

He didn't draw his sword or take a defensive stance.

His only crime was his look.

I'd been the recipient of many looks from men, mostly lust, but that wasn't it either.

This was hatred. Pure hatred.

I picked up my pace again and approached the door,

coming close, feeling his eyes follow me the entire way. I gave him a side glance, watching him as I moved to the door and got it open.

He remained, only his head turning.

I stepped into the sunlight and let the door shut behind me.

Only when the barrier was between us did I feel the stare subside.

It was probably jealousy. Jealousy that my family ruled over this great city—and he was left to guard it. My father always said being at the top was dangerous, because the higher you climbed, the more eyes were on you. The more beautiful you were, the more people wanted to be you. Perhaps that was all he wanted, to take my place.

———

I WALKED down the cobblestone streets between the shops, sloping downward as I moved farther away from the castle. When I passed the sweets shop, chocolate and caramel were in the air, and when I passed the rug shop, I saw the shop owner beating out the dust from a rug that had been in the window for too long. I made sure to cross the road to the other side to avoid it.

When I was young, my father insisted that I be accompanied at all times, but as I got older, I earned my independence. Now I came and went on my own, doing my errands and my business without permission. Some of the people in the city knew who I was, but most had no idea.

And if someone tried to cross me, my mom had taught me exactly where to shove my boot.

It was a long walk to get to the stables, at least twenty minutes from my bedchamber, and when I finally made it, my entire back was coated in sweat. My hair had been down at the start of the trek, but now I'd pulled it into a loose bun, some strands stuck in the slickness at the nape of my neck.

"Over here, Ivory." Roran, the stablemaster, was kneeling by my next patient.

A chestnut mare lay on her flank, a gruesome wound in her side near her ribs. The bite marks were unmistakable.

Roran stroked her neck to keep her calm, to ease her suffering as much as possible. "The wolves."

I kneeled in front of her right in the dirt before I put my bag beside me. "Anyone else hurt?"

He shook his head. "They ganged up on her."

I released a painful sigh as I pressed my hand to the wound. "Sorry, girl."

She gave a loud neigh when I touched her.

"Is there anything you can do?" Roran asked. "I shouldn't pick favorites…but she's a good horse."

"I'll do my best, Roran." I opened my bag and pulled out everything I needed to make this work. First, it was the disinfectant, the pollen from a flower in the wildlands mixed with distilled water. I soaked it into the wound and listened to her neigh harder at the sting. Once I let that dry, I got out my suture kit and did my best to tug the flesh back together, to get it to close and stop the bleeding. There was too much skin missing, so I had to stretch what I had, reducing the blood loss. "Almost done, girl."

Roran had to hold her down so she wouldn't buck against me. "Shh…"

Once I had the wound as contained as possible, I pressed my palms against the injury, gave a slight pressure, and then focused my thoughts. Moments of silence passed as I pushed my energy forward—but her body didn't push back.

She was too weak.

I closed my eyes and tried again. "Come on, I can't do this alone." I pushed and pushed against her, knocking on the front door to her vitality, and waited for the door to open. I didn't have the capability to fix her. No one did. But I could point her body's own capabilities in the direction they needed to go. Sometimes the body was too weak to do it on its own, like it had lost the will to even try, and I could give it the reminder it needed.

"It's okay, Ivory," Roran said. "I know you did the best you could."

"Shh…" I kept up my focus, gave her plenty of time to meet me.

And then I felt it. Like the slow growth of a stem rising from the soil, it reached up to the sun. Her heart started to beat slower, the nerves in her system sent different messages to the rest of her body, and then she began to heal.

I could feel it in my mind. "That's it, girl."

I felt her ribs pop back into place. Felt the loose flesh tighten. Felt the blood dissolve back into the tissues, where it became contained. The vibrations of her body stopped —and I knew that was the best she could do. "You're a tough bitch, you know that?"

Roran chuckled.

I opened my eyes and gave her a good rub as I looked down at her.

"She's going to be alright?" Roran asked.

"I can't promise anything." I watched her breaths become less labored, watched her flick her tail like she was restless but playful. "We won't know until tomorrow, but I think she's going to pull through."

Roran gave her a pat. "You hear that, Madeline?"

"Make sure she has plenty of rest." I got to my feet and dusted off my breeches. "And she can have as many oats as she wants—doctor's orders."

Roran rose to his full height too, a foot taller than me, his face weathered from the elements. "Where did you learn all of this?"

I grabbed my bag off the ground and inserted my arms through the straps. It was still morning, but the sun was already relentless. Sweat started at my forehead and began to soak my clothes. "Books."

"Books?" he asked incredulously.

"Yep. From the library in the castle."

"So, you taught yourself?"

"I did, thank you very much."

"Very impressive," he said with a chuckle.

"I'll check on her tomorrow. You know where to find me if you need anything else."

"Thanks, Ivory."

I went to the water basin to wash the blood off my hands, and that's when I felt it again. That stare. That penetrating stare that could see my bones beneath my flesh. When the blood was gone from my fingers, I raised my chin.

It was a brief glimpse, and all I saw was the king's steel glimmering in the sunlight. It was a flash, over as quickly as it started, and then it was gone.

But I knew exactly who it was.

I took off at a run. "Asshole!" I headed to the main road and ran up the cobblestones, my eyes scanning for the guard who had followed me all the way into town, who had continued his intrusive stare into my back when I didn't suspect it.

At a jog, I glanced into the alleyways between the buildings, searching for the steel on his chest and the sword at his side. I spun around, getting a quick panorama of my surroundings. I had no idea where he was, but he knew exactly where I was.

Because I could still feel that stare.

———

"I WANT TO SEE MY FATHER." I approached the double doors that led to his study, where two guards were positioned on either side of it.

Thomas, one of my father's personal guards, remained at his station. "He can't be disturbed."

"Yes, he can." I grabbed the handle and tugged on the door, but my hand slipped and I fell back because the door was locked in place. "I'm his daughter. I can disturb him all I want." I marched back to the door and pounded my fists into the thick wood. "Dad, I need to talk to you." I stepped back and waited for the doors to open.

They didn't.

I crossed my arms over my chest and shifted my gaze to Thomas.

"M'lady, he's very busy."

I rolled my eyes and turned away. "Well, tell him I have something important to share with him—whenever he's not busy." I crossed the great room and had entered the hallway when I heard the heavy door shift. Then whispers. I turned back, knowing he'd finally put down his scroll or whatever else he was doing to come to my call.

When I returned to the office, the doors were shut again.

Thomas approached me. "He said he'll see you in the dining hall shortly."

"Why can't he just meet me in his study?"

He stared without giving an answer.

"Fine." I escorted myself out and headed upstairs to the dining hall. It held a long table that could easily accommodate dozens of people when hosting a dinner party for fifty guests, not that we ever did.

My father wasn't a dinner party kind of guy.

I sat there and waited, and the servants came to offer me coffee and tea sandwiches. At the head of the table, I looked out the window to the city below, the summer sun causing a haze far into the distance. Outside the city gates were the fields we used to grow food and raise livestock, but most of the citizens lived within the gates. Others who preferred the wide-open spaces took their chances on their own. I could stare at the view all day, admiring the way the world just dropped off into nothing past the edge of the city.

He finally arrived, in his black breeches with a dark blue tunic on top. His cape remained on his back, held by the chain around his neck, and the symbol of the kingdom was woven into the fabric on his chest. Slightly flustered with his hair a little messy, he didn't look pleased to see me. "What is it, Ivory?"

"Nice to see you too, Father."

He lowered himself into the chair beside me, his arms immediately moving to the table, the scars on his left cheek on display in the brightness coming from the window on the hot summer day. His dark hair was the same color as mine, and he had the same green eyes too. But that was the extent of our similarities. "I'm very busy, so please get on with it."

"Grouchy today, aren't we?"

He turned his cold stare on me, barely able to contain his impatience.

"One of the guards is following me everywhere I go."

"That's their job, Ivory."

"No, no, no." I shook my head. "This is different. He stares at me like…he wants to rip me apart, piece by piece."

"Perhaps his countenance is simply set that way."

"No, it's not. I went into town to help Roran, and once I was done, he was there again. I went to confront him, but he disappeared. The guards don't follow me into town, so this was unusual."

"Has he touched you?"

"Well…no."

"Has he spoken to you?"

I shook my head.

"He could have been in town for his own business."

"On his watch?"

"Could have been moderating a dispute between the civilians. Could have been doing any number of things, Ivory. I'm glad that you're aware of your surroundings as I've taught you, but you're pulling at strands of wheat here."

"I'm telling you—I've got a bad feeling about him."

He gave a sigh as if this was a waste of time, but he would still humor me. "Which one is he?"

"I…I don't know. He has blue eyes. I'd know him if I saw him."

"Not giving me much to work with, Ivory."

"He was stationed at the front door when I left this morning."

"I'll ask Thomas to look into it, then. I'll let you know."

"Alright."

"But I think you're being paranoid."

I shrugged. "I'd rather be paranoid than dead, right?"

After a long stare, he gave a subtle nod. He rose to his feet. "I must attend to business."

"You can't stay for lunch?"

He left without looking back. "I'm afraid not."

———

I LAY on the bed with the sheets pulled to my shoulder. The lamp on my nightstand was on, and the windows to my bedroom were open so the mild breeze could dissipate all the heat we'd just produced.

Quinn sat on the couch and secured his boots in place before he tightened them by the laces. Shirtless with his hair a mess, he still had a shine of sweat on his skin. A patch of dark hair was in the center of his hard chest. "Ivory?"

My eyes opened, and I realized I'd already dozed off. With a sigh, I pushed my hair out of my face and got out of bed. My robe was at the foot of the bed, so I pulled it on and wrapped myself up in the silk.

Quinn stopped focusing on his boots to stare.

"I'll check if the coast is clear."

"Ivory." He got to his feet, the top of his breeches undone, showing the line of hair that went down and disappeared underneath the fabric.

I walked up to him, my head tilted back to meet his gaze.

"I don't want to do this anymore." His deep voice remained quiet, as if he was afraid a guard was right against the front door, listening.

"You're right. It's too risky." My father hadn't addressed my concerns about the mysterious guard with the blue eyes, and if he was watching me as intently as I believed, he would discover my affair. I might have to face some consequences, a really scalding lecture from my father, but Quinn would be beheaded right in the town square. "I haven't seen that guard I told you about, but I'm sure he's around."

"That's not what I mean, Ivory."

"Then what do you mean?"

With his arms by his sides, he stepped closer. "Becoming a member of the Royal Guard has been a dream for my family. My father is proud, and my mother uses my earnings to support the household."

My father and his associates never ventured into the town to converse with the civilians he ruled over, and he didn't spend more than a few minutes talking with the guards who would die in his stead. But I did, and it made me realize how much I had. I didn't need more in life because I already had everything. Quinn, along with everyone else, wasn't blessed with the same luxury. I hadn't even earned it. I was just born into it. "You needn't say more. I understand."

"No, you don't understand." His dark eyes became fixated on my face. "I want more…with you."

I could feel the features slip on my face, slowly sink down.

"The second I set eyes on you, I knew you were the most beautiful woman I'd ever seen. And being with you…has been an honor. I don't want to sneak around in the dark. I don't want to be clandestine lovers. I want us… to be together."

The disappointment of his words was a punch to the gut. "Quinn, I made it very clear what this was—"

"I know you did. But things have changed. Have they not changed for you?"

I wouldn't mince words. I wouldn't let him down easy. I needed him to understand—for his own sake. "No."

He winced.

"It's just physical."

"But you gave yourself to me—"

"I've given myself to men before you, and I will do so after you. I'm sorry that you feel this way, but trust me, I'm not worth it. Your family should be proud of you because you're a great man, and someday, you'll meet a beautiful girl who thinks the same. I'm not that girl. I'm not worthy of your heart."

His eyes dropped.

"This is over, Quinn. You should go."

He remained rigid, trying to recover from the way I'd ripped him apart.

"I'm sorry."

A small smile moved on to his lips before he raised his head. "Now I wish I hadn't said anything."

"I'm glad that you did."

"I'm not." The smile remained, fused with sadness. "Because I don't want this to end."

My hands cupped his cheeks, and I brought our foreheads together. "When you're old and sitting by the fire, you'll look back on this and grin to yourself. You bedded the duke's daughter—and it was a lot of fun."

Now his smile was genuine.

"Your son will ask what's the most reckless thing you've ever done, and you'll have a great story to share."

Now he chuckled.

I gave him a final kiss before I let him go. "Come on, let's get you out of here."

I cracked the door open and peered into the hallway. The sconces on the wall cast a dim light across the floor, and I listened for the sounds of heavy footsteps of a pacing guard. It was quiet. "Coast is clear…"

Quinn pulled his helmet on his head and walked out with me. We made it to the edge of my hallway so he could turn down a different hallway, and that was when we said goodbye. He gave a short nod, the sadness in his eyes, and turned to leave.

That was it. It was done.

I wasn't sad that it was over, but sad that I'd compromised his heart.

I turned around to return to my room.

But now, the hallway was blocked.

By an enormous man in full armor, two short blades at his hips, and with eyes that cut to the bone.

Blue eyes.

I didn't have my sword or my armor, and there was no escape in the narrow hallway. I could scream, but the second I opened my mouth, he would strike me down. His enormous hand could grip me by the throat and extinguish my life with a simple squeeze that would break all my vertebrae.

I didn't scare easily.

But I was fucking scared now.

To my surprise, he pulled his gaze away and moved past me.

I didn't even know where he'd come from, when he'd appeared, if he'd seen Quinn leave. "What the fuck do you want?"

He actually stopped—and then slowly turned around.

Maybe I shouldn't have said anything.

Face-to-face, his blue eyes looked down at me, wide and open, furious.

All I could see was the blue color of his eyes, not his mouth, not the lines of tension around his temples, not everything else that made a face expressive. But my imagination filled in the gaps, and I pictured a man who wanted me hung by a noose.

After the heated stare, he turned away once more.

"Asshole, I asked you a question." My response to terror was confidence, to make myself big and loud, to make myself seem like a bigger opponent than I really was. And there was a bit of rage there, because this man didn't belong in the castle, and my father would value my warning a lot more if I were a man instead of a woman.

He stilled and looked at me over his shoulder.

"Who are you?"

He stepped away and entered the hallway where Quinn had disappeared.

I was left there, my heart pounding as if the walls of the castle crumbled around me.

TWO

Ivory
_____

I SAT WITH BURKE, MY FATHER'S COMMANDER AND adviser, and told him the whole thing.

"What were you doing outside your room?" He wore a black cape like my father, a dark blue tunic, and was always in his battle uniform, his black vambraces jagged on the surface.

I ignored the flutter in my heart. "I thought I'd heard something outside."

"But if you heard him outside your door, you must always hear the guards in the hallway."

I didn't appreciate his astute observation—not when it was directed on me, at least.

"What made you go outside this night?"

"I just heard him, alright? Can we get to the part of the story that actually matters?"

He stared.

"It's the same guy I told my father about. He watches

me everywhere I go, and he looks at me like he wants to kill me."

"He had the perfect opportunity to do that last night—and he didn't."

I gave a loud sigh. "Doesn't mean he won't later. Why is this happening right now? I'm reporting an issue in the castle, and it's being disregarded. But if Ryker said something, it would be taken seriously."

"Ryker hasn't mentioned the guard with blue eyes."

"Because he has it out for me, apparently."

"We only employ the strongest and most able men to defend this castle, as well as your father. They aren't diplomats. They aren't shopkeepers. They're here for a job—and may not be pleasant company as they do it."

Okay, I officially give up.

"Can we proceed to other matters now?"

Yes, let's just sweep it under the rug and assume I'm overreacting. "Sure."

"Your presence is required in the Capital."

"And who's requesting my presence?"

"Queen Rutherford. She's hosting a retreat for all the young ladies of the court."

That meant tea parties. Gossip. Marriage proposals. I enjoyed getting together with my friends, but I didn't care for the rest of the things on the list. Occasionally, I'd meet a man I fancied, but it was too complicated to get involved with him. Sneaking guards and men I met in town into my bedroom was a lot easier. No witnesses meant no gossip. "When do I leave?"

"Tomorrow."

"That's short notice."

"Do you have prior engagements?"

I'd checked on Madeline the other day, and she'd pulled through the night. It would take some time for her to regain her strength, but she would be a powerful horse once more. "I guess not. I love the Capital this time of year. Can actually see the ocean instead of a bottomless cliff."

He shifted his gaze away.

"Burke?"

His eyes moved back to me.

"What's at the bottom of the cliff?"

After a long silence, he gave a subtle shake of his head. "I have no idea, M'lady."

―――――

"RYKER."

As if he didn't hear a word I said, he continued to feel up the servant against the wall, groping her through her dress as he kissed her like they were the only two people in the room—even though they were in a hallway.

A hallway that everyone used.

"Let the poor girl come up for air."

Ryker finally let her go with an annoyed sigh.

She scurried away back to the kitchens, and he turned to me, dressed in his tunic and breeches, his looks similar to mine because of the blood we shared. His eyes were now lifeless as he looked at me. "Yes?"

"I'm your big sister, you know."

"Your point?"

"Maybe you shouldn't feel up the servants in front of me."

"Maybe you shouldn't stare," he shot back.

"Look, I'm leaving in the morning. Just thought you should know."

"You are?" His hostility dropped, and he came closer. "Where are you off to?"

"I'm doing some lady stuff at the Capital." I walked down the hallway and took the stairs down to the next floor.

He kept my stride. "Lady stuff?"

"You know, we discuss our future husbands over tea."

"Sounds boring."

"Yeah, but I'll get to see some of my friends, so that's exciting."

"Friends?" he asked incredulously.

I nudged him in the side.

He chuckled. "I can't picture you with a husband."

"Me neither."

"Too high-maintenance."

"I am not high-maintenance. I just don't put up with bullshit. Big difference."

"Well, I want a wife who puts up with all my bullshit."

"Then you shouldn't expect a very good woman."

He looked at me, his eyebrows raised.

"How remarkable can a woman be if she's a pushover? If she accepts less than what she deserves? Trust me, you don't want that. You want a woman who calls you out on your shit and makes you a better man."

"Then let me ask this. Do you want a man who calls you out?"

"I wouldn't marry him unless he did." I made it to the double doors and stepped inside. The library was abandoned because no one ever used it. Ryker had never been interested in books, and none of my father's associates seemed to value it either. When I'd asked where all these books had come from, my father said they were from our ancestors.

"So, what are we doing down here?"

"I wanted to show you something." I moved to one of the long tables in the center of the room. There was dust in the air, but not on the surfaces because the maids tidied up every morning.

"I don't read."

"Yes, I know." I rolled my eyes. "And you're doing yourself a great disservice."

"Because I can't heal horses? They're animals, Ivory. No one cares about them."

"That's not true. I care." I grabbed all the books on the shelf that I'd stored for myself then carried them to the table.

Ryker fell into the chair, his knees wide apart, his arms on the armrests. He immediately propped his chin on his fist and looked bored. Very bored.

I took the seat across from him and opened the first book. "I was going through these and found something interesting. Interesting in that it doesn't make sense."

"Looks like I'm not the only one who doesn't read…"

I lifted my chin and narrowed my eyes. "It's a history of Delacroix, all the kings who have ruled over this establishment for thousands of years."

"If I'd known this would be a history lesson, I would have continued to feel up Amelia." His closed fist pushed into his cheek.

I ignored what he said. "The name Rolfe is everywhere. Kings, queens, stewards…"

"Your point?"

"I don't see Rutherford anywhere."

He gave a shrug. "Maybe a queen kept her maiden name."

"That doesn't happen."

"Well, what other explanation is there?" he asked irritably. "Nobody comes down here, and I don't understand why you do."

"I've always thought that was weird."

"Good, we agree on something. You're weird."

"No," I snapped. "It's weird that nobody uses the grand library. When I asked Father about it, he had nothing to say. There's so much knowledge at our fingertips right here, and nobody seems to care. I've discovered a way to heal, and still, there's no interest."

He gave a shrug.

"These history books don't mention Rutherford or our last name, Hughes. Anywhere."

"What are you implying?"

"Nothing at the moment. But I'll imply something soon."

He dropped his hand from his face and examined the bookcases nearby. His lazy eyes dragged down the shelves before they turned back to me.

"All the portraits on the wall…who are they?"

"People long dead and gone."

"Are they ancestors? When I ask Father, he says they are, but he can't give me names or information."

"Ivory, does it really matter? After a couple generations, no one is going to remember us either. The last person who might remember your name will be your grandkid, your great-grandkid if you're *really* lucky. Then there won't be a single person on this earth who's ever known you."

I held his gaze.

"Depressing, huh?"

My eyes went back to the shelves, wondering who'd been here before, what their lives had been like, the wars they'd won so we could sit on our thrones with servants at our feet.

"Be careful tomorrow."

My eyes went back to my brother.

"I know you'll have a guard, but you just never know…"

The ghosts of the people I never knew disappeared

from my thoughts. "Correct me if I'm wrong, but…it sounds like you care about me." The smile broke through my tightly pressed lips.

"Just reminding you that you aren't invincible." He looked at the shelves again.

"I'll miss you."

Now he made a face, still not looking at me.

"Ryker?"

"Hmm?"

"There's this guard in the castle——"

"Yeah, Burke mentioned it. The monster with blue eyes."

"Have any idea who I'm talking about?"

"I think I do, actually." He pulled his gaze away from the bookshelf and looked at me once more, this time his look serious.

"Do you know his name?"

He gave a slight shake of his head. "You think I know any of their names?"

"Ryker."

"When I left the castle the other day, I saw him by the door. He had a pretty hard stare."

"And that doesn't concern you?"

"It's his job to stare, right? Maybe you're just being sensitive."

"A lot of the guards stare at me. But not the way he does. It's like…" I couldn't even find the words for it. "I butchered his entire family or something."

"I think he's one of the Blade Scions."

"Blade Scions?"

"Fighters that survive the trials."

"What trials?"

"I'm honestly not sure. All I know is, most fighters don't survive it."

"Then why do they do it?"

He shrugged. "The honor? The pay? All the men who guard King Rutherford are Blade Scions."

"And you're saying this guy is one of them?"

"I think so. With all the shit he's seen…can you really blame him for being pissed off all the time?"

"The problem is, he seems to be pissed off *at* me."

"You've always been a bit self-absorbed…"

I shot him a glare.

He gave me a smirk back.

————

MY FATHER'S study was full of dark furniture, a mahogany desk with little nicks carved into the wood. He would sit there for hours and dig his dagger into the surface as he pondered to himself. It was always the same spot, a circle of abrasions. The curtains were drawn over the window, and the sconces on the wall cast a low light. His broadsword leaned against the wall, and his armor was on the stand in the corner.

He was in his chair behind the desk when I entered, his dark hair combed back and tucked in place. He was no longer in his uniform, but his clothes were still kingly.

Maps and open scrolls were across the surface of the desk, and it took him a few seconds to pull his gaze away and acknowledge my presence. "I would send Ryker to accompany you, but I need him here."

"He wouldn't want to come anyway." He couldn't feel up the other ladies of court, not the way he could with the servants at Delacroix. I took a seat in the chair facing my father's desk, my legs crossed, my boots dirty after my trek to town.

"In addition to your gowns and hair clips, bring your weapons. You can leave them in the carriage until your return."

"Why do I need my weapons?" My existence was small, just in Delacroix and the Capital. There hadn't been a war in a very long time, and the invaders had been destroyed in the last attack. As far as I knew, we were all that resided in this small world.

"The same reason I have guards throughout the castle. I don't need them, but just having them deters anyone with a hostile heart." He watched me closely. "I thought my permission would excite you."

I gave a shrug. "I'm sure I could kill someone with my bare hands if necessary."

The corner of his mouth rose in a smile. "You're definitely your father's daughter."

Our relationship was weird. One moment we were close, and then in another moment, he was too busy to give me more than five minutes of his time. We rarely sat down to dinner as a family, and he seemed to spend time with us separately. The three of us were hardly in the same room together. Ryker was given admission to a lot more conversations and meetings than I was simply because of the dick between his legs.

Infuriating.

"Give His Majesty my best."

I nodded. "Sure."

"And, Ivory?"

"Hmm?"

"Maddox. That's your target."

"You…you want me to kill the king's son?"

He gave a quick chuckle. "No. I want you to marry him."

My stomach immediately tightened in disgust. "He's not my type."

"But he's the heir to the throne. As his wife, you would be as well."

"I'm not interested in being queen—"

"But I am. The king only has sons, so this is the only way this can work."

My father had never forced me to choose a husband, and I considered myself lucky for that. But now I realized he had a plan all along.

"Maddox." He said the name again. "He's the eldest son, so his inheritance is guaranteed."

I'd lost my mother to illness when I was young, so no, I didn't believe that one bit. "Nothing in life is guaranteed, Father."

His eyes narrowed. "It is—if you make it so."

———

THE CARRIAGE WAS FILLED with my belongings, along with all my essentials to make it through the trip. It was a solid day of constant travel, so I was up and ready to depart before the sun had even risen.

I wasn't a commoner, so I didn't need to stash my weapons out of sight. My bows and quiver of arrows were placed in the carriage on the seat across from me, as well as my sword. I'd wear it on my belt, but I was dressed in a gown and matching cloak to greet the king and queen upon my arrival.

My father gave me a quick goodbye, because something more important required his attention. There was a one-armed hug and a kiss on the temple. Then he was gone, Burke and his guard trailing behind him.

I was about to leave when I had another visitor.

Ryker rubbed his forefinger into the corner of his eye as he yawned. His clothes were wrinkled like they were the same ones he'd left on his bedroom floor the night before. His sword was at his hip, and his cape dragged behind him because there wasn't even a hint of a breeze. "I was up doing my rounds, so I thought I'd say goodbye." He finally dropped his hand and looked at me, his eyes so glazed, it looked like he was still dreaming.

I grinned before my arms swallowed him in a hug. "Uh-huh. Whatever you say."

He returned my embrace, but he put most of his

weight on me like he'd fallen asleep on top of me, standing upright just like a horse.

I gave him a hard pat on the back to keep him awake. "I'll be back in a couple weeks."

He stepped back, a foot taller than me even though he was two years younger, and still had that sleepy look in his eyes. "Two whole weeks…sounds like a vacation."

I gave him a smack on the arm, but I couldn't hide my smirk as I did it.

"Be careful. You got your sword and everything?"

"Yes." My father and brother both asked about my weapons, which was odd to me. "Is there something I need to know?"

He shook his head.

"Because you and Father have echoed the same sentiments to me."

"Because we're protective of you, is all."

My eyes shifted past my brother because I saw him.

The man with the blue eyes approached, in his full armor, six-foot-something with rage targeted straight at me. Even in the presence of the other guards and my brother, he kept up the look—like he didn't give a damn.

"You've got to be kidding me…"

"What?" Ryker asked.

The man passed me, his head turning more and more to meet my look before he was gone. Once he was too far away and the connection between our eyes was severed, the tension dissipated.

I looked at my brother once more. "I'm not going anywhere with that motherfucker."

Ryker shifted his gaze past me and looked at him. "That's the guy you're talking about?"

"You know him?"

He gave a subtle nod. "Mastodon. He was a Blade Scion for King Rutherford. Asked to be transferred here recently."

"Why?"

He gave a shrug. "Didn't say."

"And you expect me to travel with him?"

"I know you're scared—"

"I'm not scared. I'm just not an idiot."

"You want to be scared of the man who protects you —because that means he scares everyone else too." His hand moved to my arm. "Father wouldn't send you off with anyone who was anything less than trustworthy."

"Father seems too distracted to know his nose from his ass these days."

"Ivory, come on. He's got a lot on his mind right now."

"And I have no idea what those thoughts are—because I'm a woman."

Ryker stared at me with tightly pressed lips, keeping his secrets. "The sun is rising. You should go." He gave me one final hug before he turned away.

I watched his retreating back for a while before I turned back to the carriage. Two horses were tied to the front, and in addition to Mastodon, there were two guards. One of the guards opened the carriage door so I could get inside. "M'lady, we should get going if we want to reach the Capitol by nightfall."

My eyes shifted to Mastodon. He stood off to the side and looked down the hillside toward the gates that marked the edge of the city. Unlike the other guards, he wore a cape, a black one. His eyes took in the landscape, as if he could distinguish something in the terrain barely lit up by the sunlight.

Something in my gut warned me about this guy, that he wasn't just some grizzled soldier who had sacrificed every joy in his life to serve the ruling class. But I seemed to be the only one who could see what no one else saw, and that made me wonder if I really saw it at all.

I had my weapons, so I'd be ready if he came for me.

I stepped into the carriage and watched the door shut behind me.

A moment later, we started to move, the carriage rocking left and right over the cobblestone street.

I didn't waste any time before I opened my bag and changed out of my gown and cloak. I pulled on my breeches, my tunic, and my boots. The sword was inserted into my belt, and the bow and quiver of arrows were pulled over my shoulder.

"Come at me, bitch."

———

AS THE SUN rose in the sky, the heat inside the carriage intensified. The roof kept out direct sunlight, so that was a reprieve, but the stuffiness couldn't be defeated. I'd have preferred to ride my own horse as I was escorted by guards, but my father said that wasn't an option if I didn't want to be seen as a swine.

My father had taught me everything I knew about the sword, about horseback riding, about anticipating an attack you couldn't see coming, but he had me lock away all those skills as if they were a dirty secret.

I would normally read a book on the journey, but they were left at the bottom of my bag so I could keep my guard up. My eyes flicked back and forth between the windows on each of the doors. The curtains were drawn to keep the sun out, but I could determine the outline of trees whenever we passed them.

There was no conversation. No small talk. Nothing.

It was as if the guards didn't even know each other.

Then I felt it.

A bump.

As if the wheels on the left side of the carriage had just run over something.

A rock. A stump.

Or a body.

Then it happened again—on the right side.

"Shit."

The carriage came to a sudden stop, and both the horses gave flustered neighs.

"I fucking knew it…"

A loud whistle rang out from the outside of the carriage. It was obviously a signal.

If only I could grab one of the horses, I could ride out of there. Mastodon would be too powerful to take down, but his weight would slow him down on a horse. I'd have the upper hand in that case.

But how would I manage that?

"Fuck...I'm a sitting duck in here." I unlocked the door and cracked it open.

No sign of the psychopath.

I left my bag behind because I couldn't manage the weight right now and slowly crept out, careful not to make a sound that would draw his attention from the front of the carriage. My boots reached the ground, and I left the door ajar behind me.

I got on my knees and crawled underneath the carriage. When he realized the door was open, he would assume I'd made a run for it and he'd missed it. With his back turned, I'd cut one of the horses free and make my escape.

Flat on my stomach, I swept my eyes across the limited view I had. The hooves of the horses shifted left and right as they tried to remain comfortable standing upright, and the one on the left released a pile of droppings.

I was too worked up to cringe.

Mastodon's boot came into view when he dropped down to the ground. Slowly, he came around, heading to the door that I'd left open. He took his sweet-ass time, every step loud and purposeful.

The closer he came, the more I shifted to the other side, careful not to let my breathing go haywire and get loud. When he stopped at the open door, I got to my feet on the other side, careful to keep my head down below the window.

So close.

I pulled out my dagger and went for it, slashing the ropes that secured the horse to the carriage.

He must have realized what was happening because now his footsteps were loud.

"Come on!" I got the last rope free and climbed onto the bare horse and kicked. There was nothing to grab because it wasn't saddled. There weren't even reins. Just the dark hair on the nape of his neck.

The horse took off—just in the nick of time.

Without direction, we just ran, ran hard.

I looked over my shoulder to peek, expecting Mastodon to do the same to the other horse.

But he just stood there and looked at me in a way he never had before.

Like he didn't hate me.

———

THE ADRENALINE WAS STILL heavy in my veins, so I didn't want to stop.

But I had no choice.

Without sunlight, I'd crash straight into a tree and kill us both.

When I was on my feet, that was when the soreness kicked in. My inner thighs hurt without the padding of the saddle. The constant friction had chafed my skin through the breeches. My back hurt too, along with my arms, and don't get me started on my ass.

That probably hurt most of all.

If I'd had any idea where I was going, I might have made it back to Delacroix, but I didn't have a clue where I was. No idea which way was north and which was south. When I didn't arrive at the Capital by nightfall, they would know I'd been compromised on my journey. Men would be sent out with horses and hounds.

All I had to do was survive until that happened.

I had only my sword, arrows, and bow. No food or water. No supplies. My stomach growled because I was hungry—I was always hungry. My horse started to munch on the grass beneath his feet, and I was a bit jealous. "Wish I could eat grass." I stopped in a thick gathering of trees because I assumed it would be more challenging to see me, but I also didn't have the luxury of selecting the right place to crash for the night.

Beggars couldn't be choosers, right?

I took a seat on the ground and leaned back against a tree. The sounds of the forest grew louder the darker it became. Now there was no illumination at all, except for the stars between the tops of the trees.

It was summertime, but it was still a bit chilly out there.

I tried to keep an eye on my horse, but if he chose to

wander away, there was nothing I could do about it. Without a rope, I couldn't keep him in place, and I wasn't going to stand there and hold on to him either.

As long as a poisonous snake or spider didn't get me, I'd be safe there until morning. If I couldn't see, Mastodon couldn't see either. I assumed he was camped for the night, but with supplies, and he'd be on the hunt at first light.

The creaking sounds of the forest were too terrifying for me to fall asleep, but I dozed off a couple times, resting intermittently. There were times when I slept long enough to have dreams, dreams of lit torches moving through the forest in my direction.

Wait, that wasn't a dream.

"Shit." I stumbled to my feet and reached for my bow.

There were five torches, all spread out in a line, coming right toward me.

I immediately turned to run, but then I realized I wouldn't get far. Fleeing would only draw more attention to myself. I stayed put and hoped my horse had disappeared so he wouldn't give away my location.

I moved to the other side of the trunk and stayed put, my arrow nocked to the string, my heartbeat like drums.

I heard them as they drew closer, but only because my ears were searching for it. If I'd had no idea they were coming, the sound would have just blended in with all the other noises coming from the forest.

I knew they were right behind me when I could see the

glow of their torches. It reflected off the leaves in the canopy and the trunks of the trees. The heat was discernible too. A few feet away from me, one of the five emerged. It was dark and difficult to see, but I knew it wasn't Mastodon. He was too short to be the guy with the blue eyes.

With my pounding heart in my throat, I kept still and waited for them to pass without noticing me. They didn't seem to discover the horse either because their progress never halted.

When they were far ahead of me, I finally took my first full breath and lowered my bow. I stepped away from the tree and slung my bow across my back as I tried to think of what to do now. If that was their direction, then it would be smart to go the opposite way, back the way I came.

But when I turned that way, the path was blocked.

I couldn't distinguish his features in the dark, but I could measure the size of his frame in the shadows, feel the angry energy emitting from every pore in his body. The shock only lasted a second. Then my instincts kicked in, and I had my bow armed and ready, the tip of the arrow pointed right at his face.

It was a silent standoff, the two of us staring each other down.

I did my best to keep my bow steady, but my heavy breaths made it rise and fall, made me lose my perfect aim.

For the first time, he spoke, his voice thick like velvet,

deep like the cliff near Delacroix. "I'll hurt you if it comes to it."

I steadied my aim. "And I'll kill you if it comes to it. Walk away. Now."

Covered in armor as he was, there were very few openings for my arrows. Just his eyes and a small part of his neck. All my hope for survival resided on this shot because if I missed, it was over. I wasn't stupid; I knew I couldn't take him in combat. All he had to do was punch me in the skull once, and I'd be dead.

He stared for a moment longer then made his move.

I held my breath for a second and fired the arrow—right at his eyes.

In mid-step, he snatched the arrow right out of the air and threw it down in a single fluid motion.

"Oh fuck." I nocked another arrow and fired, this time hitting him in the neck.

He didn't stop that one.

But he didn't go down either. As if nothing had happened, he kept up his pace right at me, my arrow sticking out of his flesh.

I dropped the bow and unsheathed my sword.

He didn't draw his, but his enormous mass was enough to terrify me.

I swung the blade, slicing at his torso.

He sidestepped it as if it was second nature, as if the darkness was as bright as daylight, and then ducked underneath another swipe of my blade. His hand gripped mine, and he slammed my wrist into his knee, making me grunt in pain as my fingers were forced to release the hilt.

Then his thick arms circled my neck and squeezed.

I tried to kick him and missed. Then I threw my arms behind my head, scratching for any piece of skin I could find. "You motherfucker!"

He squeezed me tighter until there was no breath coming into my lungs.

I struggled a bit longer, even though I knew full well how hopeless it was.

This was how I was going to die.

The blackness took me—and then it was over.

THREE

Ivory

_____

Before my eyes opened, I could hear the breeze through the leaves.

It was a subtle backdrop of noise, but I recognized it instantly once I reached consciousness. I could picture it in my head, the leaves bending to the wind, some of them coming loose and drifting to the forest floor. It was the same sound I heard through the open windows of my bedroom early in the morning, along with the songbirds greeting the new day.

Then I remembered I wasn't in my bedroom.

I wasn't even in the castle.

I was… I didn't even know.

I opened my eyes and saw the sunshine coming through the gaps in the branches. My body immediately shot up, and I looked for the man with the blue eyes, the man who had suffocated me until my brain was forced to shut down to conserve oxygen.

There he was—sitting on a log right in front of me.

But he no longer wore his helmet. For the first time, I could see his entire face. I could see high cheekbones and hollow cheeks. Could see a prominent brow that made him look subtly displeased. Could see the sharp jawline that made him look even angrier. Thick cords moved down his neck and disappeared under his armor, the black armor with the symbol of the king, the king he betrayed.

He held my gaze for a long minute, and the longer he stared, the angrier he became. "Don't fuck with me." His deep voice had a bite, a bite so hard it was like a sword against a shield. "That's the only warning you'll receive."

The arrow was out of his neck, and now a bandage was in its place. The arrow hit its mark, but it didn't hit him deep enough to fracture his vertebrae. Maybe if he wasn't so thick with muscle, it would have worked.

And I'd be free right now. "You don't want to fuck with me either, asshole."

His eyes remained steady, as if he wasn't the least bit threatened by that. He rose from the rock and turned away.

"I was right about you, but nobody listened to me."

He kept walking to his campsite, his cape fluttering at his back.

I took a look around, searching for the other four men he was in league with, but it seemed to be just us. My eyes scanned the area for my bow and sword, but those were probably long gone. After examining my wrists and ankles, I realized I wasn't restrained.

I could run for it.

Mastodon kneeled by the cold campfire with his back to me, and he seemed to be searching inside a bag.

I had questions, but I'd rather escape instead. As quietly as possible, I got to my hands and knees then pushed myself up to my feet.

"What did I just tell you?"

I turned back in his direction, like he had eyes in the back of his head.

"You can't outrun me. You can't fight me. So, just sit your ass down and be quiet." He straightened then turned back to me, those blue eyes merciless like the times he'd stared at me in the castle.

"Sit my ass down and… Wow."

He kept up his cold stare.

"Never going to happen."

He reached for a rope and marched toward me.

"Alright, alright." I stepped back, refusing to let that abrasive rope tie my wrists together.

He halted but continued to stare.

I swallowed my pride and lowered myself to the dirt.

He returned the rope to his bag and continued whatever he was doing.

"Where are the others?"

Silence.

"Where are you taking me?"

More silence.

"What do you want from me?"

"You're no longer in your castle, and I'm no longer the

servant at your beck and call." He turned around again, meeting my look. "Now, I'm the one in charge. And you will shut your goddamn mouth, or I'll force it shut."

A flush moved down my spine, followed by bumps all over both of my arms. It was a sensation I rarely felt—only had felt once, actually—and that sensation was fear. I couldn't fight. I couldn't run. I couldn't scream for help.

There was nothing I could do.

———

THE OTHER MEN were dressed in different gear. They wore all black, with no symbols or allegiance to any sovereign. All heavily armored and strong. I'd be lucky if I could take down one, let alone all five of them.

It became clear who the leader was.

Mastodon.

He was running the show, barking out orders, keeping an eye on me but also pretending I didn't exist at the same time.

I tried to size up each opponent, to glean as much knowledge about them individually as possible, because maybe I could steal a sword or a dagger, slit a throat in the middle of the night. Something.

I took Mastodon's threat seriously, so when I ran for it, it'd better be the opportune time.

They didn't have horses, so we proceeded on foot, moving back into the forest and off the main road.

The four men took the lead, while Mastodon stayed behind me.

I felt his stare in my back the entire way, felt that same piercing gaze that had penetrated my flesh in the castle. The four men in front were a bit shorter than him and definitely didn't compare in size. Mastodon was like a stone castle—and these guys were the stables.

I looked over my shoulder.

"Eyes ahead."

I looked forward again. "Shouldn't you be the one in front?"

Silence.

"You're the one in charge, right?"

"A real leader is always the last one in line. He protects the rear while looking after everyone ahead. You wouldn't know that—because your father is a piece of shit."

That made me stop in my tracks. "Excuse me?"

He gave me a hard shove. "Move."

I stumbled forward and almost fell but caught myself before I went down. "What did my father do to you?"

Silence.

"So, that's what this is about?" I moved forward, but I glanced over my shoulder repeatedly to keep him in my sight. "You want to make him pay for something?"

His ice-cold stare was on my face, his tightly pressed lips and hard jaw matching the eyes I now knew so well.

"You're the one who's kidnapped his innocent daughter, so look who's the piece of shit now…"

"Nothing I do to you will ever compare to what he's done to me."

"And what did he do?" I stopped again, turning completely to face him.

He continued his pace, headed right toward me, blood lust in his eyes. When he was right in front of me, he stopped, his chin tilted down to examine me, his breaths slow and controlled.

I wanted to take a step back, but I resisted.

His eyes shifted back and forth between mine. "He raped my mother—and made me watch."

My lungs automatically sucked in a deep breath as the repulsive accusation made my heart stop. My body gave a jolt in disgust because it couldn't process the words that were shoved in my face. "You're mistaken. He wouldn't do that…"

His eyes turned still, locked on my expression. Without a blink, without a breath, he stared.

I caved and took a step back…because I just couldn't handle it.

"When you asked him about the scars on his left cheek, what did he say?"

I breathed deep—in and out. Those scars were still visible in direct sunlight, but I was so used to them now that I didn't even notice them anymore. "He scratched himself in his sleep—"

"A lie." He stepped closer, forcing me to step back. "In a desperate attempt to stop your father from throwing her sons over the side of a cliff, my mother clawed him hard, from cheek to chin."

I could feel my head shake, feel the disbelief combating his words.

"It didn't work. With your father's seed still inside her, he threw them all to their deaths—with a goddamn smile on his face."

I couldn't stop shaking my head. "You're wrong…"

He watched me, his look maniacal. "Believe me. Don't believe me. Makes no difference to me." His large hand grabbed me by the arm, and he shoved me hard, so hard that I hit the earth with a thud that made me wince. "Move."

I pushed to my feet and stumbled forward. "That's your plan, isn't it?" I continued to walk forward, my heart dropping into my stomach. "You're going to force me the way your mother was forced…and then kill me."

"The second part. Not the first."

I turned to look at him again.

"There's not enough magic in the world to ever make me desire you."

———

AT NIGHTFALL, we reached the base of the mountains.

I knew there were mountains to the west of the Capital, so that must be our location. I spent my time sticking my nose in books, not maps, so geography wasn't my forte. But I did know there were villages between the major settlements, and Mastodon knew exactly where those were located because he expertly avoided them.

I had no idea where we were going or why he'd kept me alive this long if he just intended to kill me, but I had to keep those curiosities to myself because I couldn't ask for those answers.

We entered a cavern, and once the darkness blanketed our sight, the torches were lit. We moved forward, deeper into the cavern, the ceiling slowly rising higher and higher toward the sky.

I'd never been underground before, and the deeper we ventured, the more my heart began to pound. In the forest, I had always had the option of running if I wanted to, but down here…there was nowhere to go. "Where are we going?"

"Entitled, isn't she?" One of the five came closer to me, holding his torch up high as the oil beaded down the wood and onto his glove. He looked me over—with bright-blue eyes.

My attention had been on Mastodon this entire time since he was the leader and the others were followers. But now that I had a good look at one of them, I realized exactly who he was. "He's your brother, isn't he?"

"Stop asking questions like you're entitled to answers, *Princess*."

"I'm not a princess—"

"Really? You sure act like it." He stepped away and carried the torch with him.

When I looked ahead, I felt his stare, his cold stare.

"You need to remember I've done nothing to you and your brother—"

"Shut up." He didn't raise his voice, but his tone stunned me into silence.

I pressed my lips tightly together and tried to process the rage trapped in my chest.

Mastodon moved forward with the others, leaving me behind for the first time.

I looked behind me, daylight at the end of the tunnel.

"Go for it."

I turned back around, seeing that Mastodon was still moving ahead.

"Just give me a reason. Any fucking reason."

Every time I saw any opportunity, it was snatched away by this man who was aware of everything—and everyone.

We approached the entrance of another cavern, and once we stepped inside, I realized it was a large dome. The ceiling extended high toward the sky, and there was a break in the center, letting sunlight reach the floor.

But there was no floor.

There was a pit—without a bottom.

I crept to the very edge, my boot kicking a rock over, and I watched it tumble down until it was obscured in darkness. "What the…?" I raised my head and looked at Mastodon, as if he would give me an answer.

Mastodon glanced down before he gestured toward his men. "I'll take the lead. Ian, you take the rear."

"Whoa, hold on," I said. "We're going down there?"

Mastodon stared at me.

"Into a bottomless pit?" I asked incredulously. "For what reason?" I hoped that my father's men would search the countryside until they found our tracks. Then they would follow our scent until I was rescued. But if I went down there…they'd never find me.

It was now or never.

"You call it a bottomless pit," Mastodon said. "I call it home."

Oh shit.

Without hesitation, I went for it. I kicked the man closest to me in the back and gripped the hilt of his sword as he went down—right over the edge. I barely got a glimpse of Mastodon, but he did exactly what I thought he would do.

He chose his comrade over me.

I sprinted out of the cave without looking back, carrying the heavy sword like it was featherlight because the adrenaline was so powerful. I chose life over death, because that was all that was waiting for me in that pit, death.

I hit the sunlight and kept going, heading for the tree line. Not once did I glance behind me because that would slow me down just a second, and I didn't have a second. The sunlight disappeared once I was in the shade. I jumped over boulders and tree trunks and dropped the sword once on the way.

That was when I realized he was right behind me.

Fuck, he's fast.

I moved through the trunks, trying to find little nooks and crannies that I could sneak between and that would slow him down, but the guy was a boulder that just crashed through everything.

This isn't going to work.

Think.

I jumped over a boulder near a tree, but instead of continuing forward, I veered left and rounded the tree to get him from behind.

But the motherfucker was ready for it, his sword at the ready, his eyes more maniacal than they'd ever been. He marched toward me and withdrew his other short sword. A weapon in each hand with armor that would take several hits to hack through, he was pretty much invincible.

"You weigh like five hundred pounds… How are you so fast?" I held my sword at the ready and stayed light on my feet. My breaths came out labored and heavy because I'd just run a mile, if not more.

"Ask a horse."

The sword was heavier than I was used to, so I had to focus harder than usual. There was no chance I could defeat this guy, but maybe I could disarm him long enough to get away. Or maybe I should just fight to the death because I'd rather die than end up deep underground in that godforsaken place.

He spun one sword around his wrist, a flash of light glinting off the steel.

"I'm warning you…" I stepped back but kept my sword at the ready.

He halted in mid-step, a slight smile moving on to his lips.

"Just let me go."

"No." He moved forward.

"Even if you're right about my father, I wasn't even alive—"

One of his swords came down—aimed to wound.

I caught it with my blade like second nature, then pushed it off. I was quick on my feet just as my father taught me, getting out of the way for his secondary attack, missing the blade by a few hairs.

He dropped both swords to his sides as he circled me, his eyes narrowing in a whole new way.

"I'm sorry about what happened to you, okay?" Out of breath, I continued my movements, never allowing myself to be a sitting duck. "I'd hunt down the man responsible to the ends of the earth. But I wouldn't hunt down his daughter. I'm innocent—"

"So was my mother." He lunged at me, giving me a flurry of blows.

Muscle memory kicked in, and I blocked both hits with my sword, ducking and spinning out of all the attacks he sent my direction. I rolled out of the way, getting out of his line of fire so I could scurry back.

He stopped where he stood, the tips of both swords pointed to the ground. "You're good."

"I did warn you…"

"I'm not striking to kill. Just to make you bleed a bit." He stepped forward. "If this were a real assault, you'd have my sword straight through your eye right now. You'd be pinned to that tree behind you, and over time, your body would slide through the edge of the blade until your corpse collapsed on the roots of the tree."

"That's a really vivid picture…"

"Throw down your blade." He sheathed both of his swords.

"No."

"I will hurt you—and that's a promise."

"Let me go."

"No."

"If you really hurt me to get back at my father, you're just as barbaric as he is."

He came closer to me. "That's the point."

I lunged with my sword, aiming to swipe his neck from his shoulders.

He ducked and popped back up before I could stop the momentum of my sword. His hand gripped my arm and threw it down, forcing the blade to fly from my hand and land somewhere in the grass.

I tried to twist out of it, but his hold was too strong.

My body hit the ground, and his fingers ended up locked around my neck. He held himself over me, his fingers slack enough so just a little bit of air could make it into my lungs with every breath. "Your words are stones against a tree. Every hit makes a sound, but the tree doesn't fall. I've planned this for a very long time, and your desperate attempts to make me pity you are hopeless. All roads end at the same place—with your head off your shoulders." His fingers released me, and he stood up.

I gasped for breath, sitting up as I reached for my throat.

He scanned the forest, his eyes hollow and bored. "You're lucky I grabbed him before he fell. Otherwise, I would have thrown you in after him."

———

MASTODON MARCHED me back into the cave where the men waited, and he handed back the sword that I'd stolen from the belt of the man.

The man sheathed his blade as he kept his eyes on me. "Nothing personal."

He moved quicker than I could anticipate, and his palm hit me in the face so hard I actually turned with the hit. The skin immediately swelled with heat and pain, and my instinct was to cry out, but I kept my lips tightly shut.

I let the agony pass before I righted myself again, visualizing just how red my cheek was since I couldn't see it. Ryker had hit me before, but that was when we were kids. I'd never been smacked around like that otherwise—and that was when I realized how sheltered my life had been. I wasn't prepared for that kind of pain, but I handled it in silence because I thought that preserved the most dignity.

The man stared at me again, and when I didn't give the reaction he wanted, he went in again.

This time, I kicked him in the balls.

He cried like a girl and bent over at the waist, sucking in a deep breath as he processed the pain.

Mastodon just stood there like he didn't care what happened to either one of us. "Let's move."

I didn't drop my guard because I knew it was coming.

The man righted himself and attacked me, ready to do more than just slap me. "You fucking bitch—"

"Pyrus." Mastodon grabbed him by the arm and tugged him back. "We have a lot of ground to cover."

He tried to shove him off. "Not until I kick this bitch right in the cunt."

"I'm sure it'll hurt," I said. "Since I have bigger balls than you—"

"Enough." Mastodon yanked him all the way back until he was nowhere near me. Then he walked up to me, towering over me, his black armor making him blend in with the darkness. With the torch at his side, he stared into my face. His eyes were such a soft blue, like the sky on the first day of spring, but he could turn that beauty into ugliness when he looked at me like that—like he was picturing my head on a spike. "Let's go." He took the lead down the wooden ladder, holding the torch at the same time so he could light the way.

I approached the ladder and felt all their eyes on my back—as if one of them might kick me over the edge. They must have found the strength to resist because I stepped down the ladder and started to move.

Move deeper underground.

Initially, I didn't keep pace with the men, and a muddy boot ended up in my face countless times. "Watch it, asshole." I swatted at his boot.

He kicked my hand. "Move, asshole."

Mastodon's voice came from below. "Princess, come on."

"Don't fucking call me that—"

"Then move."

I quickened my pace, glancing down to make sure I wasn't going to put my boot directly on top of a burning torch. Keeping pace with Mastodon left me out of breath, even though he was doing all of this with a single hand.

It went on like that for an hour…and then two hours. "How long is this going to take us?"

"Days."

I stopped climbing. "I'm sorry, did you say *days*?"

"Move," Mastodon barked.

"You're insane if you think we can keep this up that long."

"No. I'm just not weak—like you."

"Wow, fuck you."

"Shut up and prove me wrong."

"I could just kick you off the ladder right now."

"Do your worst, *Princess*."

I held on to the ladder and leaned out so I could get a good look at him. "I told you not to—" The sweat from my palm greased the wood, and I felt my body swing out farther than it should. "Oh shit." The harder I gripped, the more the wood evaded my fingers, and I felt myself fall. "Ahhh!"

It all happened so fast that I didn't see what actually occurred, but Mastodon somehow managed to keep his hold on the ladder and the torch and grab me at the same time. His powerful arm snatched me out of the air just like he did with the arrow and secured me into his side, all the while keeping his hold on the ladder.

The world still spun for a second even though I was absolutely still. The scent of man was flush in my nose, of a hardworking man that worked up a sweat. There were other scents there too, like the forest after a light rain, of droplets that dripped off the leaves and fell to the earthen floor.

I stayed there, locked in place by his powerful grip, safe despite the fact that I was still on this stupid ladder miles above the bottom. When I lifted my chin from his shoulder, I came face-to-face with his blue eyes. They were closer than they'd ever been, and now I could see the details I hadn't noticed before. Flecks of white between the blue, like flakes of salt. There was more than just revenge there. There was intelligence, wisdom, and pain.

"Grab on."

His voice shattered my focus on his eyes.

"Come on."

I grabbed on to the ladder with my hands and felt him release me.

He continued his pace, his torch lighting the way for us.

It took me a moment to get a hold of myself, to let the disastrous moment become part of the past. My hands were no longer sweaty because I had turned ice-cold, so I started to lower myself down the ladder again.

"Princess, you owe my brother some gratitude." Ian's voice came from the top.

As my heart slowed back to its normal pace, I picked up speed. "What's the point if he's just going to kill me anyway?"

FOUR

Ivory

_____

JUST WHEN MY BODY STOPPED WORKING, WE CAME TO A
halt for the day.

Deep underground, there was no way to know sunrise
from sunset, midnight from midday. Based on how
exhausted I was, I assumed it was sometime deep in the
night, hours after I would normally be asleep.

Did Ryker know I was missing yet? Would he lead the
rescue party?

Did my dad feel like shit for not listening to me?

I hoped he did.

The ladder came to an end, and we hit solid rock at
the bottom. There was an opening in a cavern that led
elsewhere, and I assumed this adventure wasn't over
because the men prepared to sleep there.

How much longer did we have? And where the hell
were we going?

All my possessions had been left behind in the carriage, so all I had were my arms for a pillow. I took a spot on the opposite side of the cave, far away from the men, and watched them get settled for the night. They drank from their canteens, bit into hard pieces of bread, and made small talk before they went to sleep.

I noticed Mastodon and Ian speaking to each other quietly. Sometimes his brother would look at me across the cave, having the same light-colored hair and blue eyes as his brother.

I'd never slept in anything except a four-poster bed with a soft mattress and a down comforter filled with swan feathers. If it was winter, my sheets were heated with hot coals, and in the summertime, a large pitcher of water was placed at my bedside. Whatever I needed was at my beck and call, and now I realized how much I took for granted. My life had been luxurious simply because I was born into it. I hadn't done anything to earn it. The servants worked and lived in the castle every day of the year, but it didn't matter how much they pleased my father; they would never have what I had.

That realization hit me pretty hard in that moment.

Maybe I was a princess after all.

The men all went to sleep—except Mastodon.

He leaned against the wall with one arm resting on his propped knee. It'd been a long day, but he didn't look remotely tired. His gaze was fixed on me.

"I'm too tired to run…if that's what you're worried about."

He opened up a small canteen and took a drink, and when I saw a drop escape from his chin, I knew it wasn't water. He wiped his mouth with the back of his forearm and continued his stare.

I was hungry and thirsty, but I didn't dare ask for anything. Had too much pride for that.

I closed my eyes and decided to ignore my empty stomach and my parched mouth as best I could and just get some sleep.

Something thumped on the ground and then rolled in my direction.

I opened my eyes and saw a canteen stop just inches in front of my face. I studied it for a moment then looked at him again—as if it were a trap.

He was still drinking out of his smaller canteen.

I sat up and twisted the cap. "Holding out on me, huh?" I opened the lid and took a deep drink, the water coating my dry throat and healing the cracks that had formed in the skin of my lips.

He continued to drink.

I took another drink because I was just so thirsty. It'd been a long trek to the bottom, and if I didn't get some water in my body soon, I'd develop a headache. I returned the lid to the top and rolled it back.

He opened his bag, ripped a piece of bread off the loaf, and then threw it at me.

I caught it with a single hand and immediately devoured it. It was a bit tough, like it was a day old, but it was delicious under the circumstances. If I were home right now, I'd probably have a roast chicken with buttered potatoes and a whole loaf of bread to myself. "Do you normally fatten the pig before you slaughter it?"

His eyes shifted to the opening in the cavern and ignored me.

"We're in the middle of…I don't even know. Who do you need to watch out for?"

Silence.

I wasn't sure why I bothered.

"Where are we?"

"The only thing I should hear from your mouth is thank you and goodnight."

"You're saying I should feel gratitude toward the man who's vowed to kill me for something I didn't do just because he gave me a piece of bread?" I asked incredulously. "I'm not weak-minded like most women you know."

His eyes shifted back to me. "Choose your battles and conserve your energy."

"The battle for my life is the one I choose."

"Your best chance of survival is by not pissing me off, yet you don't hesitate to do that."

"Because I'm not a kiss-ass. I'm not going to spend the final days of my life begging for something I shouldn't have to beg for. I'm not thankful for the bread or the water. I'm not thankful that you saved me from falling to my death. The reason I'm even here in the first place is because of you, because your need for revenge blinds you to everything else that matters."

He rested the back of his head against the wall, his two short blades in the sheaths on either side of his hips, his armor molding to the movements of his body like a second skin. He stared for a while, as if provoked by my words, but then his following words were nothing but a disappointment. "Sleep. We have a long day tomorrow."

———

IT SEEMED like my eyes had only been closed for a couple minutes before I was jolted awake by a boot.

"Up." It gave me a gentle nudge in the arm.

"Get your disgusting foot out of my face." I smacked the guy away, seeing that it was Ian.

He looked down at me with a hard stare then did it again—but this time harder. "Rise and shine, Princess."

"Fuck off." I forced myself up, and the second I moved, my whole body screamed with stiffness. All the joints of my body tightened in soreness, and my muscles felt solidified in place. "Wow…that's new." I had to stretch a bit before I got to my feet—and that was a first.

Mastodon watched me from across the cavern, his eyes showing his impatience. "Come on."

"Sorry…never slept on solid rock before," I said sarcastically.

"You should have been sleeping on it all your life."

"What's that supposed to mean?"

He stepped through the opening and disappeared.

I looked up the ladder the way we came, which was

unguarded at the moment, but the thrill of escape was very short-lived. Even if my entire body weren't stiff and sore, I had no chance at outclimbing these guys. They were all strong. All fast. Especially their leader—the man who sprinted like a goddamn horse.

I joined the men, Mastodon waiting just on the other side, tall and muscular, almost like a sculpture in the palace.

I took my place in front of him and followed the guys as they moved through the dark tunnel. The air was stale like it'd been trapped there for thousands of years, and there was a mist to the air as if water seeped through the walls from a lake somewhere up above. We were slanted at an incline, going farther down.

There was one torch at the front and one at the back.

The pace was quick, not a run but a very fast walk. Hours passed, and nothing was said. Everyone focused on getting to their destination as quickly as possible...whatever that destination might be.

"Why can't you tell me where we're going?" I tired out quicker than the men, so my pace started to slacken. Mastodon always stayed behind me, though, his eyes drilling into my back. "If you're going to kill me anyway, what's the harm?"

"If I'm going to kill you anyway, what does it matter where we're going?"

"Because I want to know how much more of this torture I should expect."

"Walking is torture?" he asked with his deep voice. "Definitely a princess…"

I rolled my eyes just for my own benefit. "Answer me."

"I'm not your servant."

"Asking someone a question doesn't imply they're a servant." This time, I stopped and turned around. "I'm not acting entitled. You're acting touchy. That's the problem here. I'm sorry that I was born into power and you weren't. It's not fair, but that's how the world works sometimes."

He laughed. Actually laughed. A deep chuckle reverberated against the walls, echoing up and down the underground path. His mouth was in a smirk from his laughter, but his eyes had never looked so sinister.

"What?"

"Trust me, I know how the world works. And you're about to learn the same."

———

THE DEEPER WE TRAVELED, the colder it became. The sun could only penetrate the top layers of the soil, but down here among solid rock, there was no heat, no source of energy. The ground began to shine like glitter, the ice particles locked in place within the walls.

I started to shiver.

After a long trek with little conversation, we stopped for the night.

But there was no way I could sleep, not under these conditions, not when the rock underneath me was like a frozen piece of ice. "I can keep going if you want to cover more ground." I sat on the ground against the wall, my ass frozen.

Ian ate a couple pieces of bread with a dried-out piece of meat and stared at me as he chewed.

No one addressed what I said.

I guess I had my answer.

Mastodon whispered something to his brother before he unrolled his bedroll and lay down. He was on his back, his swords still attached to his belt.

Ian continued to eat, eyes on me.

"You mind?"

"Mind what?" he asked, his mouth full of food.

"Stop staring at me."

"Mastodon told me not to underestimate you. And I won't."

I rolled my eyes.

"Go to sleep."

"How?" I asked incredulously. "You see me shaking, right?"

He shrugged and took another bite.

"I said, stop staring."

"Mastodon stares, and you don't have a problem with it."

"Trust me, I don't like that either, but—"

"But what?"

I didn't have an answer. "I guess I'm just used to it…"

With my arms crossed over my chest, I felt my body tremble, felt my teeth chatter. This wasn't a mind-over-body situation where I could just conquer the elements by sheer will. With every passing minute, my body was being conquered, the cold moving further into my flesh.

Ian tossed a couple pieces of jerky at me.

I took them without acknowledgment and scarfed everything down like a dog that just got a bone. I was too tired and too cold to have any dignity right now, so I took it in stride. The pleasure from the food was momentary, and the cold set in once more.

I started to fade in and out, never really awake, but never really asleep either. My eyes were slightly open, and I thought I saw Ian in front of me. But it must have been a dream because I couldn't feel anything.

Then I felt a warm hand to my cheek, a touch so soothing that I sucked in a deep breath.

"She'll freeze to death." I recognized Mastodon's deep voice.

"I feel fine," Ian said. "She's weak."

"No. She just weighs a hundred pounds, and we weigh more than double that." He gripped my arms and gave me a shake.

My eyes snapped open, and I sucked in another deep breath.

His hands moved over my body, from my cheeks to my wrists to my ankles. "You're going to die if you don't do what I tell you."

"Isn't…isn't that what you want?"

"Yes, but not like this." His hands clamped down on my wrists, hot like a pot on the stove.

"Ooh…that's nice."

He pulled his hands away, and then I was immediately frozen once again. My eyes closed because I was too weak to keep them open.

"Get her up," Mastodon ordered.

I felt my body lift entirely on its own, like I could fly.

I was carried to the other side of the path, where the men were sleeping. My eyes opened and closed, somewhat understanding my surroundings. Ian lowered me to the ground, on top of a bedroll.

It was warm. Infinitely warmer than it'd been on the stone floor.

A blanket fell on top of me, and I actually felt a bit of heat in my fingertips. My eyes closed. "That feels nice…"

The blanket lifted again, and then an inferno of heat hit me. A massive arm draped over my waist, and I was smothered in the kind of heat that I felt at midday in the summer, the kind that made sweat drip down the small of my back.

"What if she tries anything?" Ian asked.

"I'll snap her neck." The voice came right at my ear. "Problem solved."

My eyes opened and looked at the muscular arm draped over my stomach, an arm that felt like a burning log in the hearth. My head turned farther, and I saw a massive shoulder, tanned skin over tight muscle, and then a jawline so hard it looked like the edge of a sharp blade. The blanket was at his chest, and I could see the muscle there too. "What…what are you doing?" I felt better, but my teeth were still chattering.

Mastodon's deep voice sounded again. "Keeping you alive."

I lifted my chin to meet his gaze.

His eyes were already closed—as if he didn't see me as a threat at all.

I lifted the blanket slightly to look underneath…and I saw it.

It.

His hard chest led to a riverbed of chiseled abs, strong abs that could take a beating, and then he had this line of hair underneath his belly button that traveled down and down…until…yeah.

His muscular thighs were tanned like his arms and covered in dark hair.

But my eyes went back to the thing that had captured my full attention.

Damn.

I dropped the blanket again and turned to make sure his eyes were still closed.

They weren't. They were wide open—and staring right at me.

For one of the few times in my life, I was actually embarrassed, so I quickly looked away, unable to handle that stare any longer.

————

THE SOUND of voices and shuffling woke me up.

Before my eyes opened, I was aware of how relaxed my body was, the way my muscles were warm all the way through. It was the first time I'd been comfortable since I'd left my bedroom in the castle.

My eyes opened, and I saw Ian beside me, leaned up against the wall as he ate his meager breakfast.

My back was swearing hot because there was a solid rock pressed to it. It slowly rose and fell, in cadence with my own breathing. Last night flashed back to me, the shoulders, the pecs, the abs of steel, the…other thing.

My god, it was huge.

And I'd been caught staring at it.

Normally, I would just own up to it without shame, but this was a little different.

The blanket shifted as he moved behind me.

He stood up, buck naked, in front of his men and started to get dressed.

I took a peek over my shoulder even though I told myself not to.

Now I had a view of the rear—a very tight rear.

His legs were lean and muscular, and his ass firm and tight. His back was a mosaic of muscles, dents in the skin between the segments, shoulders that were even bigger from this angle. He pulled on his bottoms first, then his boots. "Get up."

Did he really have eyes in the back of his head?

I let the blanket fall off me, and the cold returned to my limbs. Now that I was fully thawed, it didn't affect me as much, but if it was just as cold tonight as it had been last night, we'd have to do that again.

I folded up his bedroll nice and tight and handed it to him after he got his tunic on.

He took it from my hand, his angry stare on my face.

I expected him to make a comment about last night, but he didn't.

"Here." Ian handed me some breakfast, more dried meat and even staler bread.

I took it without complaint.

Mastodon relit both the torches, and then we were off.

Ian and the other three men took the lead while Mastodon took the rear, the heat from his torch warming my back when he was directly behind me. The scenery was more of the same, rocks, dirt, and ice crystals. I did notice small roots protruding from the dirt, and I wasn't sure how that was possible.

The slope started to descend farther, just enough that you could tumble forward if you weren't careful. It started to curve too, like a spiral staircase, round and round. "Did someone *build* this place?"

"What's the other option?" Ian asked. "It's natural?"

"But this…this must have taken—"

"More than a decade," Ian finished.

I looked behind me, Mastodon's cold stare meeting mine instantly. "Did you…do this?"

He held the torch high, his shoulders shifting with every step, the anger sheathed in his stare.

I looked forward again. "Where does it go?"

"You really can't figure that out?" Ian kept his gaze forward. "What's below your kingdom?"

"The ground?"

Ian turned around and gave me a cocked eyebrow.

Then it came to me. "The cliff…"

Ian faced forward again. "You should have figured that out a long time ago."

Now I understood. We were going to the bottom of the cliff. "What's down there?"

Ian released a laugh. "What's down *there*? Are you serious?"

Was I missing something? "Would I risk insult if I weren't serious?"

"She doesn't know." Mastodon's deep voice came from behind me. "Of course she doesn't. Too busy sneaking boys into her room and being waited on hand and foot by her servants."

So, he had seen Quinn. "You think you know me?" I turned around and met his look of wrath with my own. "You watched me for a week, and you think that's enough to tell you everything you need to know?"

He came closer, the torch illuminating his dark face. "Yes." He stopped directly in front of me. "The warm sun hits your face and blinds you to the truth right before your eyes. You're too naïve, too stupid to see the blood directly beneath your feet."

I shook my head slightly, having no idea what he was talking about. "I'm sorry about your mother—"

His hand shot out to my neck instantly, his fingers getting a good grip in a flash. "Don't talk about her." He gave me a hard shove.

I lost my footing instantly and rolled down the incline, moving between the men and hitting the curve in the wall down below. My back struck it with a thud, and then I jerked up, the world still spinning slightly.

"Do not talk about my mother." The torch in his hand illuminated the way, bringing him closer to me. "Don't speak with empathy when you have none. Don't pretend to care about the shoulders you stand on." His boots thudded every time they hit the ground, echoing against the walls. "Don't pretend you're any less vile than the bastard who took everything from me."

———

MY BACK WAS SO SORE.

But I'd let hell freeze over before I complained.

Time and distance couldn't be measured, so I wasn't sure what made them decide to stop for the night. Just general fatigue? Some internal clock? In the curve of the wall, they settled for the night, unrolling their bedrolls and getting ready for sleep.

Mastodon got his bed ready but didn't climb inside. Instead, he leaned up against the wall, an arm propped on his knee again, looking intense and bored at the same time. When I moved to the other wall, he gave a quiet whistle then nodded to the bedroll.

"I'm sorry, do I look like a dog to you?"

"You really want me to answer that?"

"Asshole."

"Get in the bedroll." He had this look I'd never seen before, with which he could command anyone to do anything by sheer force alone. He had the most intimidating stare I'd ever seen. Even on my father's worst day, he didn't look like that.

I was too cold to be defiant right now, so I got into the bedroll.

It was nice to have a warm ass for once.

The men immediately went down for the night, and Mastodon kept watch as if he wasn't the least bit tired. He pulled an apple from his pocket and took a big bite as he looked down the dark pathway.

The blanket was to my neck, locking my own body heat around me to keep me warm. It wasn't much, but it made all the difference in the world. With his eyes elsewhere, I stared at the side of his face. He had short blond hair, really short, and his look was so innately angry. Even the area where his jaw connected to his neck was tight with tension. Now that I knew what he looked like underneath his clothing and armor, I realized he didn't need the plates and vambraces to buff up his appearance. His body was a weapon in itself. "I asked Burke what was down there…and he said he didn't know."

He took another bite, ignoring what I said.

"Before I left, Ryker seemed worried…like he knew something."

"Because your brother isn't an idiot—unlike you."

All I ever received from him were insults, so I was numb to it at this point. "What's at the bottom of the cliff?"

He took another bite and chewed. "Me."

"You…live down there?"

He continued to chew.

"How?" I asked. "I was told it's uninhabitable."

"Which it is."

"Then…how?"

He turned his head back to me, his gaze cold like the ice crystals in the wall. "With a heart full of revenge." He returned to his apple and took the final bite, leaving nothing but the slender core behind.

"Why are you taking me down there? If all you want is to kill me, you could have butchered me right in front of my father. Why drag me on this escapade? How does this serve your plan?"

He tossed the core aside and ignored me.

"You must need me for something…"

There was a very subtle shift in his jawline, as if his teeth clenched inside his closed mouth. "I guess you aren't that stupid after all."

"I won't cooperate." He'd taken me from my home, accused my father of being a rapist, a murderer, and a liar, and vowed to kill me. I wouldn't do a damn thing for him, not to save my own life.

"You will."

"Torture me all you want. Won't make a difference."

"I won't have to torture you."

My eyes shifted back and forth as I stared.

He looked back to the hallway. "Because you'll want to do it."

FIVE

Ivory
———

Days passed.

Very long and cold days.

It was more of the same, long treks with wordless conversations, frozen nights when I shared the bedroll with a naked man that had more strength in his body than an ox and a horse combined.

I didn't take a peek again, but it wasn't as if I'd forgotten what I'd already seen.

How could I forget?

I'd been with a handful of men, but none of them looked like that. None of them were that size. Even the guards at the castle weren't built with the same muscularity. Mastodon dwarfed each and every one.

There was finally light at the end of the tunnel. It was subtle, but it was there.

"Oh, thank god."

Ian held the torch in the lead. "You say that now…"

"I'm confident I'm not going to miss this place," I said, eager for the summer sun on my skin.

The light grew brighter and brighter, a beacon of warmth and hope, an end to this interminable dark tunnel. The beginning of the journey had been filled with fear because I'd been captured, but then it had turned into fear for different reasons. Being underground…was torture. No sun. No trees. No sky. It was unbearable.

But as we came closer, the heat didn't carry on the breeze and hit me in the face.

It stayed cold—ice-cold.

The white light grew brighter and brighter, making my eyes wince and smart. My hand raised in front of my face to make it more bearable, to cast a shadow over my face so it was easier to see what was right in front of me.

Torches were extinguished with a quick flourish of their wrists and tossed into a bowl at the entrance to the cave. There were others there as well, ready to be used for a trek back to the top of the cliff.

I looked at the world before me—and it was nothing but snow.

A frozen tundra.

Winter.

A winter I wasn't dressed for.

I passed the men and stepped farther under the cloudy sky. Light came through the overcast atmosphere, reflective and bright, but not warm. These were the same clouds I'd stared at from above, the clouds that obscured this world below. I turned around and stepped back, looking up rocky crevasses until they disappeared into the clouds.

"Should I grab her?" Ian asked.

Mastodon shook his head. "If she wants to stay alive, she won't go far."

I looked around, the scenery expanding farther into the horizon, an endless frozen tundra. A gust of wind picked up and hit me in the face, the sting of the cold air making my eyes smart harder. "What is this place…?"

Mastodon walked past me, his heavy boots crunching against the snow, his black cape blowing in the wind. "The real world."

————

WITH THE CLIFFS BEHIND US, we ventured deeper into the wasteland of cold. Tall pines were covered with fresh powder, and the snow began to pile higher and higher as we traveled, getting all the way to my waist and soaking my flesh with the numbingly bitter cold.

I didn't complain, even though I was probably going to die.

Ian glanced at me a couple times, his height making it much easier for him to push through the snow, especially with his armor and clothing. He looked at his brother afterward but didn't say a word.

Mastodon didn't look at me, even when I tripped and landed in a pile of snow.

When my face hit the ice, I felt a shiver. "Okay…I miss the cave." I pushed myself up and back to my feet.

The men continued to move ahead, not the least bit worried about me running off or attacking them from behind. I considered myself a decent foe, but the climate had crippled me, and I was utterly useless at the moment.

It made me realize how weak I truly was. My father had taught me the blade and the bow, but those skills were useless when I was outnumbered and about to die from hypothermia instead.

Ian's voice carried to me on the wind. "You know she's going to die."

Mastodon's came next. "I already shared my bed with her."

"You're stronger than I am."

"Now you admit that…when you don't want to do something."

"Anything is better than helping that cunt."

I started to walk again, my entire body frozen.

Mastodon stopped then removed his blades and bow before he handed them to his brother.

"We should have brought her clothes."

"We don't owe her a damn thing, Ian." Mastodon turned around and faced me, his muscular arms by his sides, staring at me with utter rage.

I pushed through the mounds of snow and drew closer, knowing what waited for me when I arrived. It was the same thing that waited for me in that bedroll—searing heat. When it came to survival, I had no pride, just wanted to get into that chest as quickly as possible.

When I reached him, his arms scooped underneath my knees and back, and he lifted me into his chest like I weighed nothing.

Mastodon tied the cape around his front, wrapping it across me tightly, and then secured it so it would stay in place. I couldn't see anything except his hard chest. Dim light came through the cape, and I could see the way his body moved as he carried me, all the strong muscles of his arms as they worked to keep me against him. The heat from his body came a moment later, filling the cape and my flesh.

I finally stopped shaking. "Thank you…"

His only reply was his silence.

———

WE MADE it to a cave for the night.

I wasn't a fan of caves, but now it was preferable to the open sky. This cave was also stocked with items like blankets, dried food, warm clothing. Everything was designed for men, but I put on a tunic lined with fur and piled a jacket on top. It was a blanket on my small size, but it was warm.

But no amount of blankets and clothing would be warm enough to keep the winter air at bay. A crate of firewood was against the wall, so I grabbed a couple logs and tossed them in the cold fire pit.

Mastodon watched me from his spot against the wall. "What are you doing?"

"What does it look like?" I'd never started a fire before. I'd watched Mastodon do it, and I copied his movements to try to catch a flame. I struck the flint against the wood as fast as I could, but only a subtle spark emerged.

"No fire."

I kept trying. "It's freezing—"

"I said, no fire."

I finally stopped trying and met his look. "Why not—"

Roooooooaaaaaaaaarrrrrr.

My hands dropped everything.

The scream came from far away, but it was loud, nonetheless.

Mastodon shifted his gaze to the opening of the cave, not the least bit concerned. "That's why."

I dragged my body to the opposite wall and pulled my knees to my chest. The entrance of the cave was dark because there was no light outside, not even moonlight. The white snow disappeared after a couple feet, and the pines that were just outside were obscured in the darkness. "What was that?"

Mastodon ignored me.

"I need to know what I'm up against."

The corner of his mouth raised in a smile. "You're good, but you aren't that good."

"I'm no benefit to you dead, right? It's in your best interest to help me stay alive."

"What do you think I've been doing on every step of

this journey?" He turned his head to meet my look head on. "Do you think I like sharing my bed with the enemy? You think I like carrying you through the snow? You think I like looking at your face as I speak—when you have his eyes? If so much weren't at stake…I'd let you freeze to death."

"I'm not your enemy—"

"I am yours." His tone hardened like a block of ice. "Make no mistake."

————

WEARING the clothing I'd stolen from the cave, I didn't need Mastodon to carry me anymore. It was still freezing cold, but all the fur lining kept me warm enough to continue forward without slipping into a frozen coma.

We passed through endless trees and wilderness, and from what I could grasp, there were no villages or towns. No inhabitants. No farms. Nothing. It was just a wide expanse of uninhabitable wilderness.

I had no idea what our destination was or how long it would take us to get there, but I didn't bother to ask. I would just be met with Mastodon's stony silence.

I was a little more tense that day than I had been the night before because I knew *something* was out there. Something big. Something powerful. Something that could roar so loud I was surprised the sound didn't carry up the cliffs to my home.

Home…a place I probably wouldn't see again.

The snow started to become less frequent, and the piles along our path started to decrease in size. It was a bit warmer too, but not by much. I was relieved that the frozen tundra didn't last forever.

Our boots hit solid ground again, dark earth that I could dig the heel of my boot into. My pace matched theirs a lot easier now that I didn't have to maneuver through drifts of snow that came to my waist.

Farther we went, and just when the sun started to set, the trees began to thin and the glow of torches came into view. They were placed along a fence, a perimeter that blocked the settlement from view.

The journey was finally over.

I wasn't sure if I was relieved or terrified.

Guards covered in fur coats lined the top of the walls, armed with crossbows. Then the weapons were lowered to their sides because they obviously recognized Mastodon and the others. They gestured to the men below, and slowly, the doors started to creak open.

My deep breaths escaped as vapor and rose up my face, my heart beating so hard it hurt. This place was nothing like home, the beautiful castle that looked down the cobblestone pathways, the olive tree right outside my window.

When I lingered behind, Mastodon gave me a shove.

I responded on instinct and shoved him back. "Stop pushing me, jackass."

He didn't move because he possessed the weight of a

boulder, and he stared down at me like he didn't quite know what to make of me.

We passed through the doors, and slowly, they started to creak closed behind us.

I heard them shut—and lock into place.

I was never going home, was I?

I could tell Mastodon was an important guy because the guards immediately greeted him with fist-bumps and one-armed hugs. Others acknowledged his presence with a respectful dip of their heads.

Maybe he was their king.

But would a king leave his throne? Wouldn't he send someone else to do his dirty work? This was the man who took the rear instead of the lead…so maybe that assumption was wrong.

I watched his face change once he was home, the way his eyes lit up when he greeted his people, the way he would smile as he clapped them on the shoulder. One of his men came up with a cape lined with fur and sharp teeth and hooked it onto his shoulders, the beautiful and warm material trailing down his back. I could see people's reaction to him, awe mixed with affection, like he was unanimously loved by everyone there.

That affection was misplaced, in my opinion.

When his eyes were back on me, he was back to his old self.

An asshole.

"Come." He took the lead this time, his brother at his

side. The other three men dispersed elsewhere, their jobs complete.

I felt all eyes on me—along with their animosity.

I met their looks with my own, furious that I was judged for something I didn't do, for something my father didn't do. It was a mistake, and I knew that in my heart. But Mastodon was so focused on his revenge that he couldn't see straight.

I followed behind him, a bit warmer under the passing torches and within the enclosed area. The wind didn't make it past the walls, so it halted outside the perimeter. We passed through a sea of cabins that looked like shops and continued forward, approaching a stone mountain. There was an enormous door in the way, and as Mastodon approached, it swung open.

We seemed to be going underground…again.

When we stepped inside, I realized there was no ceiling. It was open to the elements, just warmer because of the solid rock that comprised the walls. The area was small, only big enough for a couple of buildings, and the rear had a dais with a throne made of stone.

On that throne sat a woman. With long dark hair, feathers in the strands, and bright blue eyes, she stared at Mastodon as he approached her. She wore a black fur coat with dark leggings and knee-high boots. She wasn't in a gown like Queen Rutherford, but her presence was undeniably regal.

At once, both Mastodon and Ian lowered to the ground—and kneeled.

Mastodon didn't look like a man who kneeled for anybody, so that was quite the surprise.

Both men rose and stepped away to regard me.

I slowly came forward, examining the woman who watched me with her shrewd stare. She was decades older than me, could easily be my mother, but her beauty was undeniable. Even when she looked at me like I was nothing but an insect to her, she possessed an unattainable grace while doing it.

The stare seemed to last an eternity. Unblinking. Chilling. Aggressive. It slowly started to harden, to turn angry the way Mastodon's did. "I am Queen Rolfe." She made a slight gesture with her head, her eyes moving to the ground directly before me. "Kneel."

I probably would have given a bow in respect automatically, but once it was a command, I became defiant. I could feel the animosity flow from her in waves, like the rising tide at the shore. She shared Mastodon's prejudice, clearly.

Her eyes narrowed before she raised her voice. "I told you to kneel."

I stayed on my two feet. "I've been kidnapped from my home and thrown around like a rag doll. I'm not exactly in the mood to kneel."

Mastodon turned to regard me, his eyes in disbelief.

The queen's hands curled over the edge of the armrests, and her blue eyes turned to icicles. "Huntley."

My eyes glanced around me, wondering if that was her private guard or an executioner.

Mastodon turned to me, his jaw tight in annoyance.

I met his look—and then it became clear.

He grabbed me by the shoulder and forced me, pushing down on me with a kind of strength I couldn't challenge. It was the weight of the entire sky, all on my shoulders.

I cursed under my breath then felt my knees hit the earth with a thud.

Huntley remained in front of me, his hand still on my shoulder. "My hatred doesn't compare to hers, so I suggest you keep your mouth shut if you like your head on your shoulders." He withdrew, the place where he'd touched me turning ice-cold the instant he was gone.

I took his advice and stayed in place.

The daggers in her eyes didn't sheathe. They remained blunt and sharp at the same time, as if they could cut my flesh wide open and smash my skull. The fingers of her left hand slowly started to drum, a gentle tapping that was amplified by the rock wall that surrounded us. "Good job, Huntley. You were gone too long, but it was a worthy sacrifice."

My eyes shifted to Huntley, the betrayal even deeper. He'd infiltrated my kingdom, fooled everyone, and if someone had listened to me…this all could have been avoided. He'd dragged me from my home, and now I awaited my fate.

There wasn't a hint of apology in his gaze—just more anger.

Could these people really hate me that much? "You're

making a mistake. King Rutherford will send out his cavalry until he finds me. Then he'll slaughter you all. Return me, and I'll make sure you're spared."

Her head cocked slightly, in a sickening way, as if there should be a crack in her vertebrae, only there wasn't. "Your king will never show his face at the bottom of the cliffs. I wish he would, for I would relish the opportunity to stab him in the heart then eat it clean off my sword."

That was a pretty picture.

"No one is coming for you, child."

"I'm not a child."

"It seems to me you are," she said quietly. "Thinking that knights in shiny armor are going to come to your rescue. Waiting and hoping that men will do right by you and risk their necks for you. That the Duke of Delacroix will get off his ass to save his kin." With her head tilted, she continued to stare. "Child, you can't wait for a man to rescue you. They're selfish. They're cowards. You're all you have in this world. Figure it out yourself—or perish."

"Then I'll kill you. How about that?"

She smirked, amused. "What a pity. I might actually like you…if I didn't want you dead."

"If you see me as a child, you should let me go."

She stared as if she didn't hear me.

"An innocent child—"

"You have his eyes."

The breath halted in my chest.

"I'll never forget those eyes," she said in a faraway voice. "Take her away."

Huntley grabbed me by the arm and forced me up.

I twisted out of his grasp. "I can get up, asshole."

He gestured in the direction from which we'd come.

I walked off, turning my back on the queen and her men.

Her voice followed me. "Return when you're finished, Huntley. We have much to discuss."

———

WORD HAD SPREAD like wildfire in the town square. I could tell by the way they stared at me as I passed, as if they knew exactly who I was. Huntley had left home to retrieve me, and they had been waiting for this moment until he returned.

I glanced back and forth around me, seeing men and women in wool breeches and thick coats. There were children too, but they stayed behind their parents.

Huntley remained behind me, and I continued to move forward even though I had no idea where I was going. Cabins were on either side, constructed out of wood, torches on the outside of each one of them.

"Here."

I stopped at the command of his deep voice.

It was in front of a cabin, a cabin that looked different from the others because it had no windows. I assumed it was a prison. At least it would be warm, with four walls and a roof. I hadn't slept well once on this journey, and I was so exhausted that I just wanted to go to sleep rather than try to flee.

Huntley unlocked the door then pushed it open.

Instead of crossing the threshold, I stared at him. His eyes were heartless. Empty. Devoid of everything.

"I warned you not to fuck with me. Now I'm warning you not to fuck with Queen Rolfe. You'll regret it, I promise you."

"You're threatening me?"

"Was that not clear?" His eyes narrowed.

"What the fuck is wrong with you people? This is how you handle vengeance? With the blood of the innocent? Punish the person responsible for your misfortune—"

"And I will. That's a promise." He grabbed me by the arm to shove me.

I evaded it by stepping into the cabin. "I'm not a dog. You don't need to—"

He shut the door in my face—then locked it.

SIX

Huntley

I RETURNED THE WAY I'D COME, PASSING BETWEEN THE LIT torches and ignoring the stares from the shadows. The sun had set, and the cold settled in. Everyone at the outpost would be inside having dinner with their families, but my return had shaken that normalcy.

I passed through the stone doorway and entered the cocoon of the rock, a large fire in the very center that cast off enough heat to rival the sun. I halted in front of the fire to stare at it, to watch the way the flames licked the dry wood. I was tired, far more tired than I let on, and my mind just needed a few seconds to feel nothing.

Feel nothing instead of rage. Instead of revenge. Instead of pain.

I tore my gaze away and continued to the large cabin that housed the queen. She waited for me at the long dining table, a fire in the stone hearth, the table laid out with a rack of lamb, potatoes, and a loaf of fresh bread that had just come out of the fire.

She looked at me from her seat at the table, her previous animosity absent like it'd never been there at all. Her eyes gave a squeeze, a tiny burst of emotion, something that often happened when she looked at me.

She rose out of her seat and came to me, a foot shorter in height but a mountain taller in presence. Both hands moved to my cheeks and cupped them as she admired my face, as her eyes shifted back and forth to take a good look at me. "My boy."

My eyes dropped when the look became too much.

Her thumb brushed over my cheek lovingly before she withdrew her hands. The warmth in her eyes froze over, and her posture stiffened to steel. Queen Rolfe returned, the no-nonsense ruler who had kept us alive these past decades. "Eat. You must be hungry."

We sat down together, and once the food was on my plate, I ate with my elbows on the table, devouring everything in silence, appreciating the taste of fresh meat instead of the stale bread and jerky that had sustained us on the long journey home. There was ale too, and while that wasn't as good as the scotch in my canteen, it still made my stomach warm.

"Our *guest* is comfortable?"

"Yes." With my eyes on my food, I continued to eat.

"Cameron will be her guard."

"Not Cameron."

"Why not?"

"Someone stronger."

"Are you telling me that little thing is actually a threat?" She brought her glass of ale to her lips and took a drink. There was food on her plate, but it was mostly untouched.

"She's good with the sword and bow."

"Is that why you have that scar on your neck?"

I nodded as I chewed.

She took another drink. "Little cunt, isn't she?"

"She only did what I would have done."

"Well, she doesn't have a sword or bow, so she's useless."

I'd noticed she had no experience with hand-to-hand combat. The second her weapons were stripped away, she didn't know what to do. That was something her father had failed to teach her—and that was a mistake.

"Cameron will be suitable."

I didn't make another objection. As the food entered my belly, I felt better, felt satisfied for the first time in over a week. It heated me from the inside out, cleansed me of all the rage I had to keep back in my throat.

"That's where she'll remain until you're ready. Unless…anyone wants to play."

She was out of my mind the second she was gone from my sight. She wasn't my problem anymore—for the moment.

"She's a pretty thing…despite her eyes."

I took a drink.

"That'll make it hurt him more."

"She was on her way to the Capital when I took her."

"Probably to woo the prince into marriage. That plan will be sabotaged…along with all his other plans."

The plate was wiped clean, and I was satisfied but still hungry.

"Eat. You think this is all for me?"

"Ian?"

"He was more interested in fucking his whore than a family dinner." Her hand rested on the top of her glass, and she traced her finger around the edge, her eyes watching her movements. "I take no offense. He's a man, after all."

I ate another few lamb chops and bit into the bread smothered with butter.

She turned quiet, staring off in the distance, letting me eat without distraction. Sometimes she drank her ale, and sometimes she traced her finger, her thoughts elsewhere.

After a second serving, I was finished, my tired eyes on the fire in the hearth.

The silence continued until she broke it. "How did it feel?"

It was a vague question, but I understood her meaning perfectly. "Haunting. She occupies my old bedroom. Now it's full of white curtains and linens, dressers with gold trimming, crystal vases of flowers everywhere. It feels the same—but looks different. There's still an old bloodstain in the corner from when I cut myself after training with Father, and an old slice in the wood from the edge of my sword."

She listened, her fingers still on the rim of her glass.

"The guards move about the castle in the same way, with the same rotations, like nothing has changed. Faron occupies Father's old study, and instead of spending time with his two children, he drowns himself in whores and wine."

She turned toward me, watching me with her shrewd eyes. "Our people?"

I gave a slight shake of my head. "Everything looks normal on the surface, but it's far from normal. They're plucked left and right, their families threatened into silence, and they disappear in the night without a trace. It's an open secret—fully known but never spoken."

"And they do nothing?" she asked in disgust.

"What are they supposed to do, Mother?"

"Fight back," she said quietly. "Always."

"Not everyone is as courageous as you—"

"They should be." She took another drink. "If you won't fight for yourself, fight for those you love."

In comfortable silence, we stared at the fire, watching the flames rise then fall in its unpredictable dance. "I told her what her father has done, and she doesn't believe me. Says I'm mistaken."

She slowly turned her head to me.

"I believe her."

"Does he have the scars, Huntley?"

"Yes."

"Then I'm not mistaken." She turned back to the fire.

"I believe that she believes in his innocence. She's a

smart woman, but she's blinded by love. Doesn't see that her father chooses to spend his nights with women he won't remember the next morning instead of spending time with her. Doesn't see that he uses both her and her brother as pawns in the game he's playing. Doesn't see the men and women disappear in the night. And I believe she has no idea what she really is—and what I am."

"Huntley?"

Her voice was like a hook under my jaw, and it slowly pulled my face back to hers.

"Don't pity her."

I stared.

"Because he didn't pity me. He didn't pity you or your brother. With a merciless sneer, he took everything from us —and then laughed."

I held her gaze, remembering her limp body on the bed and the way he'd thrust into her with his breeches around his knees, the way he'd thrown her over the edge of the cliff once he was finished. I remembered it all…like it was yesterday.

"Remember when you were a boy and I told you not to get attached to the pigs?"

I held my silence.

"They ended up as bacon on Christmas morning. And the same will happen to her."

———

I PASSED BETWEEN THE CABINS, the cold hitting me in the bones deeper than it had just an hour ago because it had settled in the soil now. It was quiet out, everyone returned to their cabins because the show was over.

I let myself into my cabin…and knew I wasn't alone.

The bed in the corner was occupied—by a blonde and a brunette.

Buck naked and tucked under the heavy throws on my bed, they propped themselves up on their elbows and looked at me expectantly.

I recognized them both, from different occasions. "Leave. I'm fucking tired." I unclasped my fur cloak and tossed it over the armchair by the fireplace, which was lit with a quiet fire.

"Come on, Huntley." The brunette, whose name I couldn't remember because I was too tired to think in that moment, pushed the blankets down so I could get into bed with them, her tits on display.

"I said, I'm tired."

"I'll give you a back massage," the blonde said. "My fingers like your strong back."

"Besides," the brunette said. "We've already been paid in full for the night. Shouldn't let that go to waste…"

Ian. I didn't need my brother to buy my whores, not when I could buy my own, and not when I could get laid for free.

The blonde kicked the sheets down farther. "Come on, we're cold."

They didn't look cold, not the way Ivory did when

she'd nearly died a couple times. Her cheeks had been pale, her lips blue. All of her blood was close to her heart, keeping her organs alive and warm. She'd looked nothing like the two of them, not even when she'd shared my bedroll on the floor of the cave. "Alright. Move over."

———

IT WAS SOMETIME before dawn when the bells rang.

I jolted up in bed, eyes wide open, knowing exactly what that alarm meant.

I was out of bed and dressed within seconds, my swords in my belt, my shield and ax over my back. I was out the front door and into the darkness of early morning, the cold biting my skin the second I came into contact with it. My eyes swept over the wall, looking for the position of the guards.

None were there.

People came out of their homes to see the commotion, most of the men armed with the weapons they kept in their cabins.

Ian stumbled out of his cabin, shirtless and visibly drunk.

"Here!"

I followed the voice behind my cabin and jogged up the road.

I'd already figured out exactly what had transpired before I made it to the cabin.

Cameron was dead on the ground, a small dagger

lodged in his throat. The door to the cabin was wide open, and the tray of food was spilled over the ground. The prisoner was nowhere to be seen.

I checked Cameron's belt and discovered that his sword and bow were missing. "Fuck." I checked his body for vitality, and when I felt his frozen skin, I knew he'd been dead a while. For hours. When the dawn shift had started, he was discovered.

That meant she had a head start—a big one.

"Huntley." Mother's strong voice came from behind me, low and controlled, not high-pitched with panic like everyone else.

I turned around to regard her, knowing how pissed off she was about to be.

She surveyed the scene with intelligent eyes, deducing exactly what had happened without having to ask questions. "Bring her back, Huntley. If she's going to die, it'll be by my hands—no one else's."

SEVEN

Ivory
_____

I couldn't believe I did it.

I actually got away.

I had to kill two guys along the way, but I didn't have any other choice. Queen Rolfe and Huntley made it very clear they wouldn't show me mercy, so I couldn't do that either. North was the direction from which I came, so I just had to head that way. When I found snow, I knew I was on the right path.

But with snow, there were tracks.

Huntley would come after me. He would know exactly where I was headed. He would follow these tracks and be close on my tail.

So, the only way I would be successful was if I outran him.

Or…kill him when he caught up to me. That didn't go over well last time, but if I caught him off guard, it might be different.

When I'd killed the guard, I'd taken as much of the food as I could before I ran off, so my stomach had been full at that time, but without more nourishment, I wouldn't make it far. If I found the cave where we'd rested, I could raid the storage and keep going. That was the goal... I just had to find it.

I ran for hours in the dark, using the reflection of the moon on the snow through the trees to guide my direction. The sun eventually peeked over the horizon and lit up the sky in the colors of sunrise. It was much easier to see, but if it was easier for me, it was also easier for him.

I fought to run as long as I possibly could, but my body grew too fatigued, especially with the weight of the weapons I carried. I would walk then run, alternating between the two so I could move forward at a decent pace.

I was under the cover of the trees when I heard it.

A whistle.

It made my blood go cold because I recognized what it was.

A signal.

Huntley had made the same whistle to his brother and the others once my guards had been killed. I didn't know what else to do besides hug the trunk and hope I wasn't seen. It was dark under the canopy of the trees because the limited light struggled to penetrate the branches and the snow. My breath escaped as clouds of vapor, so I tried to slow my breathing as much as possible to keep from giving myself away.

Boots crunched against the snow.

My hand went to the hilt of my sword and gripped it.

"Maybe it was just a vision. A vision of the most beautiful woman I've ever seen—running through the woods." The voice wasn't deep like Huntley's, but it was far more formidable because of the way it sounded…unhuman. "Spike, was that a dream? Or did you see it too?"

A voice far deeper than Huntley's spoke. "Yes."

Fuck. They knew exactly where I was, and they were toying with me.

"No need to be afraid, darling," the first one said. "Come out. Show us your beautiful face."

Huntley had been my biggest fear. But I'd forgotten that other people were out here. Or…other things.

I stepped out and turned in the direction of the voices. My face was hard, my eyes fearless, and I had to keep it that way even though my heart gave a jolt at the sight of them. They were both men, dressed in all black with matching gloves, swords at their hips. But their faces…I'd never seen anything like it.

Too many teeth crowded their mouths, so they protruded past their lips, looking more like fangs than teeth. It was almost as if their mouths were outside their bodies. I didn't know how they chewed. How they even spoke.

I did my best to act unsurprised, as if I'd encountered their kind many times.

The leader halted feet away from me, and with dark eyes the color of bark, he looked me over. He didn't size me up as an opponent. He sized me up…in a very different way. An intimate way. In a way that was only welcome with my explicit permission.

Spike stayed behind him, and farther back were four more, all with the same jaws.

My hand held on to the hilt for dear life. There was no doubt I'd have to draw it and fight for my life. I'd have to behead them before their teeth could pierce my flesh. Just one bite…that was all it would take to make me bleed to death, to be past the help of any healer.

He suddenly pulled his teeth back into his mouth, his mouth opening wide so he could swallow the teeth back into his throat. They must have interlocked perfectly, never perforating the inside of his cavity, spaced out just enough to let his breath pass through to his lungs. "I didn't mean to frighten you."

"You didn't."

"Really?" His hand glanced down to my blade. "Because you seem frightened right now."

"Or just annoyed." I freed my blade from the sheath and held it at the ready, to prove that I knew how to use it, that I wasn't easy prey like a bunny in the snow. "My presence is required elsewhere. Don't impede my journey."

As if I'd said something funny, he grinned. "Where is your presence required? The place from where you just fled?" He stepped forward, and just as he did, Spike and the others did too. "I recognize a runaway when I see one."

Six-to-one. Those weren't good odds.

He drew closer, but I didn't step back. "You flee from Queen Rolfe. Why?"

"I didn't flee. She's sent me on a very important mission—"

"I know who she sends, and you aren't one of them."

"My business is none of your concern. Now, step off."

He grinned, giving me a glimpse of the teeth he'd just withdrawn. "Feisty."

"I wish to part in peace—not bloodshed."

"*Bloodshed*." He spoke the word like he savored it.

Shit. "Queen Rolfe is not to be angered. And she will be angry when I don't return."

"That was the risk she took when she sent you out here. You know that." He took another step. "Or do you?"

I held my sword steady.

"You dress like a Rune. But you aren't one."

Rune? I had no idea what that even was.

"You don't look like one. You don't speak like one. But where you are from…" He inched closer, taking his time as if I wouldn't notice. "That I don't know." Now, he moved quicker, withdrawing his sword at the same time.

Here we go.

He spun then brought down his sword with all his strength, as if he expected a clean slice through my arm.

I sidestepped the blow then blocked it before I returned his attack with my own. The steel rang when it collided with his. I kicked him back and continued my assault, doing my best to overpower him before he learned not to underestimate me.

He parried blow after blow, but he did have to back up, and that was satisfying.

He lowered his blade as he retreated slightly, his dark eyes wide with undeniable surprise. "Now you're even more lovely." He gestured to Spike behind him.

I could handle one good swordsman, but not two.

Spike withdrew his blade as he marched toward me.

I had to kill one of them. Fast.

A dagger flew through the air—and impaled Spike right in the neck.

Blood stained his teeth before it dribbled over his lips to the snow at his feet. He fell to his knees as he reached for the dagger deep in his flesh.

A cloak of fur and fangs came into view. "Leave, Klaus."

Klaus lowered his blade to his side. "How romantic. His Highness comes to his damsel's rescue."

"You couldn't land a single hit," I snarled. "I'm no damsel—"

"Silence." Huntley kept his gaze on Klaus, the leader of this gang of…whatever they were. "I told you to leave."

"This is neither my land nor yours," Klaus said. "Each of us has every right to be here."

"But you don't have the right to attack my people." Huntley's broad shoulders were hidden underneath the cloak as it rose slightly in the frozen wind. A glimpse of his sheathed sword was visible on his hip, and his back held a shield and a large ax.

"She's not your people. I know the scent of a Rune,

and she doesn't have it." His eyes flicked past Huntley to look at me.

Huntley sidestepped, blocking Klaus's view of me once again.

"So, what is she?"

Huntley ignored the question. "Walk away, Klaus."

"I don't think I can now…not when I'm this invested."

Silence hung in the air, heavy silence, silence filled with lethal tension.

When Huntley reached for his ax, I knew how this was going to end.

Huntley swung for Klaus, and they became locked in battle. Spike was still on the ground, and he slowly removed the dagger from his neck and made more blood spill onto the snow.

Two rushed for Huntley, and he battled three foes all at once.

The others came for me, teeth protruding out of their mouths.

"Oh, this is going to be fun."

I had time, so I sheathed my sword and withdrew my bow. I nocked two arrows to the string, held my breath as I aimed, and fired. The first pierced one right in the neck, making him fall to his knees just like his comrade. Another flew from the string and pierced the closest one in the thigh.

That didn't slow him down at all.

My sword was back in my hand, and I blocked the blade aimed for my torso. I barely had any energy, but I mustered it from somewhere and struck back, making him trip on the snow and fall back.

That gave me a moment to address the other, who had risen, to strike his sword up and down, push him back to find an opening. If I could defeat him, I could run for it while Huntley was engaged with the others.

It would be my only opportunity to get away.

My attacker was too fast, met my blade as if he knew where it would be in just a moment. My energy was draining, the other guy was getting back to his feet, and I was running out of time.

So I did the first thing that came to mind.

I spat in his face.

He winced when the warm saliva hit him right in the eyes, blinding him momentarily.

I stabbed my knife into his gut then kicked him off.

The other grabbed his sword from the ground and rose to meet me.

But I was faster.

I slammed my sword down into his neck, deep into his chest cavity, and killed him instantly.

Huntley was still engaged, taking on Klaus and the other two. They surrounded him in a circle, and he managed to turn and meet the blows of each one before kicking them away. He moved so fast, faster than I could really see.

I'd never seen anyone fight like that.

I sheathed my sword and heard one of the guys scream.

I looked back, seeing that Huntley had narrowed it down to just two men.

I took off at a run, heading in the direction of the cave that wound up the cliff. Whoever remained the victor, I would have enough time to get inside and possibly block the opening. If Klaus was the victor, he probably wouldn't even know where to find me.

Hopefully Huntley died. He would probably run out of energy first, taking on multiple experienced swordsmen at once. I would return to the castle, report everything that had happened to my father, and this whole thing would feel like a bad dream.

"Ah!"

The scream echoed against the falling snow, made the trees vibrate with the sound. It made me halt because I knew it belonged to Huntley. I'd heard it enough on my travels, heard that rough depth of his voice day in and day out.

I looked at the trees in front of me, the piles of snow, the way back home.

But I didn't move.

Girl, don't be stupid.

Leave him.

Home. Father. Ryker.

I gritted my teeth before I turned around. I sprinted back, following my own footprints, and saw the battle come into view.

Huntley had a dagger protruding out of his side, the blood striking against his fur clothing, and he struggled to keep up the fight, barely parrying the blades that came for him. He nearly missed the next one, too weak to keep going.

Klaus grinned as he spun his sword around with his wrist. "I don't normally eat your kind. But I'll enjoy sucking the marrow out of your bones." He launched his sword, overpowering Huntley's and making it drop into the snow. "But don't worry. I'll be sure to return whatever's left to your queen—"

The arrow pierced his neck, and he stumbled back.

The distraction was enough to make the other pause the fight.

I trained my bow on him next—and struck him in the shoulder.

He rushed me, his razor-sharp teeth coming right for me.

I met his sword with my own, and we engaged in a flurry of attacks that were nearly beyond my skills. But it became instinct, my focus just as sharp as his teeth. I didn't come this close to home just to lose at the final stretch, and I wasn't letting this motherfucker take me down.

I could never get an opening because he was too fast. I was on the defensive the entire time, blocking every hit but doing no damage myself. My only chance was a distraction. I could spit on him again.

But I didn't have to, because Huntley's ax cut him down.

The guy collapsed to the snow in front of me. Klaus had vanished.

Huntley stood in front of me, out of breath, blood dripping to the snow from his wound. "You came back."

Still couldn't believe it. "Yeah…"

His eyes pierced mine, intense like usual, but without the all-consuming hatred.

"What…what are those things?"

"The Teeth."

It was nice to get an answer to a question for once. "When I said the word blood lust…the guy looked like he exploded in his breeches."

"That's what they eat. Blood. The purer, the better."

"And I'm guessing mine looks pretty pure?"

"I think they were interested in you for other reasons." His hand went to the dagger, and he prepared to yank it out.

"Whoa, hold on. If you pull that out, you'll bleed to death—"

He yanked it out with a grunt, revealing a black dagger coated with shiny blood. He let it fall to the snow. "I heal quickly."

"Not quickly enough."

His pale skin slowly started to flush, like the blood was returning to the places where he needed it most.

"How…how did you do that?"

"I told you. I heal quickly."

It was the first time I'd spoken to him as a man—not my kidnapper, not the asshole who would throw me down if I talked too much. "If you're feeling up to it, escort me to the entrance to the cave. I can find it on my own, but it'll probably take me much longer alone."

His intense gaze remained fixated on me, his blue eyes still as he absorbed my appearance.

I guess that was my answer. "Alright, then." I turned away, headed north.

"You're coming back with me." His deep voice wasn't full of unbridled anger anymore, but it did possess the kind of command that Father could never replicate.

I stilled and slowly turned around. "You're joking, right?"

He stared me down.

"If I hadn't come back, you'd be dead. You know that, right?"

His chest rose and fell with his breaths, his eyes so focused they didn't blink.

"Tell me that you know that—"

"If I hadn't come after you, you would have been raped by every single one of them—and then eaten."

"But you didn't come to save me. You came so you could have the honor of killing me yourself. That's not the same thing, and don't tell me you're too barbaric to understand the difference."

His hard stare ensued.

I shook my head, feeling like a goddamn idiot. "I told myself to leave you…told myself it would be a mistake not to—"

"Then you should have listened."

"Wow…" I shook my head in disbelief. "That's the kind of man you are?"

"Just like your father."

I was tempted to grab my sword, to fight to the death because I'd rather die out here than go back there. "No, you aren't. If your only purpose is to emulate the person that you hate, then they've won. They haven't just taken your past, but your present and your future. They've taken your identity. You're better than that. And if you aren't… you should want to be better than that."

His blue eyes were motionless as he listened to my speech, giving nothing away, not a single thought. His ax was still in his hand, the edge of the blade still dripping with droplets of blood from his final foe. "Why did you save me?"

My body's automatic reaction was to take a breath because the question was so perverse on my ears. I'd taken a gamble—and made the wrong bet. Now I had to pay the price for my foolishness. "I…I don't know."

"You don't know why you forfeited your escape? You don't know why you risked your life fighting the Teeth to save me? Such an act of bravery…and without a reason?"

"There is a reason… I just don't know what it is."

His stare darkened, like that was unacceptable to him.

"I guess it's because…I can tell you're a good man. Not to me. But I think you would be…if you didn't consider me your enemy."

A gust of wind passed through us and ruffled his short hair slightly. His cloak billowed in the wind. But the rest of him was immobile, like a mountain. Throughout our travels, the shadow on his face had darkened, getting deeper and thicker, becoming a beard. But it was gone because he must have shaved once he went to his cabin. Whether he had a beard or not, his appearance was terrifying, his features so hard—except for his eyes.

"I really am sorry about what happened to you."

His jaw tightened slightly, as if that just made him angry.

"I'm gonna go now…" I turned around and began my trek.

When he didn't say anything, I assumed I was home free.

But then his voice followed me. "I can't let you go."

My boots halted in the snow, smashing it down and compacting it under my feet. My eyes stung from the cold, and I could feel how dry my nose had become just from being out there for a couple hours. My frozen heart sank into my stomach, thinking about how worried Ryker would be, how terrified my father must be. They would never know what happened to me. They would never know how I was killed…if I was raped…if I suffered.

I turned around and pulled my sword from the scabbard.

His eyes didn't glance down at me. "I won't kill you, but I still need your help."

"Why should I help you?"

"Doesn't seem like you need a reason to do much of anything."

I gave him a blank stare. Was that a joke? I couldn't tell with this guy. He was so rough around the edges, rough to his very core.

"You spared my life, so I will spare yours. But you don't get a choice in this."

"If I help you—"

"There is no *if*. You will help me."

"Fine. *After* I help you, will you let me go?"

His answer was a hard stare.

"I asked you a question—"

Rooooooaaaaaaaaaaaarrrrrr.

My sword dropped to my side as I listened to the sound carry across the entire world, shaking the snow off the trees, making the ground unstable beneath our feet. It carried like it possessed its own energy to keep going and going.

He hooked his ax over his back and walked past me. "Come on. We have to go."

I looked past the spot where he'd just stood, as if I would see a monster emerge in my vision. "Is it coming this way?"

"Do you want to stay and find out?"

EIGHT

Ivory

————

WE RAN TO THE CAVE THAT WE HAD STOPPED IN ON THE way, the very one where I'd first heard that mighty roar. The entrance was a small crevasse that you had to squeeze past, and then the cave opened up to accommodate several people.

I eyed the firewood but didn't bother.

Huntley took a seat on a stool near the entrance to the cave, peering through the crack to the snow-covered trees outside. With his arms on his knees, he stared, looking through the falling snow and to the wilderness beyond.

I leaned against the wall, my knees against my chest. "How long do we have to hide?"

He gave a subtle shake of his head, his eyes still outside.

"What is it?"

"Yeti."

I allowed myself a couple seconds to process the word. "Yeti?"

He was motionless, his eyes focused.

"What the hell is a yeti?"

"A beast that stands nine feet tall, with claws as sharp as swords, with fur that perfectly blends into the snowy landscape so you may not even notice them right in front of you. It's happened to me a couple of times…"

"So…it's like a bear?"

He turned to me, his eyes cold.

"Can't we just shoot it with an arrow?"

Like it was a stupid question, he looked away. "If they were easy to kill, I wouldn't be hiding in a cave—with you."

"I guess I'd have to see it to understand."

"Trust me, you better hope that never happens."

"Have you ever killed one?"

"Several."

"Then why are you afraid?"

"Afraid?" He turned back to me. "What you mean is, why am I not careless, like you? It takes at least twelve strong men to take down a yeti. I have nothing to prove to anyone, so I'm not going to try to do it alone."

"Well, you'd have me."

"Same thing as doing it alone."

"Excuse me?"

He ignored me.

"I saved your ass back there. Still haven't gotten a thank-you for that, by the way."

He continued to stare outside.

"You know I'm good."

"You could be better."

"Really?" I challenged. "How?"

"You're useless without a weapon. What happens when an enemy knocks your sword out of your grasp?"

"I pick it up."

"And if you can't?" he challenged. "You can't even throw a punch."

"Wanna bet?" My fingers tightened into a fist.

He glanced at me, chuckled, and looked outside.

"What?"

"You're doing it wrong."

"No, I'm not." I examined my fingers, the way they were tightly clenched into the center of my palm.

"You'll break your thumb on the first swing."

I looked at my hands again and pulled out my thumb. "Oh…"

"Your father taught you everything else—but failed in this regard."

"Probably because I have no chance against a guy twice my size with just my hands…"

His eyes shifted back to me. "That's a terrible thing to teach your daughter. Especially since it's not true."

"I never said it was."

"The stronger fighter doesn't necessarily win. You know which fighter does?"

I shook my head.

"The smarter one."

"Like…spitting in the eye of your foe so they can't see?"

A very subtle smile moved on to his lips. "I wondered how you prevailed in that fight."

"My first time with two guys. It was a success."

His grin widened.

I rolled my eyes, understanding exactly where his thoughts ventured. "Not how I meant it…"

"As in, you have been with two guys at once? Quinn didn't slip past my watch, but the other did?"

"That's a personal question."

"Just asking for clarification."

"You better not have reported him."

He focused on the outside once more. "I don't give a fuck who you fuck."

"I don't know… You seem so intent on making my life a living hell. Reporting my lover and getting him executed is a pretty good way to do that."

He straightened on the stool and regarded me. "You love him?"

"No."

"But you care about him?"

"Of course. You don't care about the women you take to bed?"

He shook his head. "Not really."

"Damn, that's cold."

"Most of them are whores."

"Wow…you're a dick."

He gave an irritated sigh. "I mean that literally."

"Oh…"

We fell into a long bout of silence, my ass frozen on the ground of the cave. My stomach was rumbling, and I eyed the storage containers in the cave. Since we were stuck there, I decided to help myself, finding a container of assorted dried fruit and meat, along with some nuts. I returned to my seat and stuffed my mouth, feeling the satisfaction of food in my stomach almost instantly. "How do you want me to help you?"

He ignored me.

"I thought we were past this—"

He pressed his forefinger to his lips, signaling me to shut my mouth.

My eyes shifted to the crevasse, but I didn't see anything.

Was there actually something there, or did he just want me to shut up? I reached my hand inside, shoved the food into my mouth, and dropped a couple pieces to the ground. It was enough to make an echo, and the look Huntley gave me was vicious.

Then I heard it—the heavy breaths.

Heavy breaths that weren't coming from either one of us.

My eyes looked through the crack, and then I saw it, the movement.

White fur moved past my vision, looking like snow except that it was in motion. It took seconds for it to leave the crevasse—and that was when I knew how big it was.

Massive.

———

HOURS HAD PASSED since the yeti made its subtle appearance in the crack, and we didn't exchange a single word of conversation in that time. The sun came and went, and now it was getting dark.

Once the sun was gone, the shivers set in. "Are we going to stay here all night?"

"It'd be stupid to head back in the dark."

"Won't your brother worry? Will he come search for you?"

"The only reason I wouldn't return is because I'm dead, so there's no point." His eyes remained on the crevasse. "The yeti could be waiting for us to make our move. We should wait overnight, to make sure he's moved on."

"This place…is a wasteland." My life on top of the cliffs was different, and not just because I lived in the castle as one of the royals. There were no monsters that swept across our kingdom, no Teeth, Runes, or yetis.

He regarded me with the coldest look I'd ever seen.

"I don't mean that offensively…"

"It is a wasteland—and it's home to a lot of unfortu-nate people." He returned the stool to the wall and grabbed a bedroll from the crate. He rolled it out and tossed a pillow where his head would go.

With chattering teeth, I grabbed my own and rolled it out beside him.

His weapons were placed on the ground beside him—

as if he could trust that I wouldn't slit his throat in the middle of the night.

I did the same and tried to get comfortable under the thin blanket. I wasn't warm like I was when I slept next to his hot, naked body, but at least I wouldn't die overnight from hypothermia. "If he's not watching the cave, can't we light a fire?"

"No."

"Why not?"

"You never know who's watching." He lay beside me, on his back with his face to the ceiling.

"There could be people out there? In the middle of the night?"

"People. Things." My chattering teeth must have annoyed him because he took his cloak and tossed it on top of me. It was thick and heavy, and immediately trapped my body heat in place so it couldn't go anywhere.

"Thanks."

He stayed quiet.

I could hear the wind blowing outside, listen to it shriek as the temperature dropped. "Does it always snow here?"

"Yes."

"Why?"

"The climate."

"Who else lives down here?"

"Lots of people. There are different kingdoms, all independent of one another."

"Really? Why aren't you under one sovereign?"

"Because we choose not to be."

"Are there wars? Does one kingdom try to conquer another?"

"No."

"Why?"

"Because if we're fighting one another, we can't fight Necrosis."

"Necrosis?"

He gave a quiet sigh. "You really don't know anything, do you?"

"Know anything about what?"

"Necrosis is the kingdom at the southernmost tip of this continent. They're people like you and me. Or at least they were. Their immortality is conditional. Unless they feed, they'll fade to dust. Blood used to be enough, but when that stopped working, they had to find an alternate fuel source."

"Blood... Are they like the Teeth?"

"Necrosis are the originals. The Teeth are hybrids, part Necrosis and part human."

I tried to reconcile all that information but couldn't. "What's the alternate food source?"

"Souls."

My blood ran cold because that was worse than being sucked dry. You didn't just forfeit your life, but the afterlife as well. I turned my head and regarded him beside me, seeing the way he lay there with his calm breathing and indifferent expression.

"You can tell when they need to feed because parts of

their body will start to decompose. Their hand will turn black. Half of their face will look desiccated. When their food storages run low…they invade our lands."

"Fuck…"

One hand rested on his chest, while the other supported his head. "They could annihilate us, but they don't, because they need to keep us alive—until they need to feed again."

Numb. That was the best way to describe how I felt. "Can they be killed?"

"Yes. When they're weak."

"So, when they're hungry."

"Yes. When they're strong…it's much more difficult."

"How long has this been going on?"

"Forever. Long before my time."

"If you'd told me this in the castle, I wouldn't have believed you. Not when it's not in the books in the library. Not when my father never mentioned it. Not when there's never been any evidence to support such a barbaric existence at the bottom of the cliffs…"

He stared at the ceiling.

"Why doesn't everyone take the tunnel to the top of the cliffs? I don't know how many people there are, but I'm sure there's room for everyone."

He slowly turned his head back to me, his eyes open but lifeless. "And what happens when we aren't there to feed on?"

My heart sank.

"They will make it to the top of the cliff—and eat you instead."

His words were an attack on my entire system, everything going into panic mode.

"Your king has us right where he wants us. We're the barrier that stops them from invading your lands. We're the food source that keeps them satiated so they go no further. We sacrifice our lives and afterlives so you don't have to."

All I could do was breathe—in and out.

He studied me, examining every reaction on my face.

My natural instinct was to fight, to fight against anything I disagreed with, but the words remained tucked in my mouth. My entire life, I'd been told that no one had ever been to the bottom of the cliffs, that no one knew if it was land or sea. But in reality…it was an offering of souls. Sacrilege. "If we combine our forces, perhaps we could defeat them—"

"Never going to happen. At least not voluntarily."

Breathe. In and out. In and out. "Does…my father know this?"

He turned back to the ceiling.

That was my answer. "Ryker?"

Silence.

"I can't believe he never told me…"

"Your father has him under his thumb pretty good."

"My family knows Necrosis wants to destroy us all and that people are suffering, and they…do nothing?"

"More than that." He turned back to me. "The lottery

you offer? For a family to have land in the Capital? That's a lie."

"What do you mean?"

"It's just a cover-up. The families selected don't end up at the Capital. They end up here—at the bottom of the cliffs."

"What…?" I couldn't believe it. Just couldn't.

"Yes."

"No… My father wouldn't do that."

"Do you live under a rock?" Now his voice deepened with anger. "All those times you go to his study and he's unavailable? You know what he's doing?"

I didn't want to know.

"He's with his whores. He'd rather do that than give you the time of day."

As hard as I tried not to, I winced.

"I know you want to keep your head buried in the sand, but you're too smart for that." Now his voice turned gentle, like he actually pitied me for once. "They probably never told you because they knew how you'd feel about it. Easier to leave you in the dark—along with everyone else."

NINE

Huntley

AT DAYBREAK, WE SLIPPED OUT OF THE NARROW ENTRANCE to the cave and walked across the snow. I noticed them right away, the enormous footprints from the yeti that had followed us here.

She did too. She dropped her chin and stared right at them for a long time.

I scanned our surroundings, seeing no sign of the monster that thrived in the snow. He probably grew impatient and chose to find another meal rather than wait around for us. Pops of blue were visible between the clouds overhead, and the wind had died down sometime in the early hours of the morning.

Ivory was quiet. Had been quiet since I'd told her the truth.

That her father was a scumbag.

She kept my pace but didn't hit me with her usual line

of questioning. She had enough information to chew on for the moment.

I was an excellent judge of character, and I could read her innocence like words on a page. Her naïveté was infuriating, but also genuine. I hated her a little less, even though I shouldn't.

Halfway there, she broke the silence. "You never told me how you want me to help you."

"You'll see."

"Why don't you just tell me?"

"Because you wouldn't believe me if I told you."

"Maybe before…but not now. Not after I've seen nine-foot-tall yetis and men with teeth coming out of their face…"

I kept up the lead, her slightly behind me to my left. "You're a healer."

"No."

"I watched you bring that horse back from the dead."

"I knew you were watching me…"

Wasn't exactly like I hid it.

"I'm a mender. Menders only help with animals."

"Same thing."

"Trust me, they aren't the same thing. You could be on your last breath, and I wouldn't be able to help you."

My eyes scanned the landscape ahead of us, always watching for unexpected company. The trees made it difficult to see our surroundings, and the tracks in the snow made it easy to be followed.

"So, if you need me to heal someone, I can't."

"Not a person."

"An animal?" she asked. "You have an animal for me to heal?"

"Yes."

"Is this a pet or something?"

"I'll show you when we get there."

"Okay… What's with the secrecy?"

I held my silence.

She released an irritated sigh. "If it's a yeti, count me out."

I cracked a slight smile.

"So, you do have a sense of humor."

My smile dropped, my features went hard, and then I turned to regard her.

"Alright…maybe not."

An hour later, we approached the perimeter of the outpost. The guards along the wall saw my approach and immediately pulled the gates open so we could pass through. The walls were twenty feet tall—so a yeti couldn't climb over the top.

Side by side, we entered, the gates swinging closed behind us.

I could feel the difference in the outpost the second I returned. The scowls on their faces. The rage in their eyes. Ian was there, and he stared at Ivory like he wanted to murder her.

Ivory inched closer to me because she could feel it too.

My mother approached, flanked by two of her private guards, Geralt and Mace. Her fur cloak trailed behind her,

her sword at her hip, and the feathers woven into her hair symbolized her power. Every year, a new feather was added, commemorating her reign. With nostrils flared, she stopped in front of me, her eyes reserved for Ivory. "Excellent work, Huntley. Take her away."

Mace grabbed her by the arm.

On instinct, she twisted out of his grasp. "I can walk, alright?"

My mother didn't drop her stare. It intensified, making her nostrils flare, making her eyes redden with blood lust. "Cameron had a family. A wife. Two daughters."

Mace stopped, so Ivory was forced to turn around and face the wrath of the queen.

Queen Rolfe stepped forward and approached Ivory.

Ivory met her look without a hint of fear. "Who's Cameron?"

She stopped a foot away from Ivory, her muscled arms by her sides, her fingers twitching for the hilt of her blade. "The guard you slew in the middle of the night. The man who came to provide you nourishment, and you stabbed him with his own knife. His wife is now a widow—and his daughters will never see their father again. Because of you."

Ian came to my side, dressed in the same fur cloak, his gaze hardened like the edge of a blade.

Ivory held her stare, not giving a single blink, not a sign of hesitation. Strands of her long brown hair were in her face, covering part of her left eye and some of her lips. The breeze came and brushed it away, with the

146

touch of a lover. She was shorter than my mother, petite in her build, but her appearance was misleading because she was capable of more than people realized. "I'm sorry that he died, but I'm not sorry that I did whatever I could to survive. If our situations were reversed, your actions would have been no different. So don't punish me for—"

My mother slapped her hard, so hard her head turned. The clap resounded all around us. "Don't speak of punishment. Your punishment hasn't even begun." Her arm flung out and grabbed Ivory by the neck and slammed her down.

I just stood there.

Ivory hit the ground but immediately got back to her feet.

My mother came down on her, fists flying, and hit her in the face over and over.

Ivory blocked a couple hits, but she would have done a better job if she actually knew what she was doing.

"You." Hit. "Stupid." Hit. "Girl."

When Ivory was bloodied, my mother finally let up. She got off her—and spat on her face.

Blood came from Ivory's nose, but she didn't cry out in pain, and when she sat up, her eyes were full of the same rage that my mother shared.

Mace grabbed her by the arm and dragged her to her feet.

My mother returned to where Ian and I stood. "Lock up our prisoner. And this time, let's make sure she doesn't get away." The brawl concluded, she headed back to the stone keep with Geralt at her side.

I watched Ivory be taken back to her cabin before I followed Ian and my mother. I'd known there would be consequences when we returned, but I didn't warn Ivory because it probably would have made it more difficult to get her to comply. If I'd had to carry her ass all the way back, I would have. But I'd wanted to avoid that.

Everyone returned to their cabins, and we returned to the stone fortress. The warmth was trapped against the rock and immediately surrounded us. The bonfire directly underneath the sky was big and bright, and the heat radiated through my fur coat and armor straight to my skin. When Ian had left and it was just the two of us, she regarded me, looking at me with the eyes of a mother rather than those of a queen. "Are you well?"

I nodded.

"It looked like you got her to return willingly."

"Once she realized what else is out there, she knew she wouldn't make it far."

"Perhaps that stupid girl isn't so stupid after all. What did you encounter?"

"The Teeth."

Her eyes narrowed.

"They attacked Ivory first. I had to intervene if I wanted her to stay alive. Klaus fled."

"Of course he did," she said. "A coward for a king."

"There was a yeti as well…always a yeti."

The corner of her lips tugged in a smile. "I'm relieved

you returned unharmed." Like always, her hands cupped my cheeks, and she smoothed her thumbs over my cold skin. She treated me as a man in the presence of others but treated me as her son in their absence. Her warm hands pulled away, the same hands that pummeled Ivory into the ground.

"There's something I'm obligated to share."

She stared, her features hardening into her shrewd appearance.

"I was outnumbered by Klaus and the Teeth. Ivory took the opportunity to flee while I was compromised."

A flash of anger moved across her gaze.

"But she returned…and saved my life."

The anger remained, as if that didn't mean a damn thing to her.

"Just thought you should know."

There was no acknowledgment. There was nothing at all. "Go to her cabin tonight. And do exactly what her father did to me."

A chill had never crept into my bones, had never penetrated through the flesh and blood, but it did now. Everything tightened, from my stomach to my heart. I held her gaze without reaction, keeping everything contained beneath the surface. "I just told you she saved my life."

"She wouldn't have had to save it if she hadn't run in the first place."

Since the moment my father was killed, my mother had become the leader of this family. She showed me how to survive, how to adapt to the harshest changes, how to keep going even when everything felt hopeless. I watched her start over—from a peasant to a queen. And she was a damn good queen. Strong. Commanding. Fair. She punished our people, but always justly and never with glee. But this…this was heartless. "I would have run too—as would you."

She stared, her gaze hardening.

"She's not like him."

"His blood runs in her veins. That's enough."

"Her father isn't even here to see—"

"You will share every detail before I stab my dagger through to the back of his throat—just as he did to your father."

I inhaled a slow and deep breath. "That's not who we are—"

"Yes, it is. He made us this way."

"Well, that's not who I am." I was her eldest son, her golden boy, and I never defied her. I obeyed her as my queen because she'd earned my unflinching loyalty. But this… It was something I just couldn't do. "I'm not going to force a woman who just saved my life. I'm not going to force any woman—not after what I had to watch with my own eyes." Those memories were ingrained in my mind no matter how hard I tried to forget them. They were a part of me, a constant weight on my shoulders, a constant pain in my heart.

The disappointment was barely noticeable in her angry face. With an unblinking stare, she watched me for several seconds, as if her formidable presence was enough to make me change my mind.

But it wasn't.

She turned to Geralt, one of our most vicious fighters, my first pick in a battle against a yeti. "Looks like the honor falls to you, Geralt."

His lips pulled back in a smile.

"Enjoy yourself." She stepped away from me and toward her guard. "And make sure it hurts."

"I definitely will." Geralt immediately removed all his weapons as if he intended to do this right now.

Adrenaline spiked in my blood. My heart panicked. My internal systems crashed. Even in the gravest battles, I never lost my focus, never gave in to fear. But now, my breaths escalated, and my palms turned sweaty.

I walked up to my mother again and lowered my voice so Geralt couldn't hear. "Her father deserves everything that's coming to him, but she doesn't. I understand your pain. I understand your need for revenge. I feel it too— every fucking day. But how can you experience that your-self and wish it on somebody else?"

Her stare remained blank, absent of any emotion. "It's easy. Really fucking easy."

My heart tightened into a fist.

"He raped me—and made you watch." She said the words without a wince. "Your father was pinned to his throne with a blade shoved into his mouth, and your brother was running for his life through the castle. I'm as tough as steel, and a man thrusting himself inside me isn't going to break me. But you know what did? Having my boy watch. That was the worst part. That's how you hurt someone—by hurting someone they love. And that's exactly what I'm going to do."

There was nothing I could do. Her need for revenge was like mine—insatiable.

She turned away.

I did the only thing I could. "I'll do it."

She slowly turned back to me, one eyebrow cocked.

"I lost sight of what's important. I will do this."

Geralt gave a growl. "She's mine. Queen Rolfe has already given her to me."

I ignored him and kept my eyes on hers.

She studied me. "I'm glad you've come around, Huntley."

The breath slowly left my lungs, along with the panic. I would spend the evening in her cabin, but she would be in the bed and I would be on the floor. No one would have to know.

She turned to her guard. "I'm sorry, Geralt. I prefer to keep it in the family."

He sighed before he returned his sword to his hip and his shield to his back.

She came back to me. "Go."

I took the order like it was any other and prepared to leave.

"And Huntley?"

I halted, my eyes on the bonfire.

"I will check."

TEN

Ivory

I WAS BACK IN THE SMALL CABIN, THE FIREPLACE COLD, THE mattress made of old hay. With no windows, the darkness grew deeper and uglier. There wouldn't be another opportunity for escape until Huntley took me to assist him with whatever animal needed my help, so I crawled into the fireplace and looked up the flue.

It was really narrow, but I might be able to squeeze through…

The front door flew open, and the sound startled me, making me bump my head on the stone. "Ouch…"

The door shut.

I crawled out and dusted my dirty hands on my breeches. "A knock would have been nice."

It was Huntley. In one hand was a tray of food, and in his other arm were a couple pieces of firewood. He looked pissed off—like always. He stared at me for a while before he regarded the fireplace. "You'll get stuck and suffocate."

"Worth a shot…"

"No, it's not." He set the tray on the bed then set up the firewood in the hearth.

I was starving, so I took a seat and scarfed everything down.

He got the fire going, bringing it from red embers to powerful flames. Soon, the fire illuminated the entire room, casting shadows on the walls from the bed and the armchair in the corner, and the cold scurried away through the crack under the door.

He draped his cloak over the back of the chair then took a seat like he intended to stay. With his eyes on the fire, he addressed me. "How's your face?"

"It didn't seem like you cared about it when the queen went to town on it."

"You killed one of us. If you thought there wouldn't be repercussions, you're stupid."

"If I'd known there would be repercussions, I wouldn't have come back with you."

"You're under the impression I would have given you a choice." His hands curled over the armrests, and he made an old creaky chair look like a throne. With the fire reflecting in his eyes, it was like ice being on fire, blue flames.

"I don't even feel it anymore, so whatever." It had stung for a while, but the cold numbed it pretty good. I watched the fire as I ate my dinner, day-old bread, assorted fruit and nuts, and a piece of meat. I didn't know what kind of meat it was…because I didn't recognize it. I was in a world without mattresses, without servants, without hot stones between my sheets to make it warm before I got in.

I didn't complain about it, but it did suck.

He lingered, eyes still on the fire, and I assumed he was waiting for me to finish eating.

When my plate was clean, I left the tray on the edge of the bed.

He still didn't move.

"What are you doing in here?"

After a long pause, he shifted his eyes to me.

He stared—long and hard.

It was a look I hadn't received in a long time, an intense stare that was powerful and cruel. I'd never met anyone who could make eye contact the way he could, to have such confidence in his visage. "I don't need a reason."

There was something different in the air now, a tension that was hot on my skin. The relationship between us was different, but I wasn't sure what had changed. Just yesterday, I was ready to let him die so I could escape, and now…I didn't know.

The stare continued without a blink, without a break.

A man had never stared at me like that before.

It wasn't hostile, but it was intimate.

It made my heart skip a beat. Made my breath come out shaky. It felt like that charged moment before a kiss, before the guy leaned in and pushed you up against the wall. But Huntley was clear on the other side of the room —but felt right next to me.

"Why are you looking at me like that?" My voice came out weak, when it hardly ever did. I wasn't afraid. I wasn't angry. I was just provoked, provoked by that stare that had the power to move mountains.

His eyes dropped to the floor.

The connection was severed, and I suddenly felt cold.

"There's something I have to do…and I don't want to."

So, he was there for a reason. My punishment hadn't ended. It had only begun. "You said you wouldn't kill me…"

"And I won't," he said, his deep voice rough like coarse sand. "I keep my word."

"Then…what do you have to do?"

He lifted his gaze and looked at me, his stare just as intense as before.

The lit fireplace. The food. The silence. It all became clear. "No."

"I said I don't want to."

"Then don't."

He drew in a deep breath, his chest rising in his armor. "It's not that simple—"

"You said you would never desire me that way."

His eyes dropped again, his jaw tight.

"You said you wouldn't—"

"That's not why I'm here. I'm here because I don't have a choice."

"You don't have a choice?" I asked quietly, in disbelief. "You know what? Be a man and just own up to it—"

"Yes, I desire you." He raised his chin, his eyes darkening. "The moment you shot that arrow into my neck. The moment you picked up your sword and stood your ground. The moment you got into that bedroll and admired me. The moment you sliced down the Teeth and saved me. And even every moment you've run your big mouth until it made my ears bleed. Alright? There's the truth."

My mouth shut at his words.

"But that has nothing to do with this."

"She asked you to do this, didn't she?" I whispered. "What kind of barbarian gives an order like that? Especially a woman—"

"A woman who's been raped while her son was forced to watch."

Like the breath had been stolen from my lungs, I couldn't breathe.

"By your father."

He and the queen had the same eyes, but I didn't notice the similarities until now.

"I tried to change her mind. But she refused."

"Then we'll just pretend it happened. She doesn't need to know the difference."

His dismayed look told me that wasn't an option. "She'll check."

"Check?" I asked incredulously. "As in—"

"Yes."

"Fuck, what is wrong with you? All of you?" Now I grew hysterical, unable to believe this kind of evil existed in the world. "I wasn't even alive when all of this happened, but you're going to get your rocks off doing this to me?"

His features tightened, as if he was in pain. "It's not right. I agree with you."

"Then don't do it."

"As I already said, it's not that simple—"

"Then make it simple—"

"If it's not me, it'll be someone else. My mother commanded me to do this, and when I refused, she appointed Geralt, one of her guards—and he was more than happy to oblige."

He must be one of the two at her side, both huge and vile.

"I don't need to tell you how that would go."

The bile flooded my mouth. I could taste it all over my tongue. "And I should be grateful?"

"I've seen the way you look at me."

I looked away, embarrassed that I'd been caught looking at his big dick against his wall of hard abs and line of masculine hair.

"You could have let me die, but you didn't."

I kept my eyes averted.

"So, whatever this is…it's mutual."

"I wish I'd let you die out there."

"No, you don't."

My eyes moved back to his.

As if he saw the truth in my eyes, he said it again. "You don't."

My arms tightened over my chest, and I suddenly felt cold, despite the warm fire right beside me.

He remained seated, his eyes potent against my skin.

Paralyzed, I just sat there, unsure what else to do. The air felt humid, thicker on my throat, congesting my lungs. It was dry and cold outside these four walls, but within, it was a different world.

He watched me for a long time, the intensity of his stare so powerful I was forced to look at the fire. The flames licked the wood, burned the surfaces until they glowed red. That was exactly what his stare did to me— set me on fire.

He moved to the bed beside me, a slight dip occurring underneath his weight. His arms were on his knees, his shoulder almost touching mine.

I concentrated on the fire, but my breaths deepened with his proximity, and my tongue suddenly felt dry.

In my peripheral vision, I saw him remove the vambraces from his arms, the gloves from his hands, the breastplate of his armor. One by one, they came off until they ended up on the floor, along with his tunic.

I should have kept my stare on the fire, but the offering was too tempting. I still remembered the way he looked under that sheet, how hard he was, how much harder he'd been than any other man I'd seen. It was as if he lifted boulders for fun, ate an entire buck for breakfast. The muscles of his arms had cuts as if someone had sliced him with a blade.

My head turned—and I met those blue eyes for the first time.

The first time...like this.

The light from the fire blanketed his face in a handsome glow, giving shadows in the hollows of his cheeks, under the line of his jaw. His eyes were a little brighter, a little more intense as they looked at me.

There was a small amount of dark hair in the center of his chest, the same color as the shadow along his jawline and around his lips. This was the same man who'd followed me throughout the castle, but now that seemed like a whole different person.

He pivoted his body slightly toward me, his breeches and boots still on. Now the trail of hair at the bottom of his stomach was visible, leading to a significant bulge in his trousers. It was hard and defined, my mind filling out all the details I couldn't see.

My eyes lifted to his again.

It was just like the last time I'd looked at him, but this time, I wasn't embarrassed.

His deep voice had a baritone that glided right over my skin. "I'm good at this."

"Me too."

"Then show me."

I was paralyzed once again because that confidence made me weak in the knees.

He drew close, his smell coming into my nose, the heat of his body right against my skin. He did this sexy thing where he stared at my lips as if he admired me the way I admired the first flowers of spring. He came closer and closer, preparing for the landing, and then changed his direction to my neck. He pushed his mouth right into the crook, his hot lips touching my cold skin.

My reaction to the contact was instinct, and my head tilted back slightly to allow him more room to kiss me. A deep breath ballooned my lungs. My fingers dug into the fabric of my breeches. My heart fluttered like this was my first time, with a mixture of desire and nerves.

His kisses were powerful, like bites from an animal. His palm flattened against my back, and he supported me as he kissed me, as he lavished my throat with masculine kisses, making his way down to the hollow of my throat.

My arm circled his shoulders, and I felt our bodies flush together, his hard chest against my breasts, the heat of his skin so hot it was like a branding iron into my flesh. The sense of comfort came an instant later, the first time I'd felt safe since I'd been taken from my castle, the first time the world stopped.

He moved to the other side of my neck, his strong arm keeping me pinned close against him, his warm breaths drifting down my skin in sexy pants. He gave me a gentle bite right on the collarbone before he pulled away, his face returning to mine.

But there was still no kiss.

With his eyes on mine, he moved his hand up my thigh, traveling closer and closer to the apex. He watched my reaction but also guided me with his, giving me his confidence, the desire in his eyes.

My heart pounded so hard that I couldn't hear my own breaths.

His fingers slid between the very tops of my thighs and found the spot over my breeches, his thumb hitting it like he already knew where it was. He gave a gentle press, and then he started circular motions, applying just the right pressure to make my breath escape my lungs.

He could have kissed me. But he watched me instead, which was far more intimate. His stare used to be a tool of intimidation, but now it'd become my guiding star, drawing me through this, assuaging the uneasiness.

He rubbed me harder, faster.

My hands held on to his shoulders as my thighs parted slightly, giving him more room, feeling the wetness already soaking through my underwear and leaving a stain on the crotch of my pants. I breathed deeper. Harder. My nails started to make divots in his flesh, but he didn't seem to mind.

My forehead pressed against his as I enjoyed it, as he brought me closer and closer to the edge, getting me thoroughly aroused before he tried to shove that big dick inside me. Now I was hot and bothered, only living in this moment, with this man and the fire beside us.

My lips moved for his, wanting to taste them on my flesh, to feel their fullness between mine. They came into contact with a gentle collision, like two clouds that morphed into one, and he hesitated slightly.

His eyes closed and he kept his mouth against mine, but he was still. Then he met my affection with hungry lips, taking control of the kiss, leading it like he did with everything else. He was good with his mouth like he was with his hands, every embrace purposeful, with just the right pressure, with the kind of passion that made me feel like he wanted this—even if these weren't circumstances of our choosing.

The cabin was silent except for the flames in the hearth. But those were soon overpowered by our heated breaths, our lips coming together and breaking apart, the quiet moans that I couldn't keep bottled inside any longer.

He made me come—hard.

My lips couldn't continue the kiss, not when the explosion happened between my legs, right against his big fingers. My hands planted on his hard chest to brace myself in the waves of pleasure that would knock me on my backside. I moaned against his mouth, my hips bucking into his hand, my nails making scratch marks in his skin.

Too anxious to wait for me to overcome the pleasure he'd just given me, he brought his lips back to my neck, and this time, he tugged my shirt down, exposing my shoulder so he could kiss me there too.

His fingers grabbed the drawstrings of my breeches, and he tugged as he kissed me at the same time, getting them loose around my waist. Now everything happened at a much quicker pace, my boots and breeches coming off with a couple tugs and kicks. I pulled my shirt over my head and got rid of my shift, my tits bare to the air.

He got to his knees in front of the bed and tugged me against him, his lips moving to my tits to taste them like he'd already tasted the rest of me. He sucked one nipple into his mouth between his teeth as he palmed the other. I was small in comparison to his hand, but he kissed me like they were the nicest tits in the world. His hand grabbed the back of my neck, and he forced me back so he could kiss my stomach, explore my navel with his tongue, and move even farther down.

Every muscle in my core tightened when I felt the movement of his lips, when I knew the direction of his travels, where those lips would end up once they reached their destination. My breathing gave a hitch before he even made it there, when his lips kissed the insides of my thighs, when he purposely teased me to make me burn hotter than I was before.

He could fuck me any time he wanted, but he continued to work to make me writhe, to make my desire build up all over again so I would get the same grand finale he would.

He was right—he was good.

"Ohh…" My body immediately writhed when I felt his lips on me, his scruff abrasive against my soft skin, his tongue just as demanding when it had been inside my mouth as it was inside me now.

His tongue circled me just the way his fingers had, and he scooped my hips into his powerful arms so he could devour me, as if nothing ever tasted so good as I did.

It was so good that I couldn't take any more. Just couldn't. "Fuck me."

His mouth was off me instantly, and he gave me that signature intense gaze, his lips shiny with my arousal. I expected the corner of his mouth to flick up in an arrogant smirk, but it never did. My plea only turned him on based on the burn in his eyes.

He got to his feet and pulled the drawstring of his breeches so they came loose.

I sat up, his waist right in my line of sight.

His thumbs hooked into his waistband, and he pushed it down, slowly revealing the base of his cock and the dark hair until it popped free—the entire thing. Thick. Long. A swollen head with a pool of tears on the surface.

His breeches and boots were removed, and then he stood there in front of me, six-foot-something of perfection, of hard muscle and power. There were scars on his skin, an old wound where he'd been stabbed by Klaus, and a slight indentation in his chest that I hadn't noticed before.

His dick hung there, pointed right at me, and he looked down at me with a command in his eyes. His hand got a harsh grip on my neck, and he stepped closer to me, pressing the head of his cock against my lips so he could drag his arousal across the skin.

I obeyed—and parted my lips and flattened my tongue.

He slid inside immediately, his eyes closed for a long second when he felt my tongue, my wet mouth, my tight throat.

He pushed all the way inside, making himself right at home, his enormous dick taking up every single pocket of space.

I couldn't breathe. I had to hold it, which was intentional. He kept me there with his hand, looking down at me as if to prove a point, that his dick was the biggest in all the land. He finally pulled out, giving me the chance to take a breath.

But then he was back inside, thrusting into my mouth as I took it, his dick soaked with my saliva.

We moved together, and I timed our thrusts with my breaths, my eyes watering because I had the urge to gag every time he was that deep inside me. With his hand on my neck and his strong-as-steel abs in my face, I kept going, feeling that hot gaze on me the entire time.

His breathing deepened until it became audible, and then he released a moan, a deep and lengthy one, like my mouth felt so good sheathed over his length. That was when he pulled out, a string of spit connecting the tip to the corner of my mouth. His thumb swiped up, severing the connection. "Now, I'll fuck you."

He scooted me back onto the bed of hay, bringing my head to the moth-eaten pillow stuffed with sheep's hair, and then separated my thighs with his as he prepared to make his entrance.

His face hung inches above mine as he guided himself with one hand, positioning the tip of his head against my soaked opening. He gave a gentle push, but it wasn't enough to get his large size past my small gates. He gave another thrust, this time harder, and he squeezed through.

It felt like my first time, my virginal body unable to accommodate the penetration, fighting back with its tight-ness. My hands glided over his strong arms and powerful shoulders, tracing all the muscles with my fingertips, feeling like the weight of a horse was on top of me. My knees curled toward my chest, and I squeezed his torso, hoping the deeper tilt of my pelvis would make it easier to get him inside me.

He started to sink, slow and easy, pushing his way inside until there was nowhere else for him to go.

I gave a moan and a whimper at the same time because it hurt, but it hurt so good. "Fuck, that's a big dick…"

He held his massive body on top of mine with a single arm so his free hand could dig into my hair, keep me in place even though I wasn't going anywhere. Every thrust was deep and purposeful, at a quick pace that was still slow enough to appreciate every single movement. Those beautiful blue eyes were on me, but instead of angry, they were possessive, but it was practically the same look.

I expected this to end within seconds, if not a minute, because of how hard up we both were. But it kept going, as if neither one of us wanted it to end. It was hot watching his strong body work to push inside me, the way his skin beaded with sweat, the way the flesh over his muscles started to flush red from the blood.

I'd never taken a man of his size, and while it hurt, it was worth it. He amplified the pleasure with his thickness and his reach, taking up every single inch of me so he could please me in a way other men couldn't.

I felt the slow burn again, in my stomach, between my legs, everywhere all at once. My arms hooked under his shoulders, and my nails started to drag down his back, leaving marks that would last for days. "I'm gonna come again…" I said it in disbelief, more to myself than to him, because another lover had never been more generous.

He rocked his hips differently now, rubbing his pelvic bone right into my hip. "I know."

"Ooh…" I automatically bit my lower lip because it felt so good, to be full with him and be pressed by him at the same time. It was an overload of pleasure, an ecstasy I'd never reached. "Ohhhh…" I came with a moan, my hips bucking against him automatically, eyes forming tears in the corners because it was all so damn good.

His thrusts turned to pounds, and he conquered my body with his powerful hips, taking me harder than he had. Deep. Strong. Fast.

I grabbed on to his ass and tugged, pulling him deeper into me, feeling his dick harden just a little more.

And then he finished with a deep moan, the sexiest sound I'd ever heard.

With his head reared back slightly, he filled me, giving me all the evidence we needed to prove that he'd fulfilled his duty.

My body immediately slackened because it was exhausted. All my muscles relaxed, and I suddenly felt high, like I could drift off then and there for a long night of sleep.

He pulled out of me and rolled over, his skin shiny with sweat, his powerful chest rising and falling quickly as he caught his breath. Slowly, his breathing returned to normal, his lungs working less to reclaim everything they'd lost.

I reached for the blanket below, but my arm wasn't long enough.

He grabbed it for me and pulled it on top of me.

My eyes closed.

I heard him a moment later, getting dressed at the foot of the bed.

For a brief moment in time, none of this felt real. I didn't feel desolate at the bottom of the cliffs, in the company of people who wanted me dead, in the cold where winter always prevailed. It felt like I was home—sharing my bed with a man who'd earned me.

But then my eyes opened, and it all came back.

Fully dressed, he sat at the edge of the bed, his cloak secured in place. He watched the fire, his face back to its usual hardness. "Fire will last until morning. I threw on more logs."

"Alright."

He pulled his boots on to his feet then stood up.

"Thank you."

He stilled as he faced the door, his cape reaching the floor behind him.

"I'd rather it be you…than anyone else."

ELEVEN

Huntley

At the head of the table, she'd already eaten her meager meal, only eating the bare minimum so her subjects would have enough. The rest of the food was for me, but I wasn't hungry, knowing this wasn't the end of it.

Lila entered the cabin, came to my mother's side, and whispered in her ear.

"Thank you, Lila." Mother grabbed her ale and took a drink.

Lila left the cabin.

Now it was just us again.

After a minute of silence, she broke it. "You did as I asked."

I watched the fire, feeling a lot of different things. I was an asshole for fucking Ivory because I was ordered to, and I was an even bigger asshole for enjoying every second of it. It was all kinds of fucked up. "I hope this revenge is suitable to you."

"Depends." She grabbed the bottle and refilled her glass. "How was it?"

My head snapped in her direction, shocked that she'd asked.

She took a drink, not the least bit ashamed. "Well?"

"I don't want to talk about it."

"Did she cry?"

When my dick was too big for her mouth. When she came the second time.

"Did she beg?"

She begged me to fuck her. "Mother—"

"Maybe I should have just watched."

This wasn't the woman who raised me. This wasn't the woman who commanded me. I'd lived the same trauma she did, but my response was nowhere near the same. "It's done. Let's move on."

"I didn't cry—"

"She cried the entire way through. She begged me to stop. I had to tie her down." Was that enough?

Obviously, it was because she gave a quick grin before she took a drink. "Good."

———

THE NEXT MORNING, I did my rounds at the outpost, making sure everyone was exactly where they should be. Attacks were always unexpected, so we had to be prepared for anything and everything. Even an alliance between the Teeth and the yetis, though that would never happen.

Ian appeared at my side, half an inch shorter. "Did the deed, huh?"

I looked through the trees and at the frozen tundra.

It started off as a tease, but once he read my mood, he stopped. "It's over, so just forget about it."

"I'm trying."

"I'm glad she didn't ask me."

It had to be me, thankfully.

"When are you leaving?"

"Not for a while. Scouts say it's too dangerous right now."

"Who are you bringing with you?"

"Nobody."

Ian turned to me, his blue eyes just like mine. "You're going to take her to the isles—a woman who hates your guts more than she did before—alone?"

"I'll be fine."

"You'll be more fine if I come with you."

"Ian, you have to stay here. We've both been gone too long. And the queen seems…a little unhinged."

"Never seen her like that before."

"Me neither."

He faced forward again.

"You need to lead the men in my stead. We ran into a yeti out there. Camped outside the cave for most of the night, waiting for us."

"Shit."

"Things are getting worse out there."

"But you know what they say…things will get worse before they get better."

"That doesn't apply to us, Ian. When have things ever gotten better down here?"

He stared ahead like he didn't have the answer. "Just be careful with her, alright? I've seen what she can do, and after what happened last night, I'm sure she wants you dead. Don't turn your back—not for a second."

———

I ENTERED THE STONE KEEP, passed the burning fire, and exchanged a look with Geralt.

Rage was on his face, like I'd wronged him somehow.

I halted my trek to hold his gaze, to make him remember his place, and after a few seconds, he did.

He looked to the entrance.

I entered the cabin to the sound of voices.

"You'd better clean my chamber pot good—because you're eating dinner out of it." I recognized my mother's voice but not her words. I entered the dining room to see Ian sitting on my mother's left, while Ivory sat in the corner, scrubbing the chamber pot with a dirty rag. Her hair was messy, like she'd been put to work the entire day without a break.

I stilled in the entryway, my eyes locking with hers.

She stared, her gaze just as blank as mine.

The last time we'd looked at each other head on, it was under different circumstances, naked, my heavy body on top of hers, our minds, bodies, and souls connected on a different plane.

Now, we were here.

I tore my gaze away and feigned indifference.

Because I knew she was watching, Queen Rolfe.

With her drink in her hand, she shifted her gaze from me to Ivory. "Isn't life funny, child? How one day you can sit on top of a castle, and then the next day, be at the bottom of the cliffs, scrubbing the chamber pot of a woman your father once fucked."

Ivory dropped her chin and kept working.

Ian refilled his glass.

I took a seat on my mother's right and helped myself to a drink.

My mother continued to watch her. "Scrub harder. Get some elbow grease into it."

When Ivory looked up, her eyes lethal, I knew what was coming. "How about I shove this up your ass instead? That should make some elbow grease…"

Queen Rolfe smiled, like that insult was only amusing and nothing more, but I knew that wasn't the end of it. She was on her feet in a split second, glass in hand, and she rushed Ivory.

I had to sit there and do nothing.

If I helped Ivory in any way, my mother would know what really happened last night, and she would send Geralt to do the job.

Queen Rolfe shattered the glass over her head—and Ivory crumpled to the floor.

I'd wanted this for so long, but now it made me sick. "Mother, we have much to discuss. Ignore the rat in the corner."

Ivory sat up and looked at me like I'd betrayed her.

Mother came back to the head of the table and took her seat. "Yes. Let's discuss."

———

"YOU FUCKING BASTARD!" I was in my cabin when I heard it, Ivory's voice.

I gave a sigh as I looked down at the field reports on my desk, knowing that her torture had been handed off to someone else. My eyes stayed on the maps, but my thoughts were with her, unsure what orders my mother had given.

Her screams didn't come again, and that worried me more.

I left the cabin and walked down the path, approaching her dwelling at the very end.

Marcus, one of the guards who had been close with Cameron, dumped a bucket of water on top of her naked body—right in the street.

The water must be freezing because she was shaking uncontrollably.

"Marcus."

He stilled at my voice, immediately stiffening like he'd been caught doing something he shouldn't.

"I'll handle this." I extended my hand for the bucket.

He cooperated then returned to his post on the fence.

Ivory was squatting on the ground, doing her best to cover her intimate parts, shivering harder than she had in the caves on the way here. She didn't even look up at me, probably because she recognized my voice.

"Get up." I didn't offer her my cloak, not when we were in public, not when someone could see me.

She trembled before she rose to her feet, almost toppling over because she was frozen to the bone.

My mother knew we needed her, but sometimes it seemed as if she was trying to kill her. "Follow me."

"Where?" Her hands were bunched in front of her chest to cover her small tits, her head down like an ashamed animal.

I never answered and made the walk back to my cabin. My eyes scanned left and right, making sure nobody saw what was about to happen. Most of the outpost was asleep, except the guards on the perimeter, but they shouldn't see us.

I opened the door and ushered her inside quickly before I locked the door behind me.

There was a fire in the hearth, so she immediately ran to it, her palms reaching out to feel the heat.

The fire wouldn't be enough, not after what they'd done to her.

I grabbed the pot of hot stones and carried them to the tub in the bathroom. It was already full of water, and I dropped the stones inside so it would bring the tub to a comfortable warmth. The bath was meant for me, but she needed it if she didn't want to die. I tested the water before I removed the stones and returned them to the pot. "Come here."

She appeared a moment later, still shivering. "Is it warm?"

"Yes." I extended my hand, and to my surprise, she took it and allowed me to help her into the tub.

She dunked her body to her shoulders—and released a sigh so loud it almost sounded like a scream. "Oh shit… that's good." Her arms wrapped over her chest to keep the warmth next to her body, and she just sat there, her eyes closed.

I returned to the other room and got comfortable, setting my cloak on the coat hanger, along with the rest of my clothing. The only thing that remained was a pair of breeches I wore in my cabin because the roaring fire had made it plenty warm. I returned to my desk and got back to work.

Her voice reached me from the open doorway. "Can I have more stones?"

"You'll scald yourself."

"My frostbitten hands and feet sucked all the heat away…"

I dropped my quill and returned to the room. The pot of stones was on the floor beside the tub, so I carried it back to the fireplace and hooked it in place. I returned to the desk once more. I worked as the stones heated, and after a couple minutes, I carried the pot back into the bathroom. "Knees to your chest."

She moved at a snail's pace, but she did it.

I dumped the rocks on the opposite side of the tub, steam immediately coming from the surface of the water like smoke off a fire.

She closed her eyes. "Ahh…that's nice."

I returned the pot to the fireplace then sat in my chair once more.

"Your mom's a cunt, you know that?"

I stared at the map without really looking at it.

"A fucking cunt…"

The insult from somebody else would result in a bloody tub. But I didn't defend my mother's honor—not when it wasn't right.

"Good…you agree."

With a sigh, I pushed myself from the desk and returned to the bathroom. "Sounds like you're feeling better."

Her knees were still to her chest, her arms wrapped around herself, and her neck rested against the edge of the tub. Her head was slightly turned my way, her damp hair over the edge of the tub, some strands in the water. "Got any food? I'm starving."

I pulled up a chair and took a seat.

"Haven't eaten since yesterday morning…"

Which meant she'd refused to eat out of my mother's chamber pot. She'd rather starve than suffer the humiliation. No surprise there. "I'll take care of it."

"You didn't take care of it when your mother smashed that glass over my head." The betrayal was still in her eyes, even though I'd just saved her from the freezing cold and promised her food. "You just sat there…that old look on your face."

"That was for your benefit."

Her eyes searched my face.

"Because if she knew how I felt—" I faltered because that was a poor choice of words. "That our night was consensual, she would send in Geralt to do what I couldn't. If I don't publicly despise you, there will be consequences."

That answer seemed sufficient because that betrayed look started to fade. "Let me guess… She asked how it was?"

Perhaps she was as observant as my mother. "Yes."

"And what did you say?"

"I lied."

She gave a shake of her head. "She's sick…"

I still didn't come to my queen's defense because it just didn't feel right.

"Why would anyone want someone so unhinged to be their leader?"

"I don't know…your father is your leader."

She went absolutely still, her eyes locked on my face without reaction, as if she didn't know how to react.

"I know you don't want to believe me, but it's true."

She looked away, dismissing what I said.

"I'll get you some dinner." I rose to my feet.

Her head turned back to me, her eyes immediately

moving to my chest. Now she didn't play games, didn't pretend she wasn't staring.

I walked out, went to the pub across the street in just my boots and breeches, and collected my dinner on a tray. I didn't grab two because that would draw more attention than I needed, and I returned to the cabin.

"Yes." I heard her excitement from the other room.

I stepped into the bathroom, pulled up a stool beside the tub, and set the tray on top.

"It's hot." She sat up in the tub, some of the water sloshing over the edge, and inhaled her food faster than I did.

I sat there and watched her.

"You aren't going to eat?" she asked, finally coming up for air.

"Already did." I'd just given my dinner to her, but I would be fine.

She ate everything, every single drop of sauce, every crumb of bread, everything that was served to her. "I feel so much better." She relaxed in the tub again, taking a deep breath and letting it out slowly.

I cracked a smile.

"What?"

I pointed at my face. "You got shit everywhere."

"Oh, whatever. I don't care." She sat there for a minute, but then she must have cared because she wiped it away with her wet fingertips.

My smirk remained.

"Shut up."

"Didn't say anything."

"But that smile says it all…"

I should go back to work, but I knew the second I left the room, she would call me back for something else. I leaned back in the chair and watched her soak in the tub, the steam slowly fading as her body cooled the water once more. Her hair stuck to the back of her neck, and her small shoulders breached the surface of the water.

"I really don't understand how you follow her." Her eyes were on the water in front of her, the liquid blanket that thawed her organs from the cold. "I get that she's your mother, so it's complicated…but I wouldn't want to serve a queen who was maniacal."

"She's a good ruler…present times aside."

She turned to me.

"There's nothing she wouldn't do for her people. She makes sacrifices that no one knows about. She goes with less so people can have more. She can be a very loving person…if she doesn't consider you an enemy. I don't agree with her tactics at the moment, but I've pardoned them because I know there's more to her than this."

"I think you'd be better."

My eyes locked on to hers.

"You were blinded by your revenge too—but you looked past it."

I stared at her naked form in the tub, seeing a different woman from the one who snuck men into her room late at night, who had a feast for ten all to herself for dinner, who lived in a world of luxury that should have been mine.

The second she shot that arrow into my neck, I'd known she was more than what she seemed. "There's something you should know."

She watched me, trepidation in her eyes.

"Your bedroom. It used to belong to me."

A note of confusion was in her eyes, as if she didn't follow.

"I still remember waking up in the morning, opening those curtains to that breathtaking view of the city at the bottom of the hill. With the sun in the sky on a cloudless day, the light reflected off the cobblestones—and shone like gold."

Her eyes tightened, like the description was one she knew just as intimately.

"My father was the King of Kingdoms. My mother, his queen. But all that changed one night, in the middle of winter, when your father and his men made it to the top of the cliffs—and took everything from us."

Her chest rose and fell quickly under the water, making small waves that sloshed to the sides of the tub.

"They butchered my father, raped my mother, and then kicked us over the edge of the cliff. The siege was quick, killing anyone who resisted, and the transfer of power was complete. The citizens went on with their lives —as if nothing had happened. Rutherford took the Capital, his other supporters claiming other kingdoms. That was over twenty years ago now."

She experienced shock, a hardness to her features that seemed permanent. The ripples in the water stopped because she failed to breathe. The reaction was genuine, like she had no idea that her home had been taken with force and blood. "The paintings on the walls…the names in the books from the library…"

I stared.

"It never made sense…"

I shouldn't pity her, but I actually did.

"That means…this is where I'm from…"

I gave a subtle nod.

She looked away, clearly overwhelmed.

The silence seemed to last for an eternity, but I gave her all the time she needed to come to terms with the revelation. Her entire life, everything she knew about herself and her family, was a lie.

"Do you know what I am?" She slowly turned her head to regard me, all the fire gone.

"A Plunderer."

"And what are they?"

"They live on the other side of the pass. They're human—but barbaric. Rutherford and Faron left their kingdom to overthrow my family, and once they were successful, they abandoned their own people. They're still here—and still pissed."

She gave a slight nod, as if she didn't know what else to do. "How did they make it up the cliffs?"

"That I don't know."

"Nobody could climb it, right?"

I shook my head. "Impossible."

"The tunnel?"

"That wasn't there until I built it."

"You built it?"

"Took a really long time."

"I can't even imagine…"

I could feel her sunken mood, feel her despair, feel the damage my words caused. "I hope now you understand. Your father took everything away from us, banished us to this frozen hell, and it's all we ever think about."

———

WHEN THE FIRE DIED DOWN, I threw another log on top, the flames growing to a new crescendo that filled the room with a burst of heat. The sound of the roaring fire was so loud that I didn't hear her behind me.

I dusted my hands on my breeches then got to my feet.

She sat on the edge of the bed, wrapped in just a towel, her hand gliding over all the furs on top. "You have a mattress… It's soft."

Her hair was dry now, just a little damp near the scalp, and a good bath had given her beautiful skin a new shine. In the little towel, her petite figure was noticeable, but also the small muscles of her arms and thighs.

Last time we were together, I was so focused on the heat that I hadn't noticed the other smaller details, like the sun-kissed freckles on her shoulders, her little feet that barely reached the floor because of her small stature.

"How do you get out of bed every morning?" She pulled back the covers, revealing sheets underneath the fur blankets. As if she couldn't resist, she got inside, tossing the towel on the floor once she was done. Her eyes immediately closed, and she released a sigh of contentment.

"You can't sleep here."

She kept her eyes closed. "Try me."

Against my will, I cracked a smile, and I was grateful she couldn't see it.

I dropped my bottoms then got into bed beside her, the cabin dark with the exception of the fire that brightened the corners and cast shadows on the walls. It slowly burned down, the crescendo fading to a sleepy burn.

On her side, she faced the other way, the sheets to her shoulder.

I lay on my back, and while I was exhausted, I couldn't fall asleep. My skin prickled with bumps. My heart pounded harder than it should when I was lying still in bed. Heat flushed through my body, heat that didn't come from the fire.

Heat that came from between my legs.

I was so hard it hurt.

My head turned to regard her beside me, her hair on the pillow, her back rising and falling with her slow breaths.

My stare lingered, and it only took a few seconds for me to know exactly what my mind and body wanted. My body scooted closer to hers before my arm hooked around her stomach. I dragged her toward me, making her back hit my chest. My hand groped her tit as my mouth dipped to her neck, feasting on her flesh without nicking her skin.

I squeezed her tightly, letting my hard dick dig into her back as it dug into my stomach.

She turned to look at me over her shoulder. "What are you doing—"

My mouth crashed into hers, giving her a hard kiss as my hand squeezed her small tits in a single grasp.

She gave me a hard push. "Look, I just came in here because it's comfortable—"

My hand yanked her onto her back so I could get on top of her and pin her arms above her head. "Don't get into my bed with your ass and tits out and expect not to be fucked. I'm gonna fuck you good just like last time, and you're going to come just like last time. So, unless you don't want that, I suggest you put on some goddamn clothes." I released her wrists and rolled over, giving her the chance to get away if she wanted—one last chance. My dick ached against my stomach, and the rage pounded against my temples.

She lay there for a while, not moving.

I kept my focus on the ceiling. "Ten…nine…"

She lay there, the numbers counting down closer to zero.

"Three—"

She finished the last two numbers in a rush. "Two, one." Her cheeks were already flushed with arousal, and her green eyes looked at me with the same depth as the other night, when she regarded me on a deeper level. Before I could pin her down again, she was on her hands and knees, her small mouth on my dick.

I felt her tongue slide down my shaft, and my eyes closed briefly as I released a moan. "Fuck." My hand dug into her hair as I guided her farther down, bringing her to the brink of choking, and then I let her come up for air.

The firelight blanketed her in a sexy glow, showing the deep curve in her back, her perky ass in the air, her slender legs.

I loved getting my dick sucked in front of the fire, but it had never felt this good.

My arm propped behind my head, and I enjoyed it, guiding her down my length and back up again, showing her exactly how I wanted her mouth to fuck me. "I accept your apology."

Her mouth left my dick. "I didn't apologize—"

My hand forced her back on my length. "Keep going." Now I pushed her farther down on purpose, bringing her to the level of a gag, making those tears form in the corners of her eyes and drip down onto my skin.

She didn't fight it, kept her mouth wide open, her throat taking me over and over.

My hand moved to her ass in the air, and my thumb pressed against the nub that was desperate for my attention. I could tell by the way her sex glistened, shone like drops of dew first thing in the morning. The second my thumb made contact, she gave a slight buck of her hips, as if the touch was electric. Her mouth halted on my dick momentarily, but she kept going, matching the rhythm of my thumb.

Now it became a game. Who would come first?

It might be me—because she was so damn good at this.

The harder I rubbed her the nub, the faster she went. Her saliva dripped down my length, and every time she stopped for a gasp of air, I could see the string of spit that connected her lips to my cock.

Her pussy dripped and my cock throbbed.

I couldn't hold it together any longer. The muscles of my stomach tightened, my ass did too, even my balls, and I gave a loud moan as I exploded into her mouth.

She held her breath as she took it, most of my dick in her mouth, her eyes dripping with tears.

My thumb kept moving, but I wasn't aware of my movements anymore, just the incredible sensation in my groin. It was the kind that lasted forever, that was deep like a cavern, powerful like the waves of an incoming tide. So. Fucking. Good.

She swallowed it all.

"Attagirl…" My hand withdrew, and that was when I felt the moisture all over my fingertips.

She sat back on her heels, the line of spit stretching until it broke apart with enough distance. She wiped her mouth with her wrist, her eyes so wet it looked as if she'd been crying at a funeral pyre. They glistened with more tears, and she blinked them away so they wouldn't fall.

Fuck.

I threw her on her back and blanketed her body with mine. My dick was still rock hard with another load to give, and I was ready to give it to her. Her nipples were pointed straight to the ceiling, straight to my chest, but I resisted the urge to kiss them because that wasn't what she wanted right now.

She wanted the cock she'd just sucked off.

Her thighs opened to me, and she pulled me on top of her, a tear escaping from one eye and rolling to my pillow.

One of my arms pinned her knee back, and I slid inside, our wet bodies coming together much easier than last time, like my previous penetration had a lasting impression. I sank deep, as deep as her body would allow me, and I felt my cock give a slight twitch because her pussy was as warm, wet, and tight as last time.

She gave a loud gasp when she took me, my size still a surprise the second time around. The nails of one hand anchored into my back, while her other hand planted against my chest, right over my right pec.

My hips thrust at the same pace as last time we were together, lingering inside her just long enough to stretch her before I pulled out and gave another thrust, another pound into the mattress, another rock that made her tits shake.

"Yes…" Her hand moved into the back of my short hair, her fingers fisting it like a lifeline. Her wet eyes were on my mouth, her own lips parted enough to show her little teeth, her tongue pressed between them.

When her hand gripped my ass and she tugged me inside her like last time, I knew she was close, on the precipice of the same climax I'd just had. She tugged harder and harder, guiding my hips exactly as she wanted, taking more of my dick than she could handle and giving a slight wince every time she did.

And then she came, nails like claws, tears like raindrops, moans like screams.

My dick was so fucking hard.

She buried her face in my neck as she rode the high, still tugging on my ass.

I pushed her back down to the mattress so I could look at her, so I could watch every detail of her features, the way her eyes looked different in that moment, as if we weren't enemies, but something more.

Her eyes closed for a brief moment, and the final tears cascaded down her cheeks. "No…"

My thrusts continued, wanting her pussy to be as full as her mouth.

"Do it again." Her hand cupped my cheek, and she brought our lips together for a heated kiss, a mixture of her tears, our tongues, and my seed.

The two-for-one special wasn't just for anyone. It wasn't for the whores I paid to pleasure me. It wasn't for the women I met in alleyways. But now, it became an expectation. She knew what I could do—and she wanted it every time.

I pulled out of her and forced her flat on her stomach. With her hips right against the mattress and her thighs together, I slipped back inside, and it was so much tighter than it had been before. I pounded into her hard, going as fast as I could, her ass cushioning my hips as our skin clapped together.

She moaned into the pillow as her hands reached behind her to grab me.

My hand locked her wrists together, and I pinned them in place as I kept going, my back coated with sweat, my breathing haywire.

Her sex ground against the bed every time I thrust into her, and it didn't take long for her to buck as her body convulsed with pleasure, for her screams to fill my cabin once again.

I sank my hips against her ass and filled her with a moan, my cock thickening with the release. My fingers tightened on the sheets beneath us, and my ass gave a firm clench as I pumped everything into her tightness. "Fuck."

The pleasure was potent and long-lasting the second time as if there hadn't been a first. I looked down at her ass beneath me, her slender back with small muscles visible under the skin, her dark hair all over the place.

I had no idea what the fuck this was, but I didn't want it to stop.

I rolled off her and let my tired back hit the sheets. I should be starving right now, but food was absent from my mind. I let the sweat evaporate from my skin as my breathing returned to normal. The fire had died down in the meantime, just a couple flames left.

She was still on her stomach where I'd left her, like getting fucked was just as exhausting as doing the fucking.

I should get her out of my cabin and back to hers.

But my eyes were already closed, and I didn't give a damn.

The mattress shifted, and her skin came into contact with mine. Her head moved to my shoulder. Her arm over my torso. Her leg tucked between mine. Her touch was cold, like a nice breeze from an open window. I felt like the sun, blistering hot, her own personal fire. Fire and ice.

I turned onto my side to face her, hiking her leg over my hip, bringing our bodies closer together. My arm squeezed the small of her back and kept her positioned against my chest, her hard nipples sharp as nails.

She tucked her head underneath my chin, her breaths right against my exposed throat.

It was then that I realized how vulnerable I was.

That she could kill me in the middle of the night and I wouldn't even be awake long enough to know what was happening.

But I went to sleep anyway.

TWELVE

Ivory

_____

WHEN I WOKE UP, I WAS IN A COMFORTABLE BED, NICE AND warm, and the sunlight hit my closed eyelids.

For a second, I thought I was home.

I knew Huntley had moved away when the cold set in, when it pressed on me from all sides without his body there to keep it at bay. My eyes opened and saw him standing at the foot of the bed, tall, muscular, with narrow hips and humongous shoulders. He was at full mast, and it seemed like he was already ready to go.

He walked past the bed to the bathroom, and I got a view of his chiseled ass and strong back. His spine was surrounded by an array of muscles, cuts in the skin that separated each one. It was no surprise he could carry me across the tundra, could hold his swords, his ax, and his shield.

I sat up and pulled the furs closer to me, cold without the fire, cold without him.

He returned a moment later, still buck naked. "Get dressed."

"I want to stay." I didn't want to go back to that cold cabin with that hay mattress and no windows. I wanted to stay here, on the softest bed I'd ever known, with blankets that trapped the heat against my skin.

"You can't."

"What does it matter if I'm here or there? I'm not going anywhere—"

Someone knocked on the door.

He didn't panic. Just pulled on his breeches and answered the door, his body hiding me from view of the visitor. He must have issued a wordless greeting because I didn't hear a word.

"The girl is missing. Before I sound the alarm, thought I'd ask you about it…" It was Ian. I could tell by the sound of his voice, which was similar to his brother's.

There was a long stretch of silence.

Probably a long exchange of stares too.

I was in bed with the blankets to my waist, in case Ian caught a glimpse.

Huntley finally responded. "Yeah, she's here."

Ian didn't say anything for a while, probably giving his brother a long, hard look. "Well, Queen Rolfe asked me to put her to work."

Huntley sighed. "I'll bring her in a minute."

"Okay."

Huntley shut the door then turned back to me, his look angry.

"Don't look at me like that."

"You shouldn't have stayed here."

"It sure didn't seem like you wanted me to leave…"

He stood there, heavy arms at his sides, wearing a brooding stare.

I kicked off the sheets and got out of bed, the cold air hitting me right away, making my tits tighten and my nipples harden.

His gaze immediately switched to my body, taking it in, that brooding stare disappearing and being replaced by the look he'd had last night. The one that wanted to throw me down on the bed and fuck me mercilessly.

"Doesn't look like you want me to go now either…"

He made his move, walking around the edge of the bed and coming toward me.

"Nope, I don't think so." I searched for my clothes, but then I realized I didn't have any because I'd walked here naked.

He grabbed me by the back of the neck and forced me down, face first into the furs. He had the kind of power I couldn't fight. Totally helpless, I was at his mercy, completely and utterly.

He shoved my ass into the bed, where it stuck in the air, and he dropped his breeches.

I tried to fight him. "You said I shouldn't have stayed, so I shouldn't stay now—"

His cock thrust inside me with a single move, hitting me deep, forcing my legs apart to make room.

"Oh…"

He grabbed my hands and pinned them against my lower back, planted his foot on the bed, and fucked me like an animal.

With my cheek against the fur blankets and my ass in the air, I just took it, took his big dick as I rocked back and forth. Every time I tried to fight his hold, his hands tightened, constricting around me like a snake.

He pounded into me hard, balls deep most of the time, making me ache because I was sore from the night before, but it felt good…so good. My body started to rock back on its own, taking as much of that dick as I could, my moans swallowed by the blankets in my face.

His hand gripped my hair and tugged, lifting my head off the blankets, and fucked me harder. One hand held both of mine, and he controlled me by the hair, paralyzing me on the bed, showing me that I had no power whatsoever—not when it came to him.

I came with a loud moan, my face dipping back to the bed so I could stifle my cries, but he tugged harder, keeping my head up, keeping the arch in my back. Tears came from the corners of my eyes because the climax was long and hard, deep in my belly, way better than the climaxes my other lovers had given me.

Just when I finished, he released, shoving his entire length inside me and making me wince. He barely gave a moan, restraining himself far better than I did. He kept his dick inside me for a moment, let it deflate before he removed it with a swift motion. "I'm fucking you in the ass next time." He pulled up his breeches and walked away as if nothing had happened, as if he hadn't just said what I thought he'd said.

————

HE ESCORTED ME THROUGH TOWN, past the gates, and into the wild.

I hadn't said a word to him, not after what just happened, the way he'd held me in his arms as we slept, then turned on me the next morning, only to fuck me at the edge of the bed like he hadn't had me several times the night before.

He didn't say anything to me either. It was as if I wasn't there.

"Where are we going?"

"The work site."

"What's the work site?"

"Where you'll be working," he said like a fucking smartass.

I turned to him, my eyes sharp like daggers.

He met my look, his eyes even sharper. "We need fire-wood. A storm is coming."

"How do you know?"

"When you live out here long enough, you learn a thing or two."

"You don't have seasons?"

"Yes, but not the way you do at the top of the cliffs. We have cold and really cold."

"What's this?"

He looked ahead, the shadow on his face darker than it was the night before. "Cold."

"And it's like that everywhere down here?"

"No."

"Then why do you live here?"

He walked forward, moving through the thick trunks of the forest. "If you want the best, you have to fight for it. We don't want to fight for it. Besides, our goal is to take back Delacroix and the Kingdoms. We have to be close to accomplish that."

"I don't see how you're going to do that with so few men."

"Your father did it, didn't he?" He looked at me, his eyes accusatory.

I held his gaze but didn't know what to say.

"And we have more men. This is just an outpost. Our main city is farther south."

"If this is just an outpost, why are you here?"

"Because Queen Rolfe anxiously waited for my return."

"Why do you call her that?" I asked. "She's your mom."

"She's my queen first."

"Does that make you a prince?"

"It makes me the second-in-command, king-in-waiting."

We made it to the jobsite, and that was when I realized how I would spend my day—chopping down trees. "How did she become Queen of the Runes? You came here as outsiders—"

"With sacrifice and determination." He halted and looked at Ian across the way. "With a back that won't bow and a knee that won't bend." He turned back to me, his blue eyes bright with loyalty. "There's nothing a mother won't do for her children. She'll make the impossible possible. She'll make midnight daylight."

I'd never known a woman like that, and if the situation were different, maybe I would like her. Respect her. Admire her. "If you were thrown off the cliffs…how did you survive?"

"That's a story for another time." He gave Ian a subtle nod. "Get to work." He turned to step away.

"Will you come to my cabin tonight?"

He halted but didn't turn around.

"I want to stay with you."

"You don't get to decide."

"Well, then you don't get to fuck me in the ass, do you?"

He turned around, his look slightly incredulous but mostly aroused.

Ian walked up at that moment, so Huntley couldn't say anything more about it. But he stared at me with eyes more intense than they'd ever been, as if fucking me at the foot of the bed hadn't been enough. His breath released, and his nostrils flared for a moment, like he wanted to grab me by the neck and throw me down right there on the dirt.

I wasn't staying in that cold cabin with no windows. I was staying in that warm bed. I was bathing in that hot tub. I was sleeping on that soft mattress with that big man beside me. He still had the scar on his neck from where I'd shot him, and it was hard to believe where we started and where we'd ended up.

Ian shifted his gaze back and forth between us, as if he knew he'd just stepped into a private conversation. "She can handle an ax?"

"Yes." Huntley's eyes stayed on me.

"She's not going to chop me into pieces?"

He watched me. "Are you?"

I still wanted to go home, but I knew I would never make it back under the circumstances. Not when I knew about the Teeth, the yetis, and everything else I hadn't yet learned. I needed a horse. I needed supplies. I needed a chance. "No."

Huntley looked at his brother.

"Wouldn't she say that anyway?" Ian asked.

Huntley turned to depart. "Not now. Not after everything she's seen out there."

———

ONCE I STARTED CHOPPING, I wasn't cold anymore.

I was sweating.

The men worked on felling the trees, and then I had trunks to chop up. It took dozens of swings just to break off a piece of wood. And then I had to break that piece into smaller pieces. Now that I knew the amount of work that went into this, I would never take a warm fireplace for granted again.

"You're good at this." Ian appeared, in the same fur cloak that his brother wore, white with fangs along the edges. They were the only two who wore the cloaks, signifying their royalty. It was like my father and his uniform, the dresses I wore around the castle, the crest that Ryker displayed on the chest of his tunic.

"Just trying to stay warm." I threw my ax down again and finally broke off the piece I'd been chipping away at. I propped my foot on it and wiped the sweat from my forehead with the back of my forearm.

He presented a canteen.

I took it and downed it.

He reached under his cloak and grabbed another canteen. "Wait, that's the wrong one."

"Too late." Now it was empty, and I tossed it back.

He caught it, but there was a prominent look of surprise on his face. "You drank all of that?"

"Yep."

"You're going to chop off your foot."

"I'll be fine. Keeps my stomach warm."

He returned the canteen underneath his cloak and handed me the one with water.

I took a drink of that one too, washing down all the liquor that still coated my throat.

He watched me, not the same way his brother did and not the same way his mother did.

I didn't have a clue what he thought of me.

"Thanks." I handed the canteen back.

He gave a nod and returned it under his cloak.

"How did you survive the fall over the cliff?"

He stilled at the question, caught off guard. Several seconds passed as he worked through the question and considered his response. "He told you."

"Yeah."

"We got lucky. There was a lake where we landed."

"And you still survived?"

"I didn't. I stopped breathing, but my mother brought me back. She pressed on my chest and breathed into my mouth until my heart started again. Huntley carried me until we found a cave. We made it through the night because she knew how to start a fire. If she hadn't…we probably would have died."

I pictured all of it in my mind, Ian and Huntley just boys at the time. "How old were you?"

"Eleven and nine."

"I'm sorry…"

He stared with his intelligent blue eyes, absorbing my look while giving nothing away.

"I mean that."

"That's hard to believe. If it hadn't happened, you wouldn't have grown up in that castle, experienced luxuries most people don't even know about."

"A woman and her children should never be pushed over a cliff to their deaths. They shouldn't be forced to survive the harshest elements with nothing but the clothes on their backs. That's not hard to believe."

He studied me. "So, you believe us? That your father did that to us?"

It was still hard to believe he was responsible for those heinous crimes, that the same violence in his blood ran in mine, but it was getting harder to doubt. "I…I don't want to."

————

WHEN THE LIGHT was almost gone, Ian walked me back to my cabin.

"Can I have a bath first?" I didn't have a tub in my cabin. Cabin wasn't even the right word. More like prison cell.

Ian unlocked the door and didn't answer my question.

"Then how about dinner?" I hadn't gotten breakfast or lunch.

"I'll give you some dinner, sweetheart." One of the queen's personal guards approached, a man with dark eyes and a smug smile. "Just gonna cost you." He looked me over, up and down, in the same way that Huntley did, but his stare wasn't welcome.

Ian waited for me to walk inside. "I've got it, Geralt."

Shit. I walked inside the cabin, wanting the door to close and lock behind me.

"Allow me," Geralt said. "I'd love the opportunity to get acquainted with our prisoner."

Fuck.

The door shut and locked. The light was gone. Now it was just me and the darkness.

Ian's voice came through the crack. "I'm sure the queen needs you, Geralt." Their footsteps disappeared.

God, I hoped that was the end of that.

Minutes later, the lock clicked and the door opened. Ian carried a tray to my bedside.

I looked at it with disappointment. A small piece of meat and a slice of bread with a cup of water. "Is this a joke?" Huntley had brought me a much different meal last night, with a lot more food and much better variety.

Ian turned to leave.

"You can't expect me to work all day and be sustained off this."

He gave a shrug and shut the door. The lock clicked.

I sat up against the bed and ate everything in a couple bites. My back hurt. My legs hurt. Everything hurt. My hair was oily from sweating all day, and I wanted to take another bath in that warm water.

I hoped Huntley came.

I'd given him a very good reason to.

Hours passed, making it so late that I assumed he wasn't coming at all.

The door opened, and his silhouette was visible, his broad shoulders and narrow hips in the shape of an inverted triangle. I recognized him even as a shadow. Recognized his presence. Could feel it with my eyes closed. "Took you long enough…"

"Come on."

I didn't need to be told twice. I got off that poor excuse for a bed and joined him in the dirt road. The torches lit the path back to his cabin, and the road was empty except for the two of us. Both silent, we walked, entering his cabin a moment later.

The fire was roaring, and there was a tray of dinner sitting there. A real dinner. With meat, potatoes, gravy, and an entire loaf of bread. But I wasn't sure what I wanted more, a bath or food.

I walked into the bathroom and shed my clothes before I grabbed the hot stones from above the fire and tossed them inside. Once the water steamed, I got in and washed myself of all the grime I had accumulated that day.

He appeared next to my tub, dressed down in just his breeches.

"Can you bring my dinner?"

"You don't live here."

"Can you *please* bring my dinner?"

He gave a sigh as he walked out, and then I heard the front door open and close.

Did he leave?

I stayed in the tub, all my muscles relaxing from the heat. The back of my neck rested against the edge of the tub, and I closed my eyes, ignoring the pains in my stomach. A moment later, he returned, and a tray of hot food was put on the stool beside me.

"Man, this looks so good…" I sat up and ate everything, dragging the bread through the gravy, cutting into the tender meat, scooping the fluffy potatoes into my mouth and tasting their cloud-like texture.

Huntley returned to the other room.

When my tray was so clean it looked brand-new, I got out of the bath and patted myself dry before I returned to the main room with the roaring fire. Huntley sat at his desk in the corner, looking over a map I hadn't noticed before. There were little figurines on it, along with a stack of open letters.

I stood over him and examined it, realizing the world was far bigger than I realized. There were cities and kingdoms everywhere, all scattered on one side of a thick black line that marked a border. In bold lettering, it read "Necrosis."

We were far away from the border, so I guessed that was a good thing.

I turned away, noticing that his tray was empty too, like he'd eaten at his desk. The bed was calling my name, so I dropped the towel and got inside, instantly comfortable once I was surrounded by the sheets. I admired the fire in the stone fireplace and the muscular back of the man beside it.

"I know what you're doing." He finished his note with his quill then dropped it on the desk.

My gaze shifted to him.

"Fucking me for food and shelter."

My heart gave a squeeze. I didn't know why.

He got to his feet and turned around, meeting my look

with a stone-cold gaze. "Just so we're clear." He pulled the drawstring to his breeches and dropped them to the floor, getting down to his nakedness.

My gaze remained on his face, my eyes shifting back and forth between his.

He grabbed the glass of dark liquid on his nightstand and took a drink before he got into bed beside me. He lay there, one arm propped behind his head, his eyes on the ceiling. The divot in his chest was visible in the light, the way his sternum was concave instead of flat.

"But I'm not."

His head turned to me, his jaw clean because he'd shaved sometime while we were apart. "Then why?"

"I don't know…the same reason you are." I didn't have a reason. All of this just happened. It was a slow burn, but once the fire started to roar, it consumed us both. I still remembered the first time I saw him—or, at least, his eyes inside his helmet. It started off sterile and distant but turned into heated and intimate.

"I'm sure Geralt has a cabin like yours, but you don't see me running to his bed."

He propped himself up on his arm and looked at me head on.

I was paralyzed by that stare, by the strength of it, by the way it could make me cower with just its intensity. "I'm here because I want to be."

He held his silence, his eyes still burning through my skin, right to the bone.

I drew nearer, crawling toward him, my face coming close to his.

He stared at my mouth, stared at it like he had the first time we kissed, as if he needed to take a moment before the collision. His hand slid onto my cheek then into my hair, gentle rather than possessive like this morning, and he pulled me in for a kiss.

My mouth was on fire the second we were in contact, as if I'd kissed a log right in the fire. Our lips came together, broke apart, and then he gave me his expert tongue. He guided me closer with his hand, deepening the kiss.

I pushed him to his back and straddled him as I continued our kiss, my soaked sex sitting right on top of his hard cock. The second they were in contact, he gave a moan, his hot skin feeling my wetness. His hand went to my ass, and he squeezed it as he kissed me, his hips already sliding slightly, to glide through my wetness just a bit.

He was right against my clit—and it felt good.

I ground my hips too, listening to the sounds of our slick bodies as they moved together, my aching lips losing their focus as they struggled to draw breath. My hands gripped his shoulders for balance, and all the soreness from a hard day's work vanished.

He scooted back, his frame against the headboard, and he guided my hips up as he pointed his dick inside me. With eyes glued to mine, he slid the tip inside, and then he tugged on my hips to bring me down, to sheathe him like he was a blade.

My nails clawed at his chest as they made their way down, and my teeth absentmindedly bit my lower lip.

I went as far as I could, until it started to hurt. I couldn't believe something so big could fit inside me, and if I weren't always wet at just the sight of him now, this would be anatomically impossible.

Impatient, he started to guide me up and down, pull me to the head of his cock and then push me back down to his balls again. The back of his head rested against the wall, and he dropped his gaze down my body, looking at my tits and my stomach, even looking at the nub between my legs. He watched me fuck him, his face tinting with a red flush, his eyes darkening while his dick hardened even more.

I rolled my hips every time I came down, scooping his dick farther inside me before I rose again, my cream sheathing his base.

His hands came up and gripped my tits, his thumbs flicking over my nipples to make them harden. He gave them a firm squeeze and a moan before he grabbed my ass again and gave me a hard smack.

Like a horse that had been kicked, I went faster.

He hit me again, as if that wasn't fast enough.

I dropped my hips and rolled them over and over, taking in his length while I panted and sweated.

His thumb pressed against my clit, and he rubbed it, hard and fast, in a perfect circular motion.

My hips made an automatic jerk at his touch, and I gave a moan, the kind of moan that made my eyes water just a bit. It was a warning of what was to come, of the way he was going to make me come.

"You love this cock, don't you, baby?"

My arms circled his neck, and I thrust into his hand, his dick twitching inside me. "Yes…"

"In your mouth."

"Yes."

"In your pussy."

"Yes."

"In your ass."

I hesitated before I answered. "Yes…"

I clung to him as I came, my hips bucking uncontrollably, my moans muffled against his neck, my tears catching on his cheek.

He yanked me down hard, shoving his entire dick inside me as he released.

It hurt to take that much, but I didn't fight it because I liked it. I liked how big he was. So big it hurt.

He gave a satisfied moan as he filled me, his eyes glazing over slightly.

My arms remained locked around him, and we sat there together, our wet bodies slowly softening. I had his seed inside me every day now, a weight that was noticeable throughout the day, when I worked, when I slept, when I did anything.

I liked it.

He pressed a kiss to my neck then a bite to my collarbone before he guided me off him.

When my back hit the sheets, my mind and body went into a new realm of relief, like I'd finally scratched that itch on my back I couldn't reach all day. My entire body felt good, not just the sex between my legs and my pebbled nipples. The pleasure reached my fingertips and toes, took away all the stress of the day. It brought me into a dream, made me forget the truth of my reality.

He left for the bathroom and returned a moment later. "Want another log on?"

I pulled the covers to my shoulder and gave a nod.

He squatted and put another on, every inch of his body chiseled muscle. He dusted off his hands before he came back to bed and joined me. He didn't stick to the opposite edge of the bed, but came right next to me, his heavy arm draping over my body under the sheets like an extra blanket.

With him next to me, the bed was even warmer, even more comfortable.

His head was on the pillow, and his eyes were closed.

He smelled the way he always did, but now it was enhanced with sex and sweat.

"Ian told me how you survived the fall."

His eyes didn't open.

"I guess you got lucky…"

"Lucky isn't the word I'd use." His eyes opened, crystal blue, beautiful. "A part of me wishes we'd all died that day."

My eyes dropped. "You don't mean that."

"You don't know what I've endured."

My eyes were on his chest, focused on the small dent just beneath his right pec. My fingers reached out and felt it for the first time, felt the bone slant in ways that it shouldn't. "What happened here?"

His hand grabbed my fingers and directed them farther down, away from the injury.

I looked up to meet his eyes—and knew I wouldn't get an answer.

"There's something I'm confused about…"

His hand slid up my back between my shoulder blades, cradling me to him. He didn't speak, but his eyes encouraged me to ask the question.

"When your parents ruled the Kingdoms…did they know?"

"Know what?"

"About everyone at the bottom of the cliffs."

His eyes were steady as they looked at mine, but his answer wasn't forthcoming.

"You did know."

"My parents. But not Ian and me."

I stared into his gaze, picturing eyes identical to his. "They knew…but did nothing." Now their actions had a different significance because my family had been the one down below. My father. My brother. My mother. We would have been down here instead of them.

"I've questioned my mother about it. She said they were fighting a war to the north and didn't have the

214

resources to care for the population below at the same time."

"But that war couldn't have lasted forever. And what about your father's father? And his father? There were generations—but no action was taken."

He held my stare.

This changed everything. "I'm sorry for what happened to you. Truly, I am. But…can you blame my father and the others? Can you blame them for trying to survive? If the situations were reversed, wouldn't you do the same?"

His gaze hardened, like I'd said the wrong thing. "My mother deserved to be raped—"

"That's not what I'm saying."

"My father deserved to be stabbed in the throat with a knife—"

"No. I don't excuse the violent behavior. But climbing the cliffs in the hope of a better life… How can you fault anyone for doing that? For wanting to be away from Necrosis? For wanting to feel the sun on your face for once?"

His angry stare continued.

"You know I'm right."

His gaze severed, and he moved away from me. "Go back to your cabin."

"I'm not going anywhere."

"Then I'll drag your ass." He rounded on me. "How about that?" He grabbed his breeches and pulled them on but left them untied as he fetched his tunic.

"You know I'm right."

He yanked the tunic over his head. "Get your clothes on."

"No."

"You think I won't carry you like that? Because I will."

I kicked the sheets back and got to my feet. "If your father were still on the throne in Delacroix, nothing would be different down here. People would still be consumed as fuel, and they would suffer in this life as well as the after-life. You're pissed that my father has abandoned everyone down here—but your family did the exact same thing. This isn't about justice. This is about keeping the status quo. As long as you're on top, nothing else matters."

His jaw was clenched, and his eyes were merciless—like he'd never been so angry.

"That's not the same thing as saying your family deserved what happened to them, because I'm not."

My eyes flicked back and forth as I looked into his, waiting for him to come back to me. "Imagining that happening to you...it breaks my heart—"

"This was a mistake."

"What...?"

"Whatever the fuck this is. It's a mistake."

My heart ripped open with a slash, and the blood poured out.

He threw the clothes at my face. "Let's go."

THIRTEEN

Huntley

THE STORM WAS ABOUT TO HIT.

You could tell by the wind—because there was none. There was no game on the plains, no birds in the trees, nothing. Nature sensed its approach and ducked for cover. Work would cease, and everyone at the outpost would hunker down until it passed.

I sat inside the bar and drank alone, ignoring the conversations around me, all about the impending storm.

I would normally invite a whore or two to pass the time, but I wasn't interested in that right now.

Ian stepped inside, found me at my own table, and joined me.

The barmaid immediately ran over and served him his usual.

His cloak was set on the back of his chair, and he sat in his black armor, ready for battle at any moment. "You think they'll come?"

"Hope not. I'm fucking tired."

"The scouts haven't reported signs of them."

"Because they would travel in the storm, not before."

"So, you do think they're coming."

I took a drink. "Expect the worst. Hope for the best."

He turned his stare on me directly now, his eyes combing my face for clues.

"What?"

"Anything you want to tell me?"

"No."

"Nothing about the prisoner?"

I turned to him and met his look head on.

"Come on, you know I wouldn't tell her."

My hand returned to my mug, and I pulled it closer to me. "It's over now, so it doesn't matter."

"What happened?"

I gave a shrug, at a loss for words. "Reality."

"I assumed you were just fucking."

"We were."

"Then what does reality have to do with that?"

I stared into my glass, unable to find a response.

Ian dropped the subject and looked away. "Maybe I should come on your trek after all."

"I'll be fine."

"I just don't trust her not to slip a blade between your ribs."

"She knows she'd die without me, so unless she's on a suicide mission, we've got nothing to worry about."

Ian pulled his glass closer and took a drink. "How long

do you think the storm will last? Last time, it was five days."

I ignored what he said because I hated playing the guessing game. "When Delacroix was ours, we never opened our borders to the Runes or anybody else. Why?"

Ian slowly turned to me. "Could be a lot of reasons."

"Such as?"

"How would we get people up and down? There's scaffolding, but there's not enough scaffolding in the world to make that feasible."

"We could have built a tunnel—like we did. Mother didn't make that suggestion when she was up there, but it came to her pretty quickly down here."

He studied me for a while. "Sounds like this girl is putting bullshit in your head."

"I wouldn't call it bullshit…no."

"I know Mother and Father had their reasons, and I trust that. Her family could have scaled the wall and made a life in our lands without being discovered. Instead, they staged a coup, not just to overthrow us, but to rape and murder us. We have every right to seek our revenge and take back what's ours. Don't let her tell you otherwise."

———

THE WIND STARTED to pick up. The trees shook. Snow began to fall from the sky. The temperature dropped.

I sat at my desk and stared at my fire, my bottle in hand, and tried not to think about that windowless cabin with a cold hearth. Her needs would be the first thing to be abandoned. They probably wouldn't bring her food for days.

I had no idea why I cared.

I shouldn't care.

Fuck her.

I took another drink and then heard the wind howl, heard the branches bend to its bite. My door was a solid piece of wood, but it rattled on its hinges when the wind hit it just right. I looked out the window and saw the snow streak past like hail.

Fuck her.

The door rattled again, and even the flames in my hearth dimmed briefly because the wind rushed through the chimney.

"Fuck me." I slammed the bottle down and went into the mayhem outside. It was hard to see because the snow was a solid wall of white. My eyes immediately watered, and my raised hood did nothing to keep out the bite.

There was no one out, except for the few guards ready to sound the alarm on the perimeter if needed. It had happened before, and I hoped it wouldn't happen again. I made my way down the road and approached her cabin, camouflaged by my cloak and the thick snow that made it impossible to see more than ten feet ahead.

I pulled out the key and got the door unlocked.

She sat against the wall on the bed, her knees to her chest, and she looked at me with eyes that reflected the light just the way animals did in the wild when they saw the glow of my torch. It took less than a heartbeat for her to get out of bed and run to me, like she'd been expecting me this entire time.

I locked the door again and took her by the hand so she wouldn't get lost.

She stayed right against me, her grip tight.

We made it back to my place, and the wind had picked up so much that I had to use my entire body weight to shut the door again. I thrust my body against it and locked it in place.

The wind howled outside, but inside the cabin, it was silent, just the flames crackling.

I looked out the window, and now it looked as if a blizzard had struck. The storm was worse than I anticipated, and I feared we may have to take cover in the stone keep. It'd be crowded, but everyone could fit.

When I turned to the bed, she was already naked, her clothes on the floor, her tits firm because they were still cold. Bumps were all over her fair skin, and her arms were crossed over her chest, not to cover herself, but to conserve heat.

I met her look, seeing green eyes that were bright like emeralds.

She stared with the same resolve.

I felt a lot of things for her in that moment. Anger was the most prominent.

She crossed the distance between us, and her hands immediately went for my breeches. She tugged the drawstring and got it loose before she unclasped the cloak at my collarbone.

I stood there and watched her undress me.

"Keep me warm."

"Take a bath."

"Water doesn't stay warm. You do." She crawled into the bed, getting underneath the sheets and blankets, and then looked at me expectantly.

I was hard in my breeches, and I couldn't hide it. My fucking dick gave me away. I kicked off my boots and dropped my bottoms before I got into bed. Instead of going for the spot beside her, I went on top of her, her thighs already open, her hands already tugging me closer to her.

My arm hooked behind her knee, and my dick moved right to her opening, knowing her body so well that I didn't have to guide myself to her entrance. My tip leaked at our connection because she was ready for me before I'd even opened the door to her cabin. I tilted my pelvis and slid inside, pushing through her tightness until I was surrounded by her perfect warmth.

She inhaled deeply as her nails dug into the muscles of my arms. "I knew you would come for me…"

With my face above hers, I thrust into her hard. "And I know you're going to come for me."

———

THE TEMPERATURE HAD DROPPED SO low that I had to keep feeding the fire. If I didn't, she would start to shiver, even when I had her locked in my arms and against my chest. Instead of taking from our communal stockpile, I'd felled my own tree and harvested the logs. It was a good thing I had because this storm was worse than I'd imagined.

I got the fire as big as I could before I returned to bed.

She grabbed at me the second I was close, wanting me as quickly as possible. Her head moved to my shoulder, and she hugged my waist, her leg tucked between mine, the blankets pulled to her chin.

The wind was so loud it would be impossible to sleep at this point.

"Does this happen a lot?" she whispered.

"Yes."

"Are they always this bad?"

"No."

"Is this one of the worst?"

"That remains to be seen."

She turned into my shoulder and pressed a soft kiss to the muscle.

My fingers automatically moved into the back of her hair, playing with the strands that covered my arm. My eyes were on the fire, making sure it didn't die or get out of control.

"I hope it lasts a long time."

I turned back to her.

"Because I get to stay in here with you." Her eyes were on my chest, as if she was purposely avoiding my gaze.

When I first saw her, I'd recognized her beauty, but it didn't affect me, not the way it affected the other men in her life. She didn't see the eyes that followed her everywhere she went, the way they would drop to her ass the second she turned around. With her perfectly styled hair and expertly applied makeup, she looked like she belonged on a throne with a crown of diamonds. But in the elements, when all those luxuries were stripped away, was when her beauty really started to shine.

That was when I noticed it.

Her makeup had been washed away, her gown had been exchanged for breeches and a tunic, and her jewelry had been replaced by a bow and a sword. That was the moment she became the most beautiful woman I'd ever seen.

"About before—"

"No."

She raised herself slightly to look at me.

I turned back to the fire. "We don't talk about that."

Her stare was focused on the side of my face.

"Don't bring it up again." Whatever this was, it had an expiration date, a date that could come as soon as tomorrow or the following day. It didn't matter who was right. Wouldn't change anything. Nothing was going to stop me from avenging my father's death and my mother's violation…and my own trauma. I would murder her father right in front of her if it came down to it.

Without remorse.

We were just a moment in time.

Her head returned to my shoulder.

In silence, we listened to the wind and the fire, and we waited for the storm to pass.

———

"WHAT WAS YOUR FATHER LIKE?" She propped herself up on her elbow as she looked down at me, her fingers trailing over my chest in gentle caresses.

"Strong. Silent. Focused."

"I meant with you."

"He taught me the sword. Taught me strategy. Prepared me to replace him, even when I was just a boy. My childhood was spent in his shadow. I was never treated as a child, but as a man. Everything I am today…is because of him."

"I can see that."

"But I could tell he didn't do it just out of obligation— but pleasure. He enjoyed spending time with me. My brother too."

"It sounds like you were his favorite."

"I was just the eldest. Ian understands."

"You and your brother are close."

I gave a nod.

"My brother and I are close too…" Her features dropped momentarily, the stress tightening her lips and dimming the light in her eyes. "We weren't when we were younger, but after Mom got sick…we were."

Now that Ivory was gone, I was certain Faron would use his son as a pawn instead to gain entry to the Capital. That was all his kids were to him—tools. Ivory didn't see it, but I saw it as clear as crystal. "I've seen him with a lot of different women."

She rolled her eyes and gave a chuckle at the same time. "Yep. But who am I to judge…?"

"Why didn't you hold on to your virginity?"

She turned back to me, giving me an incredulous look.

"If your father wanted to marry you off to one of the princes at the Capital, that was going to be a problem, wasn't it?"

"My would-have-been husband wouldn't have cared."

I stared because I knew that wasn't how things worked.

"Trust me, when he realized his wife could fuck as good as a whore, he wouldn't have cared."

The smile that invaded my face was involuntary, and there was a lightness to my chest I hadn't felt since I was a boy.

"Will you get married someday?"

My smile faded, and I gave her a hard look. "Why would I?"

"When your mom dies, you'll be king, right? Don't you need a wife and some heirs?"

"That's not how it works. Your credibility as a ruler isn't in your blood but in your heart." But if we successfully took back the Kingdoms, that would be a whole other affair.

"I like that…"

I looked at the fire.

"Do you want to have children?"

"No."

"Really? You're so close to your family."

"I'm not interested in bringing someone into this fucked-up world. There are many days when I question the point of being alive at all…" The conversation had taken a drastic turn, starting with a smile and then crashing into a scowl.

She watched me, her eyes shifting back and forth.

"Everyone is out for themselves, and they'll do whatever is necessary to get it."

She continued to watch me.

"I know you disagree, but trust me, you'll feel differently soon enough."

"I don't disagree."

My eyes flicked back to hers.

"But I think there's a lot of good moments in between that you're forgetting. Moments like this…"

I stared.

"We're enemies, right? But here we are…wrapped in each other's arms as lovers. I think that's beautiful. Don't you?"

"We're just fucking."

Her gaze didn't flinch as I tore her down. "If that were true, you would have left me in that cabin."

I held my silence, my jaw tight, incapable of a response.

She eventually looked away, dropping her eyes back to my chest, her fingertips tracing circles on my warm flesh.

Then I heard it.

The alarm.

The horns blared, almost carried away on the wind, not nearly as loud as they normally would have been.

Her eyes flicked up as her fingers stilled because she heard it too.

I was out of the bed in a flash, donning my clothes at lightning speed.

"What's happening?" She was out of bed too, putting her clothes back on.

"We're under attack." I secured my armor in place, my black breastplate, my vambraces, my gloves.

"In a storm?" she asked incredulously, practically shrieking.

I grabbed my weapons, my swords, shield, and my ax. "It's the perfect opportunity."

"You can't see more than five feet in front of your face."

My boots were last, snug-tight.

She went for the sword I'd left behind and picked it up.

My eyes flashed. "What the fuck are you doing?"

"You said we're under attack—"

"Stay. Here."

"You know I'm good with a sword."

I didn't have time for this. "I said stay here."

"I'm not going to run!"

I stormed out the door and yanked it shut behind me. Without looking back, I ran through the wind, knowing the exact location of where the horn had blared. Shouts sounded in the outpost, commands I couldn't make out.

I made it to the stairs and ran to the top, snow and ice hitting me in the face. "What's happening?"

Dylan was at the top, lighting the fires that were contained in towers of steel. "The Teeth. And they brought a yeti with them."

Fuck.

I sprinted down the wall, calling out orders. "Boulders, now!"

Ian ran at me from the opposite direction. "There's a yeti—"

"Yes, I heard." I had to shout to fight against the speed of the wind. It was dawn, so light was limited, but it was better than sheer darkness. "You got eyes on him?"

"We did, but he disappeared."

I clapped him on the shoulder. "You take the north. I take the south. Where's Mother?"

"With the archers."

"Let's do this. And don't fucking die."

He nodded and ran past me.

Now that the alarm had sounded from all points of the outpost, the men manned the walls, prepared the boulder slingshots, and lit the beacons. Only half of the flames survived the wind, but it was better than having none at all.

The storm was too strong for arrows. Every time we fired, they were taken by the wind. That was exactly what they wanted. If we didn't take them head on, they would storm the wall and make their way inside.

That would be fine—if we could see.

Roooooooaaaaaaarrrrrr

My head turned to the main gate.

Boom.

The gate wasn't going to hold with another one of those strikes. I sprinted back the way I'd come, moving to the north where my brother was.

Boom.

The gate was open by the time I made it, Teeth pouring in, biting into anyone in their path. The blood was the only thing I could see.

Rooooooaaaaaaarrrrrr.

One of the cabins was gone, ripped apart by the monster, a streak of white in the shadow.

Then I saw it—a splash of yellow.

It was a streak, like piss in the snow.

That's when I realized what had happened. Someone had tossed their chamber pot onto the monster, and now he was visible.

I jumped down over the edge and landed hard in the mound of snow. My ax was in my hands, and I swung for the first Teeth I saw, striking him down with a quick blow of my ax. Three of them came for me at once, and I smacked one between the eyes with the hilt of my ax, knocking him out before I swung at the other. The last one got my fist right in the side of his skull.

Another streak of piss was thrown on the yeti, making him a yellow beacon in the sea of white. "Take him down!" I cut through a sea of Teeth as I made my way closer, eager to sink my blade into his foot so he would fall just like a tree.

And then I saw her.

Ivory.

With a chamber pot in her hands.

I didn't have time to scold her. Didn't have time to react. Didn't have time for anything. I swung my ax into his foot, as deep and hard as I could go.

Rooooooaaaaaarrrrr.

He spun toward me, bright blue eyes meeting mine through the snow.

Ivory emerged on the other side of the beast, stabbing him in the other foot.

He cried out again, and this time, he swung his entire body back to her, his hands reaching for her.

My ax swung again and again and again. I chopped into his ankle like a tree—until he toppled over.

"Ivory!" I called into the wind, unable to see her.

Teeth were on me again, and I knocked them out cold as I sprinted to the last place where she'd been.

The Teeth had her, arms pinned behind her back as they tried to drag her away.

Her sword was on the ground, and she tried to fight, her screams carried in the opposite direction on the wind.

Now I knew exactly why they were here.

I couldn't swing my ax, not without risking her neck, so I yanked the first one off her then went for the other.

They both came at me at once, but Ivory was free.

I engaged the first, ducking under his sword and then dodging to the left. My ax swung at his feet, but the fucker jumped over it as if he knew it was coming. He wasn't an average Teeth sent to die for the greater good. He had a much bigger purpose, so he was a greater foe. My ax was exchanged for my sword, and I met his steel with mine. We swung at each other, steel hitting steel without the echo of collision, and we guessed the position of the other's blade based on their movements—because we couldn't see shit.

A Teeth went down beside me, the blood visible from the sword in his stomach.

I knew she had my back.

I pushed the Teeth back, swinging my sword and meeting his swings, left and right.

And then a blade protruded from his stomach from behind. Blood marked his lips and dribbled down his face before his eyes glazed over and he went down face first.

Ivory appeared behind him, holding my sword, now covered in the blood of the Teeth.

I screamed and not just because of the wind. "I told you to stay in the cabin!"

"Are you kidding me right now?" Her hair whipped in

the wind, going from left to right, all over the place. "I just saved your ass."

"Baby, I don't need you to save me."

"That's the second time you've called me that—and this time, it's in the middle of battle."

The Teeth were still rampant in the outpost, so this conversation would have to wait. "Stay behind me."

"How else am I supposed to watch your back?"

I halted, just for a moment, those words ringing in my ears. Then I moved forward, back into the throng of battle, keeping Ivory on my radar in my periphery. I was back to my ax, chopping Teeth left and right, clearing out the remaining enemies until they were eliminated from the outpost.

Thirty minutes later, it was finally done, and Ivory was still behind me.

The battle might be over, but the storm raged on, whipping snow and ice into our faces.

Ivory came to my side, out of breath, looking just like one of us in fur clothing and my sword. "Is it over?"

"Yes."

Ian's face appeared a short distance away, and when his eyes widened with acknowledgment, I knew I was the person he searched for. He ran up to me, his hand gripping my shoulder. "You alright?"

"Not a scratch. You?"

"Got a nasty cut on my leg, but I'll live." His eyes darted next to me, recognizing Ivory. He couldn't hide his look of surprise, and the look he gave me was full of accusation. Unspoken accusation. "Mother is looking for you."

"Is she okay?"

He nodded. "She's got a bloody lip and a black eye, but good otherwise. Were you the one who threw the chamber pot on the yeti? That was a smart move."

I shook my head. "Ivory."

His eyes flicked back to her again. "I can't hide this from Mother."

"I'm sure she already knows." I turned to Ivory. "Go back to the cabin."

She didn't argue with me, not after she'd heard my conversation with Ian. She excused herself and disappeared after she was a few feet away.

Ian looked at me. "What are you going to do?"

"I don't know. I told her to stay in the cabin, but she never listens to me."

"Maybe it's good that she didn't. That yeti could have killed a lot more people. Could have killed us all…"

I ignored what he said. "Take me to Mother."

Ian guided me through the blizzard to where she was, guarded by Geralt and Mace. Both were banged up and bleeding. They did their job because she looked far better than they did.

When her eyes landed on me, they lightened just the way they did when I came home after a long journey, when she feared for my safety. Her hands reached out to my cheeks, and she kissed me on the forehead. "You're alright."

"I'm always alright. What about you?"

She pulled away, but her hands lingered for a few seconds, her eyes still emotional at the sight of me. "I'm fine, my boy." Her arms circled me, and she pulled me close, giving me a hug.

I hugged her back, feeling her unconditional love that had been there since my first memory. Ever since I'd opened my eyes for the first time, I'd felt it, all around me. "I'll get the gate repaired. Ian will take care of the wounded." I stepped away, knowing there was too much to do to let this moment linger. "What are your orders?"

"I have none." Her eyes darkened again, and she was back to her usual self, a queen. "Because you always know what to do. Get to work and then rest. We'll speak later."

FOURTEEN

Huntley

I MADE IT BACK TO THE CABIN HOURS LATER, THE STORM still unabated. I had to shove my entire body into the door to get it to shut, and I didn't have a clue how Ivory had managed to close it on her own. There was a fire in the hearth, and my sword had been returned to the corner.

She emerged from the bathroom, wet and in just a towel. She stopped in front of me, her eyes fixated on my face, silently asking for answers.

"We lost a lot of people. But it could have been more, so we should consider ourselves lucky."

"They came for me…didn't they?"

The attack was a distraction. Klaus had sent his men to grab Ivory while the others sacrificed themselves.

"Why would they do that?"

I shook my head. "You shouldn't have run—"

"Well, I did. No point in arguing about it."

"And what the fuck were you thinking, going out there and fighting for the Runes?"

Her eyes narrowed, her hands keeping her towel against her body. "I wasn't fighting for *them*. I was fighting for you…"

I released an angry sigh, not because of what she'd said, but how much it turned me on.

"I'm not sorry about it. Don't expect an apology."

I never would. "When my mother realizes you were out there, you will be."

"I risked my life to help you, so punishing me would be a terrible way to show her gratitude."

"But she'll realize you were in my cabin. She'll realize that I never forced you."

She rolled her eyes. "She needs to get over it."

"And when she realizes the Teeth came for you…I'm not sure what she'll do."

"How would she know?"

I stared, my heartbeat loud in my ears.

Accusation moved into her gaze. "You're going to tell her."

"I have to."

The disappointment was written into every feature of her face.

"I won't betray my people—for you."

"Then you better defend your baby against your people."

"You aren't my baby—"

"*Liar*." She dropped her towel, showing her naked

body, drops of water streaking down over small tits and her flat stomach. She called my bluff—and waited for me to cave.

My dick was hard the second I stepped into this cabin, knowing she was inside waiting for me, knowing she had more courage than most of my men put together. My breaths grew heavy, and it took all my strength not to drop my gaze down her body, to appreciate her sexy hips, her slender stomach, the freckle on the inside of her right thigh.

Her stare was pure fire, flames crackling in a hearth, a knowing glint in her gaze.

It made me want her more.

Made her fucking irresistible.

I moved toward her, my fingers yanking the drawstring to my breeches at the same time, caving within seconds.

She didn't celebrate her win with a gloating smile. She was too busy getting everything off my body, getting me naked as quickly as possible so she could take my angry dick.

I got her on her back at the edge of the bed, my dick penetrating her tightness with a hard thrust.

She moaned as her nails turned into claws, cutting into my skin.

My hands curled under her thighs and held on to them as I pushed inside her deeper than I had before, giving her every inch and watching her wince slightly when it was just a little too much. "Baby." I let her win. And it had never felt so good to lose.

———

THE STORM LASTED FOR DAYS.

Time passed in the blink of an eye, even though I hardly slept.

We fucked day and night, in every position, in every way.

She let me fuck her in the ass—and took it like a champ.

Guess she was my baby after all.

But the storm eventually passed, and reality set in.

Cold. Harsh. Reality.

I returned her to her cabin, the one without the windows or fire, and I felt like shit doing it.

She stood there and looked at me, disappointed. "This is stupid."

"I know."

"I don't want to stay in here."

"I know."

"Set your mother straight."

I couldn't make any promises. "I'll try." I shut the door and walked to the stone keep where my mother waited for me. I entered the dining room in the cabin. Ian was there, and when he didn't make eye contact with me, I knew it was bad.

She already knew everything.

And she wasn't pleased.

I took a seat and ignored the ale in front of me.

She stared at me, a stare so cold it was as if the blizzard had returned.

I didn't bother keeping my cards close to my chest. "Listen—"

"No, Huntley. You will be the one who listens. And you will listen to every damn word I have to say."

I held her gaze, my jaw tight.

Her seething look was as powerful as a blizzard. Constant. Ice-cold. Terrifying. "She was out of her cabin and wielding your sword. There's only one way that could have happened. She was in your cabin—sleeping in your bed."

I didn't deny it.

"You lied to me."

"I didn't lie."

"You told me she cried and pleaded."

"She did—just not in the way you wanted." I couldn't believe I'd said that to my mother, but I wasn't talking to my mother right now. I was talking to the queen of my people, the leader who had lost all logic and replaced it with madness.

Her eyes narrowed to slits.

Ian's eyes immediately flicked to me, shocked that I'd said that.

Her voice was controlled, and that meant she was so pissed she had to force herself to be calm. "Need I remind you what she's done to us? She took our throne—"

"*She* did nothing. Faron, her father, is the one we want.

He's the one who will be slaughtered the way my father was. He's the one who will be tortured in every way possible until he begs for death. Don't misunderstand my loyalty or my agenda. It's where it has always been—with you."

Her anger sheathed, but only slightly.

"You interfered with my plan."

"I did not. You told me to go, and I did."

"But not under my pretenses."

"Doesn't matter. Did you honestly get any satisfaction out of that anyway?"

Her face was as hard as ever. "Yes."

"When we were attacked, she could have abandoned us and run. But she didn't. She stayed—and fought beside me."

Ian shifted his gaze back and forth between us.

"How stupid are you?" Her eyes narrowed like the edge of my blade. "You don't see what she's doing? She's manipulating you. And like every man who succumbs to good pussy, you fall for it."

"That's not what she's doing—"

"She's doing whatever she can to survive. You're just a way to survive, Huntley."

"I'm not." I knew how I sounded from her point of view, like an ignorant dumbass, but I also knew it was real.

She shook her head slightly, in overwhelming disappointment.

I'd never received that look from her before, and it hurt. "We can use her in a number of ways to get what we want. Raping her and torturing her is unnecessary."

"You wouldn't care about that if you weren't fucking her."

"Then isn't that reason enough?" I challenged.

She shook her head again, her eyes shifting elsewhere. "You've lost your way."

"I haven't lost my way. Delacroix will be ours again. I will slay him right in front of her without a second thought. But she's innocent. Her only crime is being born to a man who's vile. We're better than that. You're the most loving person I know, and you're better than that."

Her eyes flicked back to me. "I have love for my people and my family—not the daughter of the man who raped me, pushed my sons off a cliff, and murdered my husband. You're weak and, frankly, stupid."

The insult was hard to digest coming from her.

"I don't trust your judgment."

Another blow. "I don't trust yours either."

Ian's eyes widened.

She stilled, as if she couldn't believe I'd just said that.

"I know why we were attacked," I said. "The Teeth came for her. I saw them trying to drag her away. The battle was just a distraction. I could have kept that to myself, but I didn't because my loyalty is always to you." I rose to my feet, finished with this conversation. "You're a commander I would follow anywhere. You're a better queen than Father ever was a king. You're the person I look up to most. I'm the man I am—because of you."

She kept her eyes hard, probably on principle.

"But in this…you've lost your way. No woman would

ever wish what happened to her to happen to someone else—especially someone whose only crime is their lineage." I turned my back and walked out, bleeding from all the places my mother had stabbed me with her words. I returned to the stone keep, to the fire that always burned, and stopped to take a breath, to let the anger leave my core.

Footsteps sounded behind me, and I knew who they belonged to without turning around.

Her voice grew louder as she came close. "We need her for the next stage of our plan."

My eyes shifted from the flames to her.

"She helps us—and I'll let her go."

I couldn't believe she'd said those words, that she'd had a change of heart.

"But justice needs to be served first."

And just like that, the relief was gone.

She nodded to Geralt.

No.

"Hold him."

Mace and another guard grabbed me, and with his head bowed, Ian watched.

Geralt grinned as he walked out. "Excited to see what all the fuss is about…"

She turned back to me, her face like stone. "This time, I'll watch—to make sure." She followed him, and they left the stone keep.

I fought both men, throwing down Mace and then punching the other in the face.

Then a metal shackle was locked on to my ankle.

I looked up, seeing Ian.

Ian stepped back, his face pale as snow.

"Take this off."

He remained still.

"Ian."

He looked away.

"Don't you fucking listen to her."

"She's our queen—"

"And she's fucking batshit crazy right now. Take this off. *Now.*"

He still wouldn't meet my gaze.

"Ian, look at me."

He wouldn't.

"You know this is wrong."

"Doesn't matter—"

"Yes, it fucking matters. I'm your goddamn brother, and if you don't let me go, I'll never forgive you."

He finally looked at me.

"Come on." I pleaded with my eyes, knowing his loyalty to me was far stronger than whatever he felt for my mother right now. "I'm running out of time…"

He closed his eyes briefly then pulled the key from his pocket.

"Hurry."

He kneeled and turned the key until the metal clicked.

I took off at a dead sprint, exiting the stone keep and sprinting down the snow-covered trail until I reached her cabin. I made it just in time because they hadn't reached the front door yet. With both swords drawn, I barred the way.

Geralt halted then looked at Queen Rolfe for further instruction.

"Geralt has protected you for years, and I'm forever grateful of his service to my queen, but I will slice his fucking head off his shoulders if he comes any goddamn closer. If you don't want me to kill your guard, you'll order him to stand down. Now."

She stared at me, her look almost bored.

"Or if he kills me, you'll lose your eldest son."

Geralt waited, prepared to fight me if he was ordered to.

After a long showdown of stares, she excused Geralt with a nod.

He fell back and retreated.

Both of my swords were sheathed in my belt.

Her blue eyes took me in without blinking for a long time, as if it were the first time she'd ever really looked at me, and then she came closer, one foot in front of the other, her boots leaving prints in the powder. She was in a thick white gown the same color as the snow, matching feathers in her hair, and wore a cloak thicker than mine. "Will you take your father's place at the top of the cliffs? Will you take back what has been in our blood for generations?"

"Yes."

"Will you avenge me?"

"With pleasure."

Her eyes shifted back and forth as she looked into mine.

"My loyalty is to my family."

"Then you understand there's no future with this woman."

"Yes."

"Yet, she's worth this stand."

"Even if she meant nothing to me, she would still be worth this stand because this isn't who we are. This isn't what we do. If it is, then we're no different from him. Surely you must see that."

Her eyes remained steady.

"You're the strongest person I know—and the most compassionate. You're fair and just. You rule with respect, not fear. You have no idea how much it hurts me to know how much this hurts you...how much it still hurts you. If only I'd been the man I am now, I would have killed all of them and protected you. I'm so sorry I didn't."

She dropped her chin. It was the first time she'd ever done that.

"I won't fail you again. You have my word."

She kept her gaze on the ground for a long time. "It wasn't your job to protect me, Huntley. You were a boy..."

"Now I'm a man. And I will slaughter him."

"I know."

"Don't ever question my loyalty to you, to our family, to what we've worked so hard for."

She raised her chin once again. "Does she know you feel this way?"

"Yes."

"Does she feel the same way about her own family?"

"I'm not sure how she feels, honestly. When I told her the truth, she didn't believe me. But I think she believes me now…"

She took in my gaze for a long time, her mind working. "You're a grown man who can make his own decisions. If this is the woman you want to sleep with, then that's your business. But you can't trust someone whose blood is the enemy to your own."

"Never said I trusted her."

"Good. Keep it that way."

I nodded.

"I will spare her. Perhaps you're right. Perhaps I've lost my mind-set. But make no mistake, she's our prisoner. We will use her to get what we need. You can't let your feelings compromise everything we've worked so hard for. Do you understand me?"

"Yes."

"Promise me."

"Yes." I said it without hesitation. "I promise."

FIFTEEN

Ivory

—————

THE DOOR OPENED—AND REVEALED HUNTLEY.

I'd only been in there for an hour, maybe two, and I was relieved it wasn't any longer. I hated this place every time I returned to it, not having anything to stare at besides the dark. Every time I lay on the bed, it hurt my back, so I chose to sit up.

"Let's go."

I didn't need to be told twice. I came to his side, and we walked back to the cabin.

He didn't look at me. Didn't acknowledge my existence. His mood was different, as if something had happened.

We returned to his cabin, and the second we stepped inside, it felt like home.

I hoped I never had to go back to that shithole. "What happened?"

He didn't take off his shoes or clothes as if he had somewhere he needed to be. "What do you mean?"

"You're different."

He stared at me, his expression hard.

"Like something upset you."

"Not upset. But I have to go. Got shit to do."

"Anything I can do to help?"

"No. You should stay here."

"So…I don't have to go back to that cabin?"

"No."

"So, something did happen…"

He kept a straight face, as if he wouldn't discuss it with me.

"Has your mother finally dropped her hostility now that she knows I'm not my father?"

"Yes, but that's not why."

"Then why?"

"Because I gave her no other choice."

Now my heart squeezed in a whole different way. "Thank you—"

"Just so we're clear, you're still our prisoner, you're still going to help me, and I doubt we'll ever let you go. Nothing's going to stop me from getting to that throne—and slitting your father's throat."

Put on the spot like that, I didn't know what to say.

"You still want to do this?"

"Do what?"

He gave me a hard stare, answering the question with his silence.

"No."

He tried to keep a straight face, but a hint of disappointment came through.

"But it's just going to happen anyway, so… Do you?"

The answer must be obvious to him because he didn't respond. "I'll be back in a couple hours. We leave tomorrow."

"Leave for where?"

"HeartHolme."

"HeartHolme… What's that?"

"Our kingdom."

So, there was more than these wooden cabins in the freezing cold. I remembered him mentioning it before, and I hoped it was a place warmer than this. "Just the two of us?"

"Queen Rolfe and her guards will travel with us."

"Oh…" I couldn't even pretend not to be disappointed.

His eyes showed a glint of anger. "She's your queen now. Remember that."

I had a good comeback, but I kept my mouth shut because of his intense mood. Now wasn't the time to provoke him. Our cohabitation had taught me things that couldn't be learned through conversation, like his moods, his unspoken desires, things I couldn't even explain.

His eyes lingered a moment longer, as if giving me the opportunity to say my final words.

"What are you doing?"

Like the question annoyed him, he walked out.

————

I TOOK a warm bath then fed the fire in the main room so it would keep it comfortable. I assumed the trek to HeartHolme was long, and it would be spent in the freezing cold, in the company of a woman who despised me.

Despised me because of the blood that ran through my veins.

Just when it turned dark, he returned with two trays of food.

I wasn't sure what I was more excited about—the food or him.

He set one tray on the table next to the armchair and then carried his dinner to his desk. He took a seat, his back to me, and ate as he pored over maps and scrolls.

I sat in front of the fire and ate, wearing one of his shirts I'd found in the closet. It was a blanket on me, and I had to roll up the sleeves several times so my hands wouldn't drown in the fabric. The fire was warm enough that I didn't need bottoms, so I sat there in just my under-wear, glancing at his back from time to time.

At some point, I fell asleep, my knees to my chest with my arms crossed over my body. The sound of the crack-ling flames lulled me under and accompanied my dreams. I suddenly felt weightless, two strong arms scooping underneath my knees and back, holding me close. I recog-nized his smell right away, recognized his heat like sun right on my face.

My back hit the mattress, and then my underwear was pulled off.

I opened my eyes, seeing his naked body on top of mine. My thighs parted with his, and then my pelvis tilted as I felt my body fold underneath him.

"I'm sleeping…"

He guided himself inside me, his entrance so powerful that it jolted me wide awake. "I don't care." With his powerful chest in my face, he pounded me into the mattress, fucking me straight to the point so we could both go to sleep.

There wasn't a single kiss, any eye contact, nothing, but my body tightened and exploded as if there'd been hours of foreplay. My open lips were pressed to his chest, my moans swallowed, my teeth clenching down for a small bite.

He came a moment later, filling me in silence, not even giving a moan.

Then he rolled off me and lay there, ready to sleep as if nothing had happened. The sheets stayed at his waist because he was warm, his skin flushed with the blood in his muscles, and his powerful chest slowly returned to its normal breathing.

Once he was cooled off, I found my place in his side, his shoulder my pillow.

"How long is the journey to HeartHolme?"

"Couple days."

"On foot?"

"Horse."

"Oh, that will be a nice change."

"Don't try to run."

I stilled at the command—because running was the last thing on my mind.

"I won't be able to protect you if she's there."

"I wasn't going to…" Honestly, the idea of escape had been forgotten. It was once my primary focus, but now… not even an afterthought. It wasn't just because of the yetis and the Teeth in my path. It was because…I didn't have any desire. "I'm dreading this, though."

"I won't let anything happen to you."

"That's not why. Come on, I threw piss on a yeti. I'm not scared."

He turned his head to look down at me. "Then what is it?"

"How are we supposed to get it on with your mom there?"

A very subtle smile moved on to his lips. "You can't wait a couple days?"

"Uh, can you?" I propped myself up on an elbow and looked down at him. "I was literally asleep, and that wasn't enough to stop you."

He moved his arm underneath his head as he watched me, wearing that hard expression that guarded everything underneath from the surface. "We'll see what happens."

"We're sharing a bedroll, right? Because I'll freeze if we don't."

"Yes. It's the best way for me to keep an eye on you."

"You really think you need to keep an eye on me?" I

asked, slightly offended.

He never answered.

"What happened today? You've been weird ever since…"

He looked away, as if to dismiss the line of questioning.

"Why won't you tell me—"

"Because I don't want to talk about it."

"Why?"

He gave an annoyed sigh.

"I'm not going to stop asking you."

"Clearly." Now he looked at me head on. "She realized the truth and sent Geralt to do what I couldn't. Ian chained me up, and then I was helpless. My brother has greater loyalty to me than her, so he let me go. I got there before Geralt entered the cabin, and I threatened to kill him if he didn't stand down. The queen didn't call my bluff because she knows I don't make threats I don't mean."

I'd sat on that bed in the dark, having no idea what was taking place outside.

"My mother and I had words… That was the hardest part."

"Why?"

He was quiet for so long it seemed like the conversation was over, like he'd shared as much as he was willing to share. "Because I realized how much it still bothers her… what happened. I failed to protect her because I was just a boy, but I still carry that guilt every single day of my life."

His eyes shifted away, to another spot in the cabin. "I'm a man now—and I won't fail her again."

As if our bodies were joined together, his pain transferred to me, hitting me right in the chest. It was a sickening feeling, like a constant weight in the pit of my stomach. My lungs hurt with my breaths. Everything hurt. "I'm…sorry."

He wouldn't look at me.

"Really. I am."

His jaw tightened slightly, the tension moving into the features of his face. "I know."

"Then…why do you look so angry?"

"Because I wish I didn't believe you."

———

I WAS FINALLY GIVEN real clothing, thick breeches made for the cold climate, a long-sleeved tunic that kept my body warm, and a cloak made of fur to survive the freezing temperatures. But I was given no weapons.

"What if we're attacked?"

"You have me."

"What if we're attacked by a horde of Teeth?"

"Then it doesn't matter."

I walked beside him, irritated that I was being denied a basic right. "In case you've forgotten, I fought for you against the Teeth. I helped you take down that yeti, and I had your back the entire time—"

"These are Queen Rolfe's wishes." He stopped beside

me, the two of us walking together toward the stone keep. He gave me a calm look, but it was packed with annoyance. "Period."

"Maybe you should be king instead."

He held my gaze, not giving any hint of a reaction.

"I think you'd be a lot better at it."

He turned away and dismissed what I'd said.

I followed him. "The thought has never crossed your mind—"

"This conversation is over."

We entered the stone keep, a place I'd visited when I'd first come here. There was an enormous fire in the center, the smoke rising in the opening between the stones. It was several degrees warmer here than outside near the cabins.

Queen Rolfe stood there, donned in her furs and feathers, her lithe body toned with muscle like she didn't just sit on her ass all day and order people around. I remembered her in the battle, her face banged up from the hits she took.

She had my respect for that.

Ian was there, a mirror image of his brother, with the same short hair, the same bright eyes.

Queen Rolfe's gaze switched to us, first landing on her son, the undertone of affection in her gaze. It was subtle, but it was there, on the surface. When her gaze shifted to me, that look was long gone, replaced by a bitter dose of indifference.

I held her stare, refusing to be intimidated by anyone, even her.

She pulled her look away then regarded her youngest son. "I leave the outpost to you, son. I know you'll protect our people." Her hands cupped his cheeks, and she pressed a kiss to his forehead. Then her arms surrounded him for a quick embrace. "I'll see you soon."

Ian gave a nod. "Travel safely, Your Highness."

Huntley approached his brother next, and they exchanged a long look, a stare packed with words that didn't need to be spoken. "Be safe."

"I wish I could come with you. Be the shield at your back."

Huntley's hand went to his shoulder. "You are—always." He pulled him in for an embrace and placed a quick kiss on his forehead.

The whole exchange made me miss my brother, even though we were never affectionate like that.

I was too busy watching them together that I didn't notice Queen Rolfe walk right up to me. My eyes shifted to meet hers, seeing the same blue eyes that bored into mine every night, but full of genuine hate. "Just remember I'm always watching you, even when you think I'm not. Give me a reason to kill you—because I only need one."

———

QUEEN ROLFE and her guards had their own horses, but Huntley and I shared one.

I didn't mind because I got to rest against Huntley's back and enjoy the scenery around us. It was mostly forest, following a weathered trail that had been traveled many times. It was still cold, but there wasn't snow on the ground, so the snow from the storm must have already melted.

That was a good sign.

Once we broke through the forest, the mountains were in view, far to the east.

When I turned around to see the cliffs, I saw nothing but a distant gray wall, like the sun was covered by storm clouds. It was hard to believe that mountains existed at the bottom of the cliffs, but their summits were still so far below that you couldn't see them through the clouds at Delacroix.

It was a long ride, all through the day, only stopping for short breaks.

At nightfall, we stopped, but only when visibility was so poor that it would be dangerous to keep going.

It was a cloudless night, so the stars were bright, and the air was cold without the blanket on the sky.

Huntley tied the horse to a tree and prepared the bedroll on the ground.

Queen Rolfe did the same with her guards a short distance away.

There wasn't a hot meal tonight, and we were back to our dried meats, fruits, and nuts. We couldn't risk a fire, so it was a cold night, and I missed the fireplace in that cabin that had been a temporary oasis.

Still in his armor and weaponry, he lay on the ground, his short swords at his hips.

I pulled the blanket to my shoulders and scooted closer to him, preferring the hardness of his skin to the hardness of his armor. His shoulder was a good pillow, but not with the metal plates there. But it was still warm, so I stayed close. "Are you really going to sleep like that?"

"Like what?" His eyes were on the sky.

"With all your weapons."

"It'd be stupid not to."

"It's stupid that I can't have my own weapons, considering I could just grab yours in your sleep right now."

"That sounds like a threat."

"Just a point."

His eyes remained on the sky.

"Can I ask you something?"

He kept his deep voice low, just loud enough for me to hear. "What?"

"It seems like you're her favorite…"

He was silent.

"Why? Is it because you're the oldest?" My father preferred Ryker, but I assumed it was because he was a boy. If I had a dick between my legs, I suspected I would be the favorite since I was a lot more adventurous and reckless.

"No."

"Then why?" I saw the way she looked at him, the way she abandoned her position as a queen and became a mother instead. She grasped his cheeks with a lot more affection than she did with Ian, and her hug was much longer. I wondered if Ian noticed it too.

"Because I tried to save her—and Ian didn't."

So, he knew full well of her favoritism.

"Ian isn't a coward. He did what he was supposed to do, what I should have done too. But I stayed…and that changed our relationship forever."

"Does that bother Ian?"

"He says it doesn't, but I know it does."

"Yeah…"

"I feel guilty that I didn't protect her. He feels guilty for not even trying."

"You were both so young at the time."

"Doesn't matter."

We turned quiet, both of us looking at the blanket of stars. One streaked across the sky, a trail of light shining behind it. His body had warmed the blanket that was draped over us both, and that made it easy for my tired eyes to close, to fall asleep with him next to me.

———

ON THE SECOND DAY, I was sore. Really sore.

I'd never ridden a horse so long. And I'd never slept on the ground the night afterward either.

As if he didn't experience the same discomfort, Huntley didn't mention it, and he climbed back on that horse, ready for another day. Queen Rolfe and Geralt and Mace were the same way, not giving a complaint before they set out again.

The mountains remained on our left, and the landscape started to thin out into open fields with green grass, weeds, and occasionally flowers. The air was still cold, but at least now it was mild, not burning your nose every time you took a breath.

It was too challenging to talk on the ride, so we didn't say anything, and I sat behind him with my arms locked around his waist. We stopped for the night, had a meager dinner, and slept hard because we were so tired. The third day was more of the same, and I was relieved this trip was only a couple of days rather than weeks.

I knew we were close to our destination when we approached enormous stone gates. They were so tall I could see them from leagues away. With the height of a mountain, they must have taken decades to complete.

"Is that it?" I said into his ear.

"Yes."

The gates were attached to a rocky outcropping, the rest of the city hidden from view by the stone. It was a lot more fortified than the outpost, which was surrounded by a simple wooden fence that was just tall enough so a yeti couldn't climb over.

I wondered if they had yetis out here.

Geralt pulled a flag from his saddle, bright red, the color of blood.

That must have been a signal to open the gates because they slowly started to move.

A queen should be escorted by an entire army, not just three men and a woman who wasn't allowed to carry weapons, but maybe that made her trek across the open safer since she would look like a nobody instead of a somebody.

"Yetis aren't going to be able to get inside there…"

He gave a chuckle.

"Did I just make you laugh?"

"Hardly a laugh."

The gates fully opened before we arrived, and the horses rode through the open doorway and brought us into HeartHolme. The stables were first, along with sling-shots fitted with enormous boulders, quivers of arrows all along the walls, ready for use. It was a battle station rather than an entryway.

HeartHolme immediately felt different from the outpost, just by the way Queen Rolfe and Huntley were treated. The horses were taken away, and men in uniforms with a feather crested on their chests came forward to assist her. They gave her water, a tray of cheese and fruits, and removed her fur cloak, replacing it with a regal one. Huntley was treated the same way, like royalty.

They weren't sure what to do with me.

Queen Rolfe and her guards stepped into a carriage waiting for her arrival that took her away, down a stone pathway between buildings and shops. It couldn't have been more different from the outpost, which was earthy and open. This was a city hidden away by the stone, opening into several streets with homes and shops, a place established long ago. People walked the pathways, women carrying bags of fresh baguettes and produce. Kids played in the street, chasing one another into alleyways.

It reminded me of Delacroix.

Huntley walked up to me, his fur cloak and thick breeches replaced by an outfit far more kingly. Dressed in all black with gold chains across his chest, he carried his short swords at his hips and his ax across his back. Even in the city, he was armed, ready for anything.

I looked him over, liking the way the sleeves covered his thick muscles snugly, the way his clothes fit his body like they were made just for him. A black cape hung behind him, flowing over his broad shoulders nicely.

He gave a nod in the direction we were going. "Come on."

I joined him, still in the clothes I'd arrived in. "So… this is HeartHolme."

"Not what you were expecting?"

"It's…big."

"I told you there were a lot of us."

We walked through the streets, moving up a slight incline as we went higher from the ground level. When the road curved a different way, I saw it. The castle was at the highest part of the mountain, visible because of its grand size, but also its elevation above the rest of the city. The blue sky was behind it—and nothing else. "Is the castle on the edge of a cliff?"

"Yes."

"How high is this cliff?"

"Very."

"So, it can't be attacked from the ground?"

"Not unless they can fly."

"Is that where you live?" I asked. "In the castle?"

"No." He gave a slight chuckle. "I'm too old to live with my mother."

"Well, it looks big enough for all three of you."

It was a long walk through the city, moving down the different streets until the castle came closer into view. I didn't realize we'd reached our destination until Huntley stopped in front of a gate in a wall. A two-story building was behind it, mostly hidden behind the stone and the ivy that grew over it.

He pulled out a key and opened the door.

"This is where you live?" I stepped inside, seeing a small garden with flowers, plants, and trees. There was a sitting area next to a fountain, even though he seemed like someone who didn't take time to socialize.

He locked the gate behind us. "I like my space. And I don't like bullshit."

"Is there a lot of bullshit at the castle?"

"Like you wouldn't believe." He walked to the front door of his home and unlocked it next.

"Where does Ian live?"

"You ask a lot of questions about my brother." He stepped inside, emerging into a kitchen with a dining table.

"I know you guys are close. Reminds me of Ryker and me." There were counters, a stove, pantries probably filled with food. The dining table could fit four people comfortably. Everything was made of dark wood, which suited his personality perfectly.

The next room was the living room, several couches all arranged around a large fireplace, nearly three times as big as the one in the cabin. Down the hallway was the bathroom and his office.

That meant the upstairs must just be bedrooms.

I guided myself up the banister and emerged into one large bedroom. The bed was bigger than the one at the cabin, and the fireplace was just like the one on the bottom floor. Candles were everywhere, probably to light up the rooms after the sun went down. "Am I staying here with you?"

"Yes. But don't get comfortable. We're leaving in a few days."

"Why?" It would take me a few days just to recuperate from the ride here.

"Because we have shit to do."

"What shit?"

He gave me an irritated look. "You agreed to help me, remember?"

"I thought that was why we're here."

"No."

"Oh…" I suspected where we were going would be a major step down from this.

He studied my expression. "You like it here."

"Yeah. Reminds me of home."

His expression hardened for just a second.

Sometimes I forgot that we had the same home. It was still there waiting for me—but it had been savagely taken from him. "Sorry…"

He brushed it off. "Stay here. I'll be back later."

"Can I walk around—"

"No."

"You really think I'm going to run? Climb over that gate like a fucking spider?"

"I said stay."

"I'm not a fucking dog!"

His nostrils gave a slight flare.

"I'm not asking your permission—"

"You forget who you are now. You aren't the Duchess of Delacroix. You're my fucking prisoner, and if I tell you to stay, you fucking stay. Your entitlement is fucking obnoxious—"

"Demanding to be treated better than a dog is obnoxious to you? Then I'm glad I'm obnoxious. I'm going to be so fucking obnoxious—"

His hand was on my neck, and then he crashed our mouths together, silencing my protest with his crushing kiss. His body backed me up, kept making me go until I hit the wall. He cornered me, pushing me into the surface like it was a mattress. One hand reached into my breeches and found my nub, and he rubbed it as hard as he kissed me, one hand still on my neck.

It was like the fight had never happened, totally absent from my mind, and my hands dug into the back of his hair like I'd wanted to do for the last three days. I'd had to lie beside him two nights in a row, only able to sleep and do nothing else, which was so hard considering he was the sexiest bastard I'd ever seen.

My mouth devoured his as I fell into the oblivion that only he could give me. He swept me away in a passion so hot, it was like nothing else existed. I wasn't far away from home. I was at home—with him. It made everything better.

The climax hit me unexpectedly because he had complete control of my body. He rubbed me just the way I liked, thoroughly acquainted with my body by this point, and he released my lips so I could moan, so my hips could buck against his palm as the tears formed in the corners of my eyes.

With his face hard and flushed with heat, he watched, watched the climax hit and enjoyed the show until the curtains closed.

My arm hooked around his neck, and I rested my face against his shoulder, breathing, feeling my body go weak as if someone snuffed the life right out of me.

His hand left my pants, and he forced my head back so I'd look him in the eye. "Feel better, baby?"

I was too tired to be angry. Too satisfied to care.

He let me go and stepped away. "I'll fuck you when I get back."

I watched him walk away, leaving me against the wall. "You better."

He stilled before he stepped out of the bedroom. His body became rigid and tight, like all the muscles of his back squeezed his spine. He drew in a breath, let it out, and found the strength to keep going.

SIXTEEN

Huntley

_____

WHEN THE GUARDS SAW ME APPROACH, THEY SIDESTEPPED out of my way, allowing me entry to the cobblestone path that led to the large double doors of the keep. There were more guards there, and they both opened the doors so I could pass.

The castle was made of stone, far more bare than the one I'd grown up in, but there were rugs to cushion my boots, vases of flowers on the tables, heavily armored guards positioned throughout the castle to defend their queen.

I took the stairs and moved to the next floor, walking down a corridor until I reached the grand room where my mother had her meetings. A large table stood in the middle of the room, the double doors to the balcony open because it was an unusually warm day.

Asher was already there, sitting in his large, cushioned chair with the maps on the surface of the table in front of him. He grabbed a pawn, his thumb rubbing over the chess piece before setting it back down onto HeartHolme. He didn't look at me as he addressed me. "Good to be home, Huntley?"

I sat in the chair across from him. "I'll be gone before I can even enjoy it."

His eyes flicked up, and he regarded me, his look slightly cold. He was in the garb of the queen, the feather on his chest. His head was bald, his skin was tight over his thin body, and he had eyes that could see through everything.

"Have something to say, Asher?"

He straightened in the chair, drawing a slow breath. "Queen Rolfe told me about your…interest in our prisoner."

"Captors fuck their prisoners. This isn't revolutionary."

"Captors *rape* their prisoners. That's not what you're doing."

Sometimes I wished I were king just so I could bash his head in. "Where is she?"

"She'll join us when she's ready." He grabbed the pawn again, rubbed his fingers over it. "Her Highness informed me about the attack on the outpost. Very concerning."

"Another day, another yeti…"

The silence trickled by, the two of us exchanging stares, the tension stretching.

Commander Dawson came next, dressed in the armor

that signified his rank, a broadsword on his hip. "It's good to see your return, Huntley. This castle was quiet without the two of you."

"Nice to be back, Commander."

Commander Dawson took his seat, the strong and silent type, much more my style.

Minutes later, my mother finally made her entrance, her hair done with brand-new feathers, her makeup painted on her face, in her royal garb that made her look like a true queen. She fought alongside her people as one of them, but she could also occupy a throne like it was made just for her.

We all rose when she entered the room, and once she sat down, we followed suit.

Her eyes went to me first, and instead of a glimmer of motherly affection, there was just callous coldness. "You think it's wise that our prisoner is unattended this very moment?"

"What's she going to do?" I asked incredulously. "Go on a killing spree? To what purpose?"

Her eyes remained cold.

"And she can't escape, so we don't have to worry about that."

Mother turned away, as if the conversation was dismissed. "I'm concerned about the two of you traveling alone together."

"Why?"

She turned back to me. "She can slit your throat in the middle of the night."

"She won't."

"You said you didn't trust her—"

"She'd die without me, and she knows it. Unless I personally deliver her to Delacroix, she'd never make it back—at least not alive."

My mother's frozen eyes held my gaze, processing my words without a hint of reaction.

"We don't need to worry about her—at least, not right now." Once she got me what I needed, I wasn't sure what would happen next. We couldn't let her go, but we couldn't kill her either. At that point, it would get complicated…really complicated.

Asher stared at me with that obnoxious look on his face, like he didn't find any merit to my words.

She addressed the table. "As was already stated in my letter sent with the emissary, the outpost was attacked. The Teeth recruited the help of a yeti and nearly destroyed our camp. Huntley believes they were there for Ivory."

Commander Dawson turned to me. "Your evidence?"

"I watched them try to take her. Everyone else was attacked, but she was spared."

"But why would they want her?" Asher asked. "How would they even know who she is?"

I explained the story. "After I took her to the outpost, she escaped. I went after her, but the Teeth found her first. They attacked us, and we killed them all except for Klaus, who got away."

"That doesn't explain why they would want her,"

Commander Dawson said. "However beautiful she may be doesn't make her worth bloodshed with the Runes."

"She told me Klaus suspected she's from the top of the cliffs," I said. "He said she didn't look like a Rune or anything else down here."

Commander Dawson stiffened, his fingers gently closing into a fist.

Asher was still too, like he understood exactly what that meant.

Mother addressed what we were all thinking. "If he knows she's from the top of the cliffs, that means there's a way up, and she knows how to get there."

I nodded in agreement.

"They know our history, so if she's in our company, that means she's probably someone important," Queen Rolfe continued. "And that's why they attacked us, and probably why they'll attack us again."

"They'll assume she was taken to HeartHolme," Commander Dawson said. "If she's important, she wouldn't stay at the outpost."

"True," Mother said. "That means we need to be prepared for war."

The tension in the room was palpable, heavy like a cloud, fog in our lungs.

"If that cunt hadn't run away, we wouldn't be dealing with this." She turned her stare on me, as if I were somehow to blame.

"You would have done the same thing—"

"You should have killed Klaus." She wasn't my mother

right now. She was a queen desperate to protect her people and her agenda. "You let him get away."

"I didn't let him get away. He overpowered me, and when Ivory came to my aid, he took off."

"Then you should have hunted him down." Her eyes were blue flames.

"Ivory rescued you?" Commander Dawson asked. "If you were the person she was running from, why didn't she leave you to your fate?"

I kept my gaze on my mother. "Because she has a heart." I could see straight through a lie, smell bullshit from a league away, and I knew every word out of Ivory's mouth was the truth. I knew she cared about what happened to my family. I knew she cared about me. I knew she cared about the animals she helped.

Mother held my look for a long time with an angry stare. It wasn't clear what pissed her off more—the fact that I allowed Klaus to escape or that I defended Ivory's character. I was definitely on her shit list right now.

She withdrew her stare. "We have a few options. We prepare for a war that might arrive on our doorstep. We hit the Teeth now while they don't expect it. Or we give them Ivory and avoid bloodshed altogether."

"The last one isn't an option," I said. "We need her."

"But what about when we don't?" She kept her eyes on Commander Dawson. "She gives us what we need, and then we throw her to the wolves."

My heart hadn't pounded like that in a long time. A

really long time. "I told her I wouldn't kill her if she helped me."

"And you would be keeping that promise." She turned to me. "She'll be alive when we hand her to the Teeth. She may not be alive much longer after that, but…" She gave a shrug, the situation inconsequential.

I could actually feel my chest vibrate with every beat of my heart. It was fear—and I hadn't felt fear since I was a child. "If we hand her to the Teeth, we can't use her against Delacroix."

"If she's successful in your mission, we don't need her against Delacroix," she countered. "We can do the rest ourselves."

"If you hand her over to the Teeth, she'll tell them everything if she thinks it'll spare her life, and then we'll have competition on top of the cliffs. That would be a mistake."

"And it would be a mistake to go to war with the Teeth when Necrosis can strike at any moment." Now her voice rose when it hardly ever did. She could command a room with silence. She never needed to yell to maintain control. "We can't take on all three at once. We need to eliminate one—and this is the best way to do it."

———

I WALKED down the cobblestone streets at dusk, the torches already lit to prepare for the imminent darkness.

The streets turned empty, and the windows of the pubs and eateries started to glow with activity.

I approached the door to the Golden Horse and stepped inside.

The bar was already occupied with its regulars, enjoying the fresh-brewed ale with a bowl of stew and a side of bread. I made eye contact with a couple people I recognized and made my way to the petite figure in front of the dart board.

She held the dart between her fingertips, closed one eye to aim, and then threw it at the board.

Bull's-eye.

One of the guys groaned before he pulled out a pouch of coins.

Elora took the pouch and tossed it in the air a couple times. "Nothing better than robbing a man right in front of him." She gave him a wink then strutted toward the bar.

I stepped in front of her because she hadn't noticed me. "Looks like you're buying me a drink."

She'd just tossed the bag into the air when she stopped. She caught it without a glance as her jaw dropped open. "I didn't know you were home."

"Arrived a couple hours ago." I couldn't suppress my smile, not when she lit up like that.

She jumped into my arms and gave me a bear hug. "I'm so glad you're back. You were gone for so long."

I squeezed her back, my chin resting on her head.

"It sucked. Don't do that anymore."

I pulled away. "Well, I've got bad news… I'm leaving again in a couple days."

Her eyebrows furrowed in her anger then she stuck out her tongue. "How long?"

"I don't know…but probably a while."

"Ugh." She turned to the bar. "Let's get that drink. Now I really need one."

We took seats side by side, ordering a couple of ales and some stews. She pivoted in the stool toward me, her legs crossed, her breeches tight, with thick boots on her feet. "So, did you grab the girl?"

"I did."

"That went smooth?"

Smooth wasn't the word I'd use. "A hiccup here and there…"

"Now what?"

"I'm taking her with me to the isles in a few days."

"Just the two of you?" she asked incredulously. "Gonna have her tied up the entire time?"

I shook my head.

"Then how do you know she won't try to kill you?"

"Because she knows she'd be dead without me."

"What's she like?"

I shrugged. "A pain in the ass…"

She turned to her stew and took a couple bites. "Is she in the dungeon?"

I held her gaze for a while, unsure what to say. "Yes."

She continued to eat. "How was the outpost?"

"Cold. Got attacked by the Teeth and a yeti."

"Oh shit. What happened?" She dropped her spoon back into her bowl.

I told her the story—and left out Ivory's part in it.

"They haven't attacked in forever," she said. "Why now?"

I told her that story too.

"Wow, you're right." She took a drink of her ale. "She is a pain in the ass."

I noticed the way the other men in the bar looked at her, always had her in the corner of their eye, as if they had any chance with her. If a stare lingered too long, I stared back until they backed off like a fucking pussy.

"Ian?"

"He's fine."

"Are you worried about him being at the outpost alone? Now that we know what's going on with the Teeth?"

I always worried about him. He was my little brother. It was my job to worry. "I'm confident in his abilities."

"I hope you mean that…because now I'm worried."

I washed down my fear and brushed it off. "He'll be fine, Elora. What's been going on with you?"

———

I ENTERED my house behind the gate and made my way upstairs. The glow from the fireplace was visible, shadows on the walls, so I knew she was there. Hoped she was naked in bed, because I'd been thinking about her since I'd walked out the door.

My eyes immediately went to the bed, but she wasn't there waiting for me.

My eyes flicked to the open doorway that led to the bathroom. "Ivory?"

She came out of nowhere, and with a dagger in her hand, she stabbed me right in the stomach.

My guard was down. Otherwise, that wouldn't have happened.

Her hand was still on the hilt as she held it inside me, her eyes more vicious than my mother's on her worst day.

I didn't grimace or wince, didn't make a single gesture of discomfort.

She yanked it out of me, the blade red with my blood.

I could feel my body immediately begin to heal once the weapon was gone.

"Is she your girlfriend? Or is she your wife?"

My eyebrows furrowed.

"I followed you—and now I know why you wanted me to stay here."

Elora.

"Sure didn't look like a whore to me."

Now it all became clear.

"You were away from home a little too long and couldn't say no? What were you going to do? Never tell her about me?" Furious, she walked away and threw the bloody knife on the dresser. "You're a fucking piece of shit…"

My eyes watched her movements, aware of the blood that had soaked into the fabric of my tunic and splashed onto the floor. The blood stopped as quickly as it started.

She paced around the room with her arms crossed in front of her, her chest heaving with her anger. When I didn't say anything, she turned to regard me. "That's it? You have nothing to say?"

I unbuttoned my tunic then removed it, tossing the bloody shirt on the floor so it wouldn't stain anything else. The wound had already healed over, leaving a small line as a scar. "Not really."

Stunned, she just stared at me.

"I don't see why it matters if I'm fucking her or not."

Her eyes widened at my declaration. "Wow…you're an asshole."

"Whether I'm committed to her or not, it's none of your business. And why would you care?"

"Why would I care? Because I don't sleep with married men."

"Not married."

"Whatever. You still belong to somebody else."

"I don't belong to anybody." Never had. Never would. "And don't pretend to have this righteous moral compass. That's not what this is about."

She stopped in front of me, her arms still crossed over her chest.

"You don't want me to sleep with anyone else. That's what this is about."

Her eyes brightened in anger. "I couldn't care less—"

"Are you my baby or not?"

She shut her mouth and went still.

"I like a woman who tells me what she wants and how she wants it—so fucking tell me. Stab me with that knife and tell me that you want me all to yourself. Stab me and tell me that you're my baby and you're the only woman who gets my dick every night."

All of her anger drew out of her features. Now she stood there and stared, at a loss for words.

"I speak my mind. I tell it like it is. If there's something you don't want to know, you shouldn't ask, because I'll tell you the whole goddamn truth with every minor detail. That's what you get from me. You want to be my baby? Then you better do the same."

She stared for a long time, all the anger now out of her eyes, a calm serenity on her delicate features. "I'm your baby…"

My body flushed with heat, my skin on fire, my dick hard in my pants.

"And I don't want to share you."

I could feel my muscles tighten the same way they did before battle, an intensity that I couldn't shake until every last foe was dead. I could feel the adrenaline drop into my stomach, feel my heart race like I was running rather than standing still.

I stepped closer to her, seeing the way she drew breath when I came near, the way my proximity affected her, scared her a little bit. With my chin tilted down to regard her and my eyes locked on to hers, I reached for her clothes and started to pull them free. Her shirt moved over her head, her breeches came loose; it all happened while I kept my eyes locked to her face.

She breathed hard like my mouth stole her breath along with her kisses, and her hands went to my breeches to get them loose, her green eyes still on me. Clothes fell to the floor, boots were kicked away, and then I got her on the bed.

I took her at the foot, her ass hanging over the edge, my arms locked behind her knees.

She couldn't handle all of me, so I always gave her most but not all, but this time, I didn't hold back. My thrusts were hard, my shaft went deep, and I made her moan and wince at the same time. "Can you handle that?"

Her hands held on to my arms as her nails dug into me, her eyes glistening with unshed tears. "Yes…"

"That's my baby."

———

THE FIRE BURNED in the hearth at the foot of the bed, filling the room with heat that was almost too much after all the fucking we just did. The sheets were pushed to my waist, and she was all over me, the heat not strong enough to keep her away.

"You never told me who she was." Her hair was on my shoulder and my chest, her leg tucked between mine under the sheets. Her soft fingertips lightly traced my hard body, following the river between my abs.

"Elora. My sister."

Her fingers halted on their venture down my stomach. "You never mentioned you had a sister."

"Because it was never relevant."

Now she sat up, propping herself up on her elbow. "But you said when you were exiled from Delacroix, it was just the three of you."

"And it was."

"Then…where does she come into this story?"

"She was born afterward."

Her questions stopped, as if it finally made sense to her. "My half sister."

"I saw the way you looked at her…like you loved her."

"And I do."

"I guess that was why I thought you were married."

"If I were married, you wouldn't be here right now."

"So, you would be faithful to her?"

"If that's what she wanted."

"That's not just a given if you're married?" she whispered.

"Probably not, since I wouldn't marry for love."

"Then why would you marry?"

"Duty."

Her fingers started to trail down my stomach again. "Your mom is unmarried."

"She has children. I don't."

With one hand propped under her head, her fingers ran up and down my chest, her skin glowing beautifully in the firelight. "You only get to marry once, only get to bind your soul with another one time, and it seems like a waste to do it for an obligation…"

I turned to regard her. "Are you just realizing this now?"

"I've always known. I just…never really thought about it before." She turned away, her eyes growing lost in thought. "My father wanted to marry me off to a prince so we could be closer to the throne, and I always assumed that was the right move. But now…I don't know. It just seems like a big sacrifice." She turned back to me. "Does that bother you?"

A monk performed the ceremony in the eyes of the gods, binding their souls permanently—or, at least, until one of them passed on. Divorce wasn't a real thing because there was nothing that could be done to unbind the two souls—except death. That was how some marriages ended, in murder, because there was no other option. But even if it did, you couldn't remarry at a later time because the soul had already been used. "I never thought I'd marry for love anyway, so it doesn't matter to me."

She turned her gaze on me and stared for a long time.

I held her gaze, expecting her to say something, but nothing was forthcoming.

She broke the trance and looked elsewhere.

Then we sat in silence.

After a while, she spoke again. "Are you close with your sister?"

"Yes."

"What does she do in HeartHolme?"

"She's a citizen."

"She doesn't serve your mother?"

"No."

She looked at me, like she knew there was more to that story that I didn't want to share.

"Elora and my mother aren't close."

"Why?"

I never answered.

She didn't press me. "What's on the agenda for tomorrow?"

"I'll be gone all day."

"And you expect me to *stay*?" Her eyes flashed with accusation.

"Yes. But I'll give you a tour in the morning."

"Good." That momentary look of anger faded quickly once she got what she wanted. Her head returned to my shoulder, and she snuggled into my side, taking the exact position she usually did right before she fell asleep.

I listened to her breathing change and recognized the moment she slipped under. I stayed awake and stared at the fire a while longer, unsure what my next move would be.

SEVENTEEN

Ivory

_____

"Up." His deep voice punctured my dreams of sunshine and flowers.

I kept my eyes closed. "Nuh-uh."

"Baby."

I turned over and ignored him. This bed was too comfortable, and I wasn't moving for anything.

He forced me onto my back, the sheets slipping away and exposing my naked chest to the cool air. Then the mattress dipped with his weight, his heat smothering my skin like a blanket, and my thighs started to separate.

I felt it—hard and hot.

He gave a firm thrust, burrowing inside me and waking me up that way.

My eyes opened, and I saw his blurry chin, his hard chest, and powerful shoulders.

He did all the work, kept my knee pinned back, rocked into me in a nice, slow pace.

My arms wrapped around his shoulders, and I held on as I buried my face in his neck, waking up in the most pleasurable way possible. My teeth sank into his collarbone, and my eyes closed, enjoying the way he felt buried deep inside me, lighting up my body like a new fire. My mind was still fuzzy, so it made everything more enhanced, and the orgasm came quickly, even quicker than usual.

I moaned against his chest as my nails clawed the back of his neck. "Huntley…" It was the first time I'd said his name in bed, but it was well deserved because he was the best lover I'd ever had.

He gave his final pumps and released, giving a sexy moan as he filled me with another load to go with all the others from the night before. He stayed on top of me as he breathed through the pleasure he'd just received.

"Okay…I'm awake."

He placed a kiss on my neck before he got off me.

"And you can wake me up like that every morning…"

His back was turned to me as he gave a chuckle. "Good to know."

We both got dressed, and I put on the clothes he retrieved for me. They were mostly in neutral shades with a jacket on top, nothing like the dark colors he wore to symbolize his status. He left his weapons behind, and it was the first time I'd seen him without them—other than when we were in bed together.

We walked through the cold streets in the morning, people everywhere as they got their days started. He took me through the farmers market where everyone converged to get their food for the day, and he led me past a couple pubs and restaurants that he liked. A lot of people stared at us. And I mean, a lot.

As if they knew I didn't belong there.

Strong, tall, and proud, he walked beside me, feet between us like we weren't lovers in the slightest. "Hungry?"

"You should know me better than that by now."

He hardly ever smiled, and whenever he did, it was a half smile, just a subtle change in his lips. But the smile he showed me now lit up his entire face, gave him a boyish charm that was so handsome it hurt. "Then let's get breakfast." He walked up to a small building with a slanted roof, the windows showing the tables full of patrons. The waitress seemed to know him the second we walked inside because she was eager to rush over and help him.

She was pretty too.

I felt that ugly green monster rear its head inside me again.

This time, I kept my shit together.

She took us to a table and told us what they had. "Two orders?"

"Yes," Huntley said. "And coffee."

She took off to the kitchens.

We were beside the window, and I noticed the people behind him turning their heads to look at him, recognizing his face or the symbol on his uniform. She brought the coffees a second later, and then the breakfast of pancakes, bacon, and eggs wasn't far behind.

I stared at my food for a second, my eyes practically popping out of my head. "I don't think I've ever seen anything so beautiful…"

He was already eating, taking big bites of everything and scarfing it down.

We ate in silence, but it was a comfortable silence, the kind I had with my brother. "I've never done this before."

He looked up as he chewed.

"Gone out to eat in town. The only time I'd go into town was to help with the animals. Never gone out with a guy either."

"I'm happy to be your first." He gave a playful look before he dropped his attention back to his food.

I ate everything on my plate, every single crumb, and felt my belly stretch my pants when I was finished.

Whatever. Worth it.

We left and took a long route back to the house. HeartHolme rose from the gates at a slight incline, climbing higher and higher until it reached the edge of the cliff. That was where the castle stood, and I imagined the view was breathtaking. Huntley didn't offer to take me there, and I was certain the area was off-limits to me.

We approached his home, and he unlocked the gate. I could tell he didn't intend to come inside because he lingered in the street. "When will you be back?"

"Not sure. Before dark."

"Well, I'm gonna need food. Don't expect me to stay put and starve."

He gave a quiet sigh as if he'd expected that. "Don't draw attention to yourself, alright? Queen Rolfe wanted you in the dungeon, but I dissuaded her. Don't run. And don't kill anyone."

"Uh…why would I kill anyone?"

"Don't ask me."

"Your mother thinks I'm a psychopath, doesn't she?"

He gave a shrug.

"Alright. I'll *try* not to kill anyone."

"The pub next door serves the best steak I've ever had. If that's what you're in the mood for. There's money in the nightstand." He shut the iron gate, still visible through the sections of the bars, and locked it. "I'll see you later."

———

THERE WASN'T much to do while he was gone. He didn't have any books, which didn't surprise me because he didn't seem like the kind of guy who spent his free time reading. I took a long bath, kept the fire going, and then when my stomach started to growl, I decided it was time to get that steak.

I opened his nightstand and found the money he'd referred to. Some of it was made of paper, and the rest were coins. I took a bit of everything and headed for the stairs.

Then someone knocked on the door.

I stilled at the sound—because Huntley hadn't mentioned anything about visitors. And obviously, it wasn't him because he wouldn't knock on his own door. Whoever it was, they were there for him and not me, so I decided not to answer it.

The knock sounded again. "Asshole, open the door."

It was a woman.

And that piqued my curiosity.

She knocked again, making a beat like she was recreating a song. "Huunnntttlllleeeey."

I should ignore it, but now I wanted to know who it was that was so desperate to get his attention. I opened the door and came face-to-face with a brunette. A very pretty brunette.

She stilled when she saw me, as if she was just as thrown off by my appearance as I was by hers.

Dark hair. Green eyes. Fair skin.

I saw the resemblance instantly.

She must have too, because she was dead quiet.

There was a long bout of silence, a long exchange of stares.

I was the first one to regain my footing. "Um…are you Huntley's sister?"

Her eyes shifted back and forth as she looked at me, as if her mind was trying to determine whether this was real or not. "Who are you?"

"Ivory."

"That didn't answer my question."

"Huntley took me from Delacroix. We've been traveling together for a while."

That seemed to be enough information for her to put it together, as if she knew about the mission Huntley had set out on. Her eyes had this knowing look, and the surprise slowly faded. "Tell him I came by. He knows where to find me."

———

I NEVER GOT DINNER.

I sat in the armchair near the fire upstairs, replaying the interaction over and over in my head, her face still fresh in my mind even though hours had passed. I had an unsettling feeling in my stomach, a discomfort that gnawed at my insides.

My heart hadn't stopped racing.

I heard the front door open and close, and then I heard his footsteps on the stairs a moment later. He appeared after a few seconds, already removing his tunic as if he couldn't wait to get it off the second he walked in the door. Hard and chiseled, his skin was a second set of armor.

He regarded me in the armchair by the fire, and as if he could read my mood like every word was spelled out for him, his eyes shifted back and forth between mine.

I pushed myself to my feet and met him head on. "Your sister came by…"

His eyes immediately narrowed.

"You want a woman who says what she wants? Then tell me who she is."

His eyes hardened the way valleys did after the sun had passed. The shadows invaded and hid their sight from view.

"Who she really is."

He sidestepped me and moved to the edge of the bed. He took a seat, his breeches and boots still on, and rested his arms on his knees. His chin dipped, and he regarded the rug that cushioned the hardwood floor.

I pivoted my body to look at him and waited for my answer.

"I think you already know."

Instinctually, I turned away, faced the fire because his face was too much right now. It gave me a chance to hide my composure, to hide all the emotions that flowed through my body in a rush. I felt my head shake automatically, giving a pointless disagreement. "Why didn't you tell me?" My arms tightened over my chest, and I felt sick. Sick to my fucking stomach.

"To spare you."

I shook my head again, my eyes watering.

"That's not how I wanted you to find out—"

"Does she know?" I kept my eyes on the flames, watching them consume the wood.

"No."

"What are you going to tell her?"

"The truth. The time has come."

I felt the tears fall down my cheeks, felt my heart break

in the most inexplicable way. There was no way to convey the way I felt, the disgust, the betrayal. My world had been shattered.

He came up behind me, his hands moving to my arms.

The touch felt good initially, but then it made me ache. I pushed his arms off. "Don't touch me."

He grabbed me again, and this time, he forced me to turn and meet his gaze.

With tears splashing on my cheeks, agony on my face, I felt so ugly.

He stared, his eyes shifting slightly to take in my appearance.

I averted my gaze because his stare was too much. I just wanted to disappear. Crawl under the bed like a child.

His fingers loosened on my elbow, and they traveled up my arm, over my shoulder, and then cupped my cheek. His thumb brushed across my bottom lip then over my cheek, swiping at a tear that was sitting there. "I'm sorry."

My eyes found the courage to meet his again.

"Really. I am."

EIGHTEEN

Huntley

At first light, I slipped out of bed and grabbed my pants.

She felt my absence the second I was gone, and her hand automatically reached out to find me. When she felt nothing but sheets and air, she opened her eyes to a squint. "Where are you going?"

"I'll be back in a couple hours." I pulled my shirt over my head and shoved my boots on.

"That wasn't what I asked." Now she sat up in bed, her hair all over the place, her tits hard from the cold air. Her eyes remained in a squint, a little glassy because they were still tired.

I came back to the bed. "To talk to Elora."

She didn't give a hint of surprise, so that must have been what she suspected all along. "I want to talk to her too…if she's willing."

That conversation was inevitable. "Let me speak to

her first."

"Okay."

"Go back to sleep."

She lay down again and pulled the sheets to her shoulder. "I'll try. Hard to sleep without you…"

I left the house and felt the cold air hit me right away. It was a lot more tolerable than the winter winds of the outpost, and it didn't freeze my lungs on contact. I walked down the cobblestone streets until I arrived at her doorstep.

She wasn't a morning person, but after what had transpired yesterday, I had a hunch that she was awake. I knocked, and after a moment, she answered.

She was in the comfortable breeches she wore around the house, along with a loose sweater with sleeves that were too big, as if it used to belong to someone who wasn't in her life anymore. Instead of speaking her mind as usual, she was quiet.

I was quiet too.

She eventually left the door and walked into the house, giving a silent invitation.

I shut the door behind me and joined her in the living room. The fire burned in the hearth, and there was a cup of coffee on the table.

With her arms crossed over her chest, she regarded me with her shrewd gaze. "What the fuck, Huntley."

Both women had figured it out the moment they saw each other. They looked like different people, but their eyes were identical in shape and color. They possessed the same high cheekbones, the same color hair. When I first saw Ivory, I noticed the similarities, but the more I interacted with her, the more I saw someone else entirely. "Mother didn't want me to tell you. I honored her wishes."

"Tell me what?" She stepped closer. "You haven't told me shit, remember?"

"She's your sister. Half sister."

Her eyes hardened, as if she knew that was the truth but still reacted to the revelation. "We must have the same father. Otherwise, that would just be disgusting."

I gave a subtle nod.

"You're telling me my father is the Duke of Delacroix?"

I moved to the armchair near the fire and took a seat. "Yeah."

"And…how did that happen?"

I didn't want to say. Didn't want to open the vault to those memories. "When Faron took over Delacroix and exiled us to the bottom of the cliffs…he raped her."

Her gaze remained hard, not giving a sign of a wince.

"We survived the fall, and she carried you to term."

She drew a deep breath, looking away as she did it. "Now I know why she hates me…"

"She doesn't hate you—"

"Cut the shit, Huntley." She turned away and looked at the fire for a while. "I can't really blame her. I'm not sure if I would react any differently. How is she supposed to have a connection with me when every time she looks at me, she sees the man who forced her? Who took away everything from her?"

I drew a deep breath and let it out slowly. "It gets easier…in time."

She turned back to me, her eyes absorbing my stare and my words. "You told me she was in the dungeons."

"Well, I lied."

"I thought you didn't do that."

"It's a delicate situation, Elora."

She moved to the couch and took a seat, her arms still crossed. "You aren't treating her like a prisoner, so what is she?"

"It's complicated."

Her eyes grilled me. "Huntley."

"She had no idea what her father did to us. When I told her, she didn't believe me. But once we came down here…she saw the world differently. Her small little world suddenly became bigger, and she lost her place in it. When I told her what happened to Mother, her sorrow was genuine. That's the kind of person she is… Genuine. What's going on with us…it just happened. We don't really talk about it. Neither one of us really thinks too hard about it. I'm not sure of her allegiance at this point, but I know she doesn't mean any of us harm. Now that she's seen you, she knows the truth…and that might change things."

"In what way?"

"She always insisted it was mistaken identity, that her father wasn't the culprit. Maybe she just said that to make herself feel better, to hold on to the perfect life she once had. But now that she's seen you…there's no mistake."

"He's still her father."

"But he killed my father and took our home from us. It's barbaric—and she agrees."

She crossed her legs, her face still tight with anger. "I don't think that's enough reason to trust her."

"Not saying I trust her. But I know she's not like him."

"You sleep beside her every night when she could slit your throat. That's trust, Huntley."

"She wouldn't hurt me."

She stared at me in disbelief. "You've got to be kidding me."

"She saved my life. She could have kept going, but she came back for me."

Her stare continued. "Family is everything. At the end of all this, don't expect her to pick you. Because she probably won't. Doesn't matter if her father is a rapist and a murderer. He's her blood."

Her blood. Her family. "You're right."

"Damn right I'm right."

She'd even justified what her father had done in some ways. Because my parents had sat on the throne, while everyone else was abandoned at the bottom of the cliffs. They could have helped, but they chose not to. Our places could have been reversed, and nothing would have changed. She would have been the one stuck down here instead of me.

It was either her or me.

That was what it came down to…in the end.

———

EVER SINCE THE moment we'd met, she'd been a roaring fire, a fire that snow and rain couldn't put out. But now, her flames were doused, and she was as cold as ice. It was the first time I'd seen her that way.

She sat in the armchair near the fire, in one of my shirts she'd fished out of the drawer, with a blanket over her legs. Her arms were crossed, and her eyes were glazed over, as if she wasn't really looking at the fire.

She knew I was there but didn't acknowledge me.

I grabbed a bottle, filled two glasses with my favorite liquor, and set them on the table between us.

She immediately reached for hers and took a big swallow.

I felt like I was drinking with Ian.

"How is she?"

I turned my head in her direction, my fingertips on the rim of my glass. "Shaken up."

"I can only imagine…" She swirled her glass as she looked inside, her eyes heavy as if she'd cried after I left. "Now I know why she's not close with your mother."

"My mother has always been distant…unfortunately."

"That doesn't surprise me."

I watched her from the side, stared at her cheek and the deep shadow under her jawline. "I don't always agree with her, but it's wrong to judge her for this."

"I don't, actually." She took a drink. "So, I have a sister… I've always wanted a sister."

"Having the same blood doesn't make you family."

She looked at me for the first time.

"She's my family—not yours."

"I wasn't implying anything, Huntley."

I turned back to the fire.

"I'm guessing you're the one who took care of her?"

I watched the flames with the glass in my hand. "Yes."

"What about Ian?"

I gave a shrug. "He's like my mother. Not invested."

"Why aren't you that way?"

Because I'd had to sit there and watch my mother abandon her. Elora always had food, but nothing else. No attention. No love. Nothing. She didn't even have a name until she was four. My mother didn't care enough to give her one. "I pitied her."

"That's not enough reason."

"I loved her." I could feel her stare burning into the side of my face, feel it like the sun. "I'm her brother, but sometimes I feel like more than that. Ian and I are friends, not just brothers, but the relationship is different with Elora because I raised her."

After a long stretch of silence, she spoke. "You're nothing like your mother."

I tore my gaze away from the flames and looked at her.

"You can let things go. She can't."

"I haven't let a damn thing go." I would butcher her

father like livestock for dinner.

"Then you have a bigger heart than she does."

I looked at the fire again. "I'm just weaker than she is…"

"No." Now her voice rose as if offended. "You're stronger than she is."

I watched the flames dance, watched the logs turn red and smolder.

"You're the one who should be king."

"And I will be—someday. When your father is dead at my feet and my homeland is reclaimed." I felt the bitterness in my voice, felt the throbbing of the agony that had been inside my chest for decades.

She was quiet.

I turned back to her to see her reaction, to see if anything had changed.

Her eyes were empty. She was a cold morning, fog in the air, frost on the ground.

I almost wished she were angry instead, just to see that fire that drew me to her in the first place. "I'm sorry." Not for what I'd said, but that she was the daughter of a murderer, a descendant of monsters.

Her eyes dropped. "I didn't want to believe it. Refused to believe it. I admit my father is a bit cold and distant at times, but…I never imagined he would do such a thing. Now I tell myself that he's a different man, that when he met my mother and had us, he changed. At least, I hope…"

I had a callous retort, but I kept it to myself.

"But even if that's true, it doesn't excuse what he did." She suddenly turned her gaze to the fire and took a deep breath, like it was all she could do to stop herself from crying.

The anger left me whenever I saw her like that, because I saw how much it hurt her.

I wasn't the only victim in this.

If my father had done something as heinous, if he had been anything less than the honest and admirable man he'd been my whole life, it would change everything. I wouldn't be the man I am today.

"I just can't believe he would do that…" She sniffled. "Were there others?"

Most certainly.

"I want to confront him about it…but what would I even say?"

She wouldn't have the chance because I'd kill him the second I laid eyes on him.

Her fingers moved to her cheeks, and she wiped away the tears that had escaped. "I can't even imagine everything your mother has been through, surviving down here and protecting her sons while her stomach grew bigger with a child she was forced to have…"

"It's one of the reasons I revere her. She's a good leader. My father would be proud if he could see how far she's come, everything she's defeated to be where she is now. She never stopped to pity herself. She never broke down in tears. She just kept going…and she's still going."

Her arms crossed over her chest, and she turned quiet,

her eyes on the fire, her tears dry. "Do you think I could talk to Elora?"

"Why?"

"I know you said we aren't family, but we are…"

"Your only connection is your father, and I don't think that's enough reason to kindle a relationship."

She turned to me. "Why don't you want me to talk to her?"

"Because I don't."

She held my gaze, the disappointment on the surface of her eyes. "I'm sure she's curious—"

"The answer is no."

"I think she deserves to make this decision herself. She doesn't need a man to do it for her."

"I'm not a controlling jackass—"

"Then ask her."

I felt my teeth grind when I clenched my jaw.

"If she says no…I'll understand."

I turned away and looked at the fire. My hand grabbed the glass, and I tilted my head back as I downed everything in a single swallow.

———

IT WAS the only time we'd slept side by side and didn't fuck.

I could tell she wasn't in the mood. Otherwise, her hands would trail down my stomach underneath the sheet while her lips pressed kisses to my shoulder. She always had this look in her eye too, a low-burning fire that warmed the entire room.

Now, she was cold.

We faced each other, sharing a single pillow, her leg hiked over my hip. The sheets were at our shoulders, and her palm was flat against my chest as if feeling my heartbeat. Her eyes were closed at the moment, her eyelashes down over her cheeks.

Normally, I'd be hard as a rock right now with her looking like that, beautiful in the dying light of the fire. But I didn't feel anything for her, not when I knew her chest was a void at the moment.

Not when I could feel her sadness.

She must have felt my stare because her eyelashes lifted, and she met my look.

My fingers automatically dove into her hair, pushing it back from her face as I touched the soft strands. They dropped to her shoulder a moment later, the rough pads of my fingertips feeling her rose-petal skin.

"Does she know about us?"

I gave a slight nod.

"How does she feel about that?"

"The same way everyone else does."

She didn't look surprised but a little hurt. "Then why do you keep doing this?"

My mother was disappointed in me. I could feel it in her stare, in the hostility that surrounded her. I could feel Ian's disapproval. I could feel Elora's judgment. This was stupid—plain and simple. "Because I can't stop."

NINETEEN

Ivory

———

I was numb.

Even the next day, I still felt that way.

Heartbreak. Betrayal. Hatred. I felt it all.

Up until this point, I'd never confronted Huntley's accusation. I put it to the back of my mind and forgot about it.

But looking at Elora's face, I had no choice but to accept the horrible truth.

There was no benefit of the doubt anymore.

Fuck.

Huntley left in the morning and didn't wake me up before he was gone. I had no idea when he would be back, but I was in no mood to explore HeartHolme or do anything else except imagine the conversation I would have with Ryker…if I ever saw him again.

He wouldn't believe me. Of course he wouldn't. I hadn't believed it either.

Not unless he saw Elora in the flesh.

The door opened and closed downstairs, and I knew he was home.

Home…or whatever this place was.

His voice emerged from downstairs. "Come here."

"Hello to you too," I called back.

"Ivory." His voice deepened with annoyance.

He hardly ever said my name, so it was weird whenever I heard it. "Baby" had become a second skin, an identity I wrapped around myself like a thick blanket. I headed downstairs and saw him standing near the couches.

That was when I spotted her—Elora.

I paused on the staircase with my hand on the banister as I looked at her. I overcame the surprise and continued.

She was on the armchair, her dark hair pulled off her face, tied in an elastic cloth, her similar features on display.

I walked right past Huntley like he wasn't even there because she was all I cared about in that moment. I took a seat in the other armchair and looked at her, knowing her curiosity would be too much to ignore.

Huntley stared at us for a while before he walked up the stairs and gave us our privacy.

My eyes were on hers, seeing the same green eyes that I possessed, the ones we'd both inherited from our father. I could see Huntley's mother in her face as well, the way her features would naturally set in a tense fashion, the way her mind seemed to be working constantly.

I'd asked for this conversation, but now I didn't know what to say. "I'm Ivory… Nice to meet you."

"Elora."

"I know this is…awkward…and I appreciate your coming here today."

"It seemed important to Huntley, so…"

Because it was important to me.

"I never really believed Huntley's accusation until I met you. Now that I have…the sky has crashed on my shoulders. My whole world is…different. I can't imagine how it must feel for you."

With her legs crossed and her hands in her lap, she was quiet, taking and not giving. "My entire life, I assumed my mother hated me because I was a girl instead of a boy. But now I know the truth, and I don't blame her for her hatred. I would hate me too."

"I can't even imagine how difficult it was for her, but you're still her daughter, and I don't think hatred is the right response to the situation. Huntley doesn't hate you. I've seen the way he looks at you. Honestly, I thought you were his wife or something…"

She released a laugh, a big, booming one. "Now that's funny."

"He speaks highly of you, too."

"He does not," she said with another laugh. "Tells me I'm a pain in the ass every day."

"Well, he's lying. Says I'm a pain in the ass too, but I know it's bullshit."

Her smile faded, and her eyes turned serious once again.

"I know this doesn't mean much…but I'm really sorry about what happened. I know it's not my fault, but I feel so terrible, like I'm responsible for my father's behavior. I thought I knew him, and then I find this out, and I'm just…not sure of anything anymore."

"Your father is a piece of shit. Plain and simple, sweetheart."

I sucked in a breath between my closed teeth, the action involuntary.

"He's not sorry about what he did, and he would do it again in a heartbeat."

It was another punch to the stomach.

"You can give your pity and your apologies, but at the end of the day, it doesn't matter. He's your father. You would choose him over us in a heartbeat. It doesn't matter how barbaric he is—family is everything, and I'll never trust you. Huntley may be fucking you, but he doesn't trust you either."

She sure knew how to lay it on thick. "It doesn't matter if he's my father, I'll never condone what he did to your mother. It's disgusting…and it breaks my heart."

She gave a shrug. "We're still enemies as far as I'm concerned."

"But we aren't. I don't think what he did is right—"

"But if he hadn't taken Delacroix and the Kingdoms, you would be the one down here, forsaken just like us. Always at war. Always vulnerable. And always fucking cold. In this world, there is no morality. There is only survival. You may not believe that right now, but you will once my family takes back what's ours."

I felt like I'd been slapped in the face.

She got to her feet. "One more thing. You stab my brother in the back, I'll stab you in your goddamn face."

————

"I WARNED YOU." Huntley was shirtless at his desk, his muscular back covered in scars from the wars he had fought. The mosaic of trials and injury was a testament to his bravery, and while the scars made me sad, they also turned me on a bit.

"I still have no regrets."

"Then you got a mild version of her."

I sat on the edge of the bed and removed my shoes. "She reminds me of your mother."

"Me too." He pivoted in the chair so he could look at me, his jaw cleanly shaved, his hair a little damp from the bath he'd taken recently. His blue eyes locked on me, reminding me of a blue sky I hadn't seen in a long time.

"Well…thank you anyway."

He left his desk and approached me, his breeches low on his hips, the drawstring untied. "We're leaving tomorrow."

"We are?" My head tilted back to look at him because he towered over me as I sat on the bed.

"First thing in the morning."

"Is it just the two of us?"

"Yes."

"And where are we going?"

"West."

"Still won't tell me where we're going or what we're doing?"

He tucked his thumb into his breeches and pulled them down, letting his hard dick emerge. My question was clearly the last thing on his mind. Without his bottoms to support his shaft, his dick plopped down right on my face, his tip resting against my lips.

His thumb grabbed my chin, and he traced my bottom lip with his finger, enticing my lips to open.

"We're in the middle of a conversation—"

He guided his length inside me, pushing inside my mouth until I nearly choked.

He thrust inside me as he supported the back of my head, his dick hitting my throat deep and hard. "And I'm changing the subject."

———

I WOKE up that morning to kisses on my collarbone and a hand between my legs.

My body was stirred from sleep quicker than my mind, immediately responding to the circular pressure between my legs. My back arched. My hips bucked. My lips released a quiet moan.

My eyes finally opened, and that was when his

muscled mass got on top of me, his arms locked behind my knees. His smell was masculine and natural, like fresh air when you walked out the front door. His skin was warm, like a blanket against mine. My body naturally opened for him, and now that my body was used to being ready before I was even awake, I took his thrusts without resistance.

"God…" My nails scratched down his back as I felt him fully inside me, hurting me just a little bit.

It was slow and steady, his sleepy eyes locked on me, his hair a mess from where I'd fisted it the night before. He gave a moan from deep in the back of his throat like an animal, and his dick got just a little harder when he did it.

I lay there and enjoyed it, just as I did every morning. I was woken up by this gorgeous man in the best way possible, his fat dick inside me, his heavy body pinning me to the mattress and making me his.

It only took a couple pumps to make me come, to make my toes curl because his dick hit me in the perfect spot from the start. My hands planted against his chest, and I dragged my nails down, making marks against his skin because I dug so deep. Tears formed in my eyes and streaked down my cheeks to my ears. "Huntley…" It was so good, the best I'd ever had, making me forget every man I'd snuck in to my bedchambers.

His eyes darkened as he watched me come, his face flushing with arousal and adrenaline. He shoved himself deeper inside me before he came, making me wince from his size, which made him enjoy it more. "Fuck, baby." He gave one of his animalistic moans as he finished, his dick throbbing inside me as it dumped all his seed.

It was better than a fresh cup of coffee. Better than a hot fire in the hearth. Better than a big breakfast of pancakes and bacon. It was my favorite part of the morning, the best way to wake up.

He rolled off me and got straight out of bed.

I rolled over and went straight back to sleep.

"Get up."

"Mmmm…"

"Baby, come on." He tugged the sheets down and gave my ass a hard smack.

"Ugh…"

"If you don't want a dick in that ass, get moving."

I stayed still. "Can I go back to sleep afterward?"

He was quiet—because he was seriously tempted.

I closed my eyes.

"I told you we're leaving."

Oh shit. Forgot about that. Back to the elements. Back to the cold, hard ground. "No…I don't want to go."

His knees hit the mattress, and then he was on top of me, his dick hard and in between my cheeks. "You had your chance, baby." He licked his palm then wet the head of his cock before he pushed against my tight entrance and started to sink.

––––––

I WAS IN THICK BREECHES, heavy boots, a tunic made of wool, and then a jacket on top.

I didn't want to leave, not when this place was so comfortable, when the bed was so soft, when there was a fireplace in every room, when we could sleep together naked and feel hot like a blazing inferno.

He pulled out a couple weapons and set them on the bed.

"Take this." He grabbed a bow and quiver of arrows and held them out to me.

I didn't take it, as if this was a test.

He continued to hold them up to me, his eyes narrowed.

"I thought I wasn't supposed to carry weapons."

"Not when it's just me."

I placed everything over my shoulder.

"I need you to watch my back. Can't do that if you aren't armed." He grabbed a dagger next and handed it to me.

I took it out of the scabbard and examined it before I secured it to my belt.

Then he grabbed a broadsword. "Can you handle this?"

"Psh…can I handle this." I took it from him, trying not to falter when I realized just how heavy it actually was, a little too heavy for a single hand. "If I can take your broadsword up my ass, I can handle this."

The grin that came over his face was so cocky, but so handsome too. He took the broadsword out of my hand

and handed me one about half the size, a short sword to him.

"I just said I could handle it."

"You can barely hold it."

"With one hand, but it's a two-handed sword."

"For you." He continued to hold out the other sword to me. "Now isn't the time for this stubborn bit. I need you to have my back out there, and you can't do that if the sword is too heavy for you."

"It's not too heavy—"

"Come on." He forced the hilt into my hand then grabbed the rest of his supplies. Food, water, compass, and a bedroll. "Ready?"

I gave a shrug. "I'll never be ready to leave a soft bed and a warm fireplace."

"The bed won't be soft, but it'll still be warm."

"Thank goodness for that."

———

WE WALKED through HeartHolme to the gates where we'd originally entered. The sun was slowly rising over the horizon, chasing away the frost that took the leaves in the middle of the night. Both dressed for the wild, we looked out of place compared to everyone else.

We made it to the bottom of the incline, back to the stables and battle stations. The rest of the city wasn't manned with cannons and quivers of arrows, so all the attacks on HeartHolme must come here—to this enormous stone gate.

I didn't see how anyone could conquer it.

A beautiful chestnut mare was waiting for us, saddled and ready to go, supplies in her saddlebags. Huntley added his things to the compartments.

But there was only one horse. "Where's mine?"

"We'll share."

"She's going to take both of us *and* all our stuff?"

"It's a horse."

"We'd go a lot faster on two."

He stopped preparing for departure and faced me head on.

"You still think I'm going to run?" I asked incredulously. "Really?"

"You can get pretty far on a horse."

"Not when I don't know where I'm going."

"Don't play stupid with me. I know you're a lot more resourceful than that."

"Yes, I can just head north, but what will I come across along the way? Sure, I can piss on a yeti again, but I don't think it would work out like last time…"

He didn't crack a smile.

"I'm not going to run, Huntley."

"That's exactly what you would say if you were."

"Not me."

He watched me, his eyes observant.

"I said I would help you. Let's do that…and then figure out our next plan."

The stare continued, as hard as stone. Then he addressed one of his men. "Saddle another horse."

They got to work.

He gave a sigh and turned away.

The carriage arrived, and Queen Rolfe emerged in a long-sleeved dress with the feather crest in the center. A chain dropped at her neckline, the clasp to her black cloak. Black pants were underneath, along with dark boots. The feathers were in her thick hair, dark ones that looked as if they had once belonged to a crow.

I looked at her differently now.

Her eyes were focused on Huntley entirely, my presence excluded. She approached him, and her hands reached for his arms with a delicate look of a mother. "Please be careful."

A foot taller and a hundred pounds heavier, he was a monster in comparison. Hard to believe that he was born of her womb, that her body could sustain the boy that would become this man. "I will."

"Don't trust the wilds. And don't trust her either."

It was like I wasn't there at all.

He gave a subtle nod.

Her hands cupped his cheeks, and he automatically dipped his head to her so she could kiss him on the forehead. "I love you, my boy."

"I love you too, Mother."

She embraced him with a warm hug, her face moving to his shoulder, the emotion visible in her eyes. "You have my full confidence. You will prevail."

"I will."

She stepped away, and when there was space between them, she was cold once again. Her eyes turned on me, and I knew I would be the recipient of her wrath.

I held my ground and held her stare.

She walked to me, shoulders back, head held high.

Huntley didn't turn to watch.

She moved right into my personal space, her nose just inches from mine. Out of nowhere, she withdrew a dagger and placed it at my throat, so close to cutting an artery and bleeding me dry. "Do anything to my son, and I'll carve your eyes out of your goddamn face. Understand me?"

I did my best not to swallow, to hardly move when I spoke. "Yes."

She yanked on my hair and bent me down, bending me over the knife. "What did you say?"

I spoke louder, the dirt up close. "Yes."

She withdrew the knife and shoved me to the ground.

My knees hit the dirt, and my palms planted against the earth so I wouldn't topple over.

As if that wasn't enough, she kicked me in the ribs.

That made me topple over.

I saw her boot aiming for me again, ready to kick me in the stomach.

"That's enough." Huntley's deep voice steadied her foot, stopped it from swinging right into my stomach and making me lose my breakfast.

She gave me an angry look before she walked away.

She entered her carriage then took off, heading back to the castle at the top of the hill.

I groaned before I pushed off the ground to my feet.

A hand appeared, a hand that touched me every night, that brushed the hair from my face.

I swatted it away. "I got it." I got to my feet and brushed all the dirt from my palms and knees.

His eyes shifted back and forth as they looked at me, with a tone of apology in his gaze.

"It's fine. My mom was a mama bear too… I get it." I turned to the mare that was brought for me, white with patches of gray dots. "Let's go."

––––––––

RIDING my own horse in unfamiliar territory was a lot different from holding on to Huntley as he controlled the reins, but I got used to it almost immediately, ducking my body forward slightly like he did, running fast down the trails and through the valleys.

Huntley glanced at me often to make sure I hadn't fallen off the horse and collapsed along the way.

It was a hard ride, but Huntley seemed to know exactly where he was going, as if he recognized markers we passed. A pile of boulders here. A copse of trees there. Indications that meant nothing to me.

At sunset, we entered a forest, the light even dimmer under the canopy of trees.

He tugged on the reins and brought his horse to a walk.

I followed close behind him, the horses giving neighs in the quiet.

The darkness crept in further, but he kept going, like he knew the way even in the dark.

Then I heard it—the sound of a stream.

My horse seemed to see better than I could because he came to a stop.

A moment later, there was light. Huntley lit a torch and guided his horse forward by the reins, leading him to a stream so he could drink.

My horse did the same, not waiting for me to dismount.

I rubbed the back of her neck as she bent down to drink. "My kinda girl…doesn't wait for nobody."

Huntley's hand reached for my waist and started to guide me down.

I swatted at his hand. "I can get down myself, alright?"

"Sure about that, Princess? Can you even see the ground?"

"Ooh…don't start with that princess nonsense."

"Answer my question."

I ignored him and started to dismount.

And because I had the worst luck ever, I slipped on the way down and almost landed on my ass.

Of course, he was there to catch me, his large arms a powerful net.

Thankfully I faced the other way, so he couldn't see my embarrassment.

His arms remained locked around my waist even though I was stable on the ground, and his smile was right against my ear. "Guess not, then." He finally let me go and pulled out his bedroll from the saddlebag.

The torch burned on the ground where he'd left it, tipped up on a rock. It was a beacon of light in the dark forest, but the circumference of illumination was limited, plunging the rest of our world into darkness.

He got the camp ready while I ran my fingers through my horse's hair, giving her a nice rubdown after riding so hard to get me there. She continued to drink from the stream, her front hooves in the water.

"Do you have any oats for them?"

"They're horses." He finished the campsite, a single bedroll and a single pillow. "They can eat grass."

"They worked their asses off to get us here."

"And they're fed regularly and sheltered from the elements the rest of the time." He grabbed his horse by the reins and tied them to a long rope hooked to the trunk of a tree. That way, he had ample room to graze and reach the stream.

I did the same to my horse.

We sat together in front of the light of the torch and ate our dried dinner, both of us too tired for conversation. Without four walls and a bed and a fireplace, it was just us and the elements, and that joy we had was long gone. We exchanged looks from time to time, but we didn't have the same heat as we did before.

"How long until we get there?"

"Couple days." He bit into his dried meat and chewed, his arms on his knees as he sat on a rock.

"Are you going to tell me where we're going?"

"What difference would it make?"

"Well, does it have a bed and a fireplace?"

He gave a slight smile. "Not a princess, my ass…"

"Don't act like you're enjoying this trek through the wilderness."

"I don't mind it."

"Liar."

He took another bite.

"You'd rather be fucking my brains out in a four-poster bed, and you know it."

His grin widened. "You've got me there."

"So…how am I helping you? Because if you have an animal that's needed my help this long…it's probably dead by now."

"I'm sure they're fine."

"They? As in there are several?"

"Three."

"Wow… This is going to be a big job."

"You have no idea." He chewed his piece, his eyes on me.

My heart tightened just the way my stomach did. "What are they?"

He took another bite, as if he had no intention of answering my question.

"Really? I'm just going to walk in there and find out?"

"I'm not sure you would believe me if I told you."

"You wouldn't lie to me." The words flew out of my mouth on instinct, like they came right from the heart.

He finished chewing before he closed up the sack and stuffed it back into his pack. With his arms on his knees, he looked at the torch between us, the fire slowly died as it ran out of fuel to consume. "Dragons."

My body hardened like I was frozen in place.

My face must have been pale and my eyes in shock because he said, "Told you."

TWENTY

Huntley

SHE SLEPT ON TOP OF ME IN THE BEDROLL, THE TOP blanket completely over her head to trap the heat against her skin. My arms locked around the small of her back, and I felt her hair against my chin and neck all night. She was out like a wet torch, knocked into oblivion without a care.

I was only half asleep, part of my brain always awake, always listening. When the dark sky lightened slightly, I knew dawn had arrived, could feel it through my closed eyelids. That was when I stirred Ivory. "Time to wake up, Princess."

"Mmmm…" She didn't move, totally limp against me.

"Baby, come on." My hand moved underneath her shirt in the bedroll, gliding up her back between her shoulder blades.

Her eyes remained closed. "Fuck me if you want me to wake up…"

Kinda hard to do in a bedroll when we were both fully clothed. "Later."

"Then I'll wake up later."

"You're already awake."

"Oh, I could go back to sleep so fast…"

I rolled her off me then left the bedroll, knowing the absence of heat would freeze her to the bone shortly. I packed our things, took a drink from the stream, and got the saddles ready.

A couple minutes later, she was fully awake, the cold too uncomfortable to sleep through. Her hair was all over the place, her eyes were squinting with a hint of malice, and she looked a little maniacal.

"Not a morning person, huh?"

She released a growl as she got up and got ready.

I chuckled then prepared the horses.

With sleep still in the corners of her eyes, she walked to her horse. "I'm so fucking tired."

"You don't know what tired is, Princess."

She gave me a smack on the arm then turned back to her horse.

I gave her a hard smack on the ass.

She turned back to me, pissed off but adorable at the same time. "I'm warning you…"

"Do your worst, baby." I grabbed the reins to her horse and pulled her away along with mine.

Ivory followed behind me. "What are you doing?"

"We're walking for a while."

"Why?"

"Because we're getting into dangerous territory. We have to be quiet."

"What kind of dangerous territory?"

"We're crossing a trail that the Plunderers often use."

"Plunderers?"

"The other human clan."

She went quiet, clearly remembering when I'd told her the name before.

"After we cross, we can ride again."

She came to my side and took the reins of her horse. "My father was a Plunderer, right?"

"Yes."

She looked ahead as she pulled her horse along, suddenly quiet.

"Are they enemies to the Runes?"

"We're all enemies to one another. But war is uncommon because of the constant threat to the south. If Necrosis were defeated, it would be a different story. It'd be constant bloodshed until there was only one victor."

"You have no allies?"

He shook his head.

"And no one else has allies?"

"I guess the Teeth are allies with the yetis now…"

She remained quiet.

"We're allies in a loose sense. Once Necrosis descends, we fight shoulder-to-shoulder. It's us versus them. But once that passes…it's back to our old ways. If we find one another in a compromising situation, it usually ends in blood. If they found us traveling alone, they would kill me and take you."

"That's lovely…"

"But don't worry. That won't happen."

"Damn right it won't. I'd shoot my arrows into their eyes."

We traveled deeper into the forest, the shadows changing as the sun moved overhead. It broke through the openings in the canopy, warming the forest floor underneath our boots. The sound of the stream grew quieter and quieter until it disappeared altogether. The journey could have been completed in half the time if we could ride, but it wasn't worth the chance of exposure.

And going around would take even longer.

When we drew close to the trail, I could hear it.

Footsteps. Hooves. Neighs.

I stopped.

She stopped too, taking notice of my mood. Her eyes watched me, waiting for some kind of signal.

The sounds grew louder.

I pressed my forefinger to my lips as I held her gaze.

The trail was fifty feet in front of us, trampled dirt between two lines of trees. I could see through the opening in the trunks, see the men pass by with their carts and horses. On their heads were the cattle skulls, the large horns of the bulls reaching high above their heads. Necklaces made of teeth hung around their necks. Their skin was marked with permanent black ink, words in their language, images of battles.

With wide eyes, Ivory watched them pass.

Our horses stayed quiet and flicked their tails, releasing occasional neighs that the Plunderers couldn't detect. There was a long string of them, several dozen, along with their horses and carts.

They passed, but we remained hidden in the woods, waiting long after their footsteps retreated before we moved forward.

She was pale as snow. "Why do they dress like that?"

"Intimidation."

"What are they like?"

"When Necrosis comes, they sacrifice the weakest members of the herd. The elderly. The injured. The disabled. They also sacrifice children because the younger you are, the purer your soul is. And the purer your soul is…the more energy it has."

She halted in her tracks.

It took me a few steps before I realized she'd fallen behind.

She stood there, breathing hard, practically panting. "Nobody would do such a thing…"

"I've seen it with my own eyes."

"And you did nothing?"

"When Necrosis hits, there's not much you can do but try to survive."

"But children aren't weak. They grow. They raise the population."

"But one child is the equivalent of four adults. It's fewer lives."

She shook her head like she refused to believe me. "That's not where I come from…"

It's exactly where she came from.

"My mother would never have allowed that."

"When you're at the top of cliffs, safe from Necrosis, you don't have to worry about it. Your morality isn't tested. You don't have to make hard decisions because you aren't faced with hard decisions. Your parents may seem like true north on a moral compass, but that's only when the sun is shining, when there's food on the table, when peace reigns."

She shook her head slightly, her eyes about to burst with rage. "My mother would never have supported such barbarism."

"I'm sure she didn't. But it probably wasn't up to her."

"My father… He wouldn't do it either."

He was probably the one who had suggested the idea in the first place.

She stared me down, as if she dared me to challenge her.

I should take the opportunity to rip her to pieces, to tell her exactly how horrible her father was, but I couldn't do it. It would bring no satisfaction, just guilt and pain. "We should keep moving."

"Can you get them to stop?"

"No." I kept going.

"What do you guys do?"

"We send our army out to war to protect HeartHolme."

"How many times have you fought them?"

"Four."

"And what was it like?"

A living nightmare. "No words can describe."

"Is it possible to defeat them?"

I didn't surrender. I didn't lay down my sword. I kept going until death stopped me. "No."

"You really believe that?"

"Yes."

"So…what, then? Some die while others feed? And then they retreat back to their lands?"

"Exactly."

"And they spare everyone else so they can eat you later? Like leftovers?"

"Yes. I've already told you this."

"But…I just can't believe that. I can't believe that it'll be this way forever. That we just give up?"

"There're too many of them."

"So, your solution is to go to the top of the cliffs?" she asked incredulously.

"Go?" I turned on her, my anger rising. "You mean *return*. Because it's my home."

She went still, meeting my fury with her own. "And then abandon everyone else down here. Just like my father has. Because you're no better."

My hand released the reins of my horse, and I turned on her, unable to believe she'd just said that to me.

"That's exactly what your family did—and they'd do it again. Don't pretend to be righteous saviors when you're no different from my father. My father did some really fucked-up things, but the Runes, Teeth, Plunderers would all still be stuck down here suffering if your family was on the throne. This isn't about doing the right thing. This is about climbing to the top and saving your own ass."

It didn't matter if she was right. I wanted to grab her by the neck and throw her down to shut her mouth, but my hand wouldn't reach for her.

"The only way this works for everyone is if we defeat Necrosis."

"And then the Kingdoms will just turn on one another down here."

"Not if a truce is signed. Not if we make peace. Not if there's one king who rules over them all." Her eyes drilled into mine. "If your plan works and you take back Delacroix, those innocent children will still be sacrificed. People will still lose their lives and their afterlives. This is bigger than your need for revenge. This is about *all* of us."

All I cared about was myself—not anyone else.

"You know I'm right."

I dismissed her by walking away.

"Huntley."

"This conversation is over."

"And if everyone makes it to the top of the cliffs, then Necrosis will scale the walls and come for the Kingdoms. But if Necrosis were gone, some people wouldn't mind being down here. You said it's not freezing cold every-where, that some places are more hospitable than others."

I kept walking.

"Don't ignore me."

That's exactly what I did.

"I know you're not so closed-minded as to think I'm wrong."

I halted and turned back around. "No, you're exactly right. That's what we should do. But I've spent the last twenty years fighting those monsters, while that mother-fucker fucked his whores in my father's study. I'm taking back Delacroix, and everyone else can be damned to eternal hell."

Her entire body was still, with the exception of her eyes. They shifted back and forth between mine, bright with disappointment. "And what about me?" There was a bitterness to her voice, like ale that had sat out too long. "Am I down here too? Pissing on yetis and fending for my life?"

I hadn't thought that far ahead.

"And what about other people like me? Sacrificial lambs? This doom just continues indefinitely? You take Delacroix from my father and the Kingdoms from King Rutherford, and then a decade later, someone does the same to you? The cycle just never ends?"

"I lost my kingdom once. I won't let that happen again."

Now she gave a slight shake of her head, looking at me in a way she never had before. She took her horse by the reins and walked around me. "You're no better than he is."

———

WE SLEPT TOGETHER in the bedroll, but it wasn't with the same affection as our other nights. She used me to stay warm, but she didn't actually want me. I could feel it in the way she touched me, the way she kept her hands to herself rather than on my body.

After a long ride, the air became colder, saltier. A fog made visibility poor, and I took my directions based on instinct. The grass beneath the hooves of the horses turned to harder soil, and soon we were on rock.

"Where are we?" she called from behind me.

"The coast." I tugged the reins, and we came to a walk as I approached the outpost. Now that it was close enough, I could make out the details, the earthy structure that blended well into the landscape. My fingers jammed into my mouth, I gave a loud whistle.

"Who are you whistling to?"

I dropped down from my horse and took her by the reins, and Ivory did the same behind me. We approached the dwelling, the details becoming clearer as we moved through the fog.

The gates opened.

"I didn't even see it…" Ivory came to my side, her cheeks freckled with drops of moisture.

We guided our horses inside, and the doors closed behind us.

It was instantly warm, the cold air restricted to the exterior. Torches lit the walls, showing the stables.

Grayson, the commander of the outpost, came up the stairs and greeted me, dressed in a beige tunic and breeches. "You made it in one piece, Huntley." He embraced me as he grasped my hand and gave it a squeeze. "Any trouble out there?"

"No."

Grayson's eyes shifted to Ivory next, and his stare lingered longer than it should. She hadn't showered in days and she didn't look her best, but nothing could hide the fairness of her cheeks, the intelligent twinkle in her eyes. "She's not a Rune."

"Long story. We need passage across the fold."

His eyes shifted back to me. "You're going back?"

"I must."

"The winds are strong today. You'll have to wait until tomorrow."

"We need to rest anyway."

"Then I'll show you to your quarters." He turned to the stairs.

"We require just one room."

He turned back around, glanced at Ivory behind me, and then looked at me again with a ridiculous smile. He gave a wink, even though Ivory could see, and then walked off to prepare for our stay.

Ivory came to my side and gave a loud sigh. "Please tell me they have actual soft beds here."

"No."

"Ugh."

"But it's better than sleeping outside."

"You got me there."

We were escorted to our room a moment later, the same size as my cabin at the outpost. It was just four walls, a bed, and a bathtub. I knew she was more anxious than I was, so I let her fill the tub with hot water then slip under the surface.

From a chair in the corner, I watched, eating from the plate of hot food Grayson had delivered.

She didn't touch hers. That was how uncomfortable she was.

She scrubbed her hair of oil then washed the dirt from her skin and underneath her fingernails. She focused only on herself, eventually resting the back of her neck against the tub to relax.

I enjoyed my food as I watched, appreciating the silence, appreciating the way we didn't need to fill every quiet moment with words. It was different between us, though. There was an underlying tension that seemed permanent now.

When she was finally finished, she drained the tub and stepped out in her bare skin, drops of water hitting the stone floor. Her lithe body was fair like her cheeks, with perky tits, hair between her legs, and a flat stomach I'd kissed just like everywhere else.

She wrapped her body with the towel and dried off, squeezing the drops from her hair into the tub. Like I wasn't even there, she didn't look at me, ignored my presence entirely. The food was right next to me, but she didn't make a move for it.

"Don't expect me to change the circumstances of our world. I can't—nor can anyone else."

She turned to me, her damp hair flat against the back of her neck.

"My birthright was taken from me, and I must take it back."

She rubbed the towel between her thighs, down her legs, between her breasts, catching the drops everywhere. "People are sacrificing their eternal souls so Necrosis will maintain their immortality, and you care about keeping your ass warm on a throne? Children are the first line of defense for the Plunderers, and your one and only concern is a crown? I'm sorry about what happened to you, but there's nothing so cruel that would justify your selfishness."

Now I was on my feet, stripping off my clothes so I could bathe next. "And you would do anything different? If I returned you to Delacroix, you would be back in your villa, your servants waiting on you hand and foot, appreciating the warm sun on your face. You wouldn't do a damn thing for the people below—and don't pretend otherwise."

"I would do something—"

"What? Piss on Necrosis?"

"I would tell my father that something needs to be done."

I released a laugh, a genuine one, but also a sarcastic one. "And what would that do? You really think your father would agree with you? Go to King Rutherford and pitch this wonderful idea, and then in a week, all the armies of the Kingdoms would march on Necrosis? How naïve are you?"

She inhaled a breath, like that was a slap to the face.

"It is what it is." I grabbed the bucket and filled the bath with water, dismissing this conversation.

"It is what it is?"

I dumped another pail full of water into the tub and looked at her.

"If believing that everyone has the right to live free of suffering makes me naïve, then I'd rather be naïve than heartless like you."

———

"I'M GOING to ask for another room." She headed to the door.

"No, you aren't."

"There's no reason to share a small-ass bed if there are other rooms."

"I just said no."

She turned back to me, murder in her eyes. "I do what I want and don't need your permission."

"You do, actually. Because let's not forget our circumstances. You're my prisoner."

"Oh, that's right." She gave herself a tap on the forehead. "Prisoner first. Fuck buddy second. Got it." She turned to leave.

I crossed the room and planted my palm against the wood, barring it shut so she couldn't open it again. "They don't get a lot of women at the outpost. Understand me?" I had to look down at her every time I spoke to her because she was a head shorter, but her scathing eyes made up for her lack of height. "This is for you, not me." I released the door once I knew she'd stay put and headed back to the bed.

She stayed there, even after I got under the covers. There wasn't a fireplace, so it was dark, the fog outside casting a glow through the windows.

She finally gave a sigh and came to the bed, getting on her side of the small hay mattress, pushing herself to the very edge.

It was warmer inside than it was outside but still not warm enough for her liking. I could tell by the way her muscles spasmed in her back, the way her body gave small convulsions to create heat.

"You're that stubborn?" I asked, my eyes on the ceiling.

She pulled the sheets tighter against her body. "Damn right."

My arm hooked around her waist, and I dragged her to me, pulling her right to my chest, my face against the back of her head.

She rocked her hips into me, as if trying to buck me off like a horse. "Get off me."

"You'll be warm." I kept my arm secured over her body, planting her right against me.

"Well, I'd rather be cold than close to you." She bucked again.

I rocked with her as I kept her close to me. "Are you trying to get me off or turn me on?"

"Oh, fuck you." She grabbed my hand on her waist and tried to pry it off.

My fingers curled underneath her body against the mattress, secured in place so she couldn't move them. "Just go to sleep. We have a long day tomorrow. You can be stubborn all you like then."

"You bet your ass I will."

My face was in her hair, breathing her scent, my dick hard against her ass. "Would expect nothing less."

TWENTY-ONE

Ivory

When we took the stairs, we headed deeper into the rock down below. The fog was still pressed to the windows the whole way down, trying to get inside and freeze us all. The closer we came to the bottom, the more I heard it, the sounds of waves lapping against rocks.

Then I smelled it, the heightened scent of salt.

We reached the bottom and came to an enormous cavern, with docks that anchored ships. Some had three sails, some had two, and some had only one. But they were sailing ships, destined for deeper waters.

I'd seen them at the Capital, all in the harbor, their white sails glimmering in the sunshine. The castle was in the center of the Capital, but high on a rise so it had breathtaking views of the ocean. Summer was swelteringly hot, hot enough to take a dip in that bright blue ocean. Luncheons and events were held by the sea, full of gardens of white lilies and colorful flowers.

It wasn't like this—cold.

Grayson was there to meet Huntley. "The sloop is ready for voyage. Stocked with enough food and water to get you there and back. Our scouts say the ocean is calm, but we both know that can change at a moment's notice."

We were sailing? Uh, where?

"Thank you, Grayson." Huntley was in the same thick clothes he'd worn on our adventure here, covered in all his weapons, looking like a true adversary. "I'll be sure to return her in the same condition."

Like last time, Grayson shifted his gaze to me. "They say it's bad luck to have a maiden on a ship…"

Huntley clapped him on the shoulder before he headed down the dock. "I've had nothing but bad luck, and I've made it this far."

We walked to the smallest ship at the dock, lightly bobbing up and down on the waves. It had a single white sail, and there wasn't much room, even for two people. Huntley jumped on board then extended his hand to help me over the edge.

I jumped across on my own and ignored him.

"How long is this going to go on?"

"Indefinitely." I set my bag down on the deck.

"I highly doubt that." He got to work on the sail, lowering it and turning it to the right. Then he untied all the ropes that moored it to the harbor. "You're going to need to get laid eventually."

"I can do that myself, and I'm pretty damn good at it."

He dropped the ropes and turned to me, his bedroom

eyes coming out. They were dark and intense, like his arousal made his skin flush to just the right color to make him appear angry. The stare lingered for a long time, like hot coals directly against my skin.

Maybe I shouldn't have said that.

He finally pulled his gaze away and turned to the wheel. "Ever sail before?"

"Do you know many princesses who sail?"

The corner of his mouth quirked up in a smile. "If we're going to survive out here, you need to do what I tell you. No questions asked. Alright?"

"Yeah…we're going to die."

"Baby, come on."

"Don't call me that anymore."

"Fine. I'll only do it when I'm fucking you."

"Fine by me—because that ain't gonna happen again."

A smile pulled at the corner of his mouth then he took over the wheel, steering us out of the cave and into the open ocean. "We'll see about that."

———

AFTER WE WERE past the initial waves at the coastline, the water was smooth as glass, and the wind in our sail pushed us forward at a quick speed. The land where we'd come from was immediately swallowed by the fog, so all I could see was a solid gray bar across the horizon.

Huntley stayed at the wheel, checking his compass

from time to time and making the necessary adjustments. When the wind changed, he ordered me to change the direction of the sail. Since it was life or death out there, I did as he asked without attitude.

Hours passed in silence, just us on the ocean, the wind ice-cold against my cheeks.

The fog cleared away, and we saw more of the horizon. It was a never-ending ocean, going forever. Whenever I found myself getting a little seasick, I focused on the horizon and tried to clear my mind, letting the fresh air cleanse my lungs. "How long will it take to get there?"

"If nothing goes wrong, three days. But at the speed we're going, probably two." He turned the wheel then secured it in place with a rope so it wouldn't turn left or right in the wind. "We'll be going this direction for a while, so now is the time to rest if you're tired."

I'd been tired since we'd left his home in HeartHolme. The constant travel made me weary. I never once complained because I was above that, but I definitely appreciated those times we stayed still, when we slept in the same bed several nights in a row. "Alright." I headed below deck, seeing two beds against the opposite walls. "Oh, what a relief…" I left all my soiled clothes on the floor and found something clean to wear before I got into bed.

He came down a moment later and washed his face in the water basin. He brought out his razor too, shaving without cutting himself during the unexpected bumps of the ocean. Then he got into bed buck naked—as if he expected to get some.

Not gonna happen.

He'd lit one of the lanterns below deck, casting just enough light so we weren't submerged into total darkness once the sun went down. He lay in bed against the opposite wall, the hatch closed to conserve heat.

It was so cold, especially on the open ocean. I tried not to shiver, but it was impossible, not with the bumps all over my skin, the tightness in all my muscles. When I glanced across the floor, I saw him lying there with a huge smirk on his face.

"Hop in." He pulled back the covers, revealing his hard-as-rock chest, his tight abs, and his tree trunk of a dick.

I didn't let my gaze linger. "I'm good."

"You're freezing."

"The blankets are thin."

"I'm just fine." He kept the blanket off, his hard dick against his stomach. "Get your ass over here."

I wasn't going to get any sleep like this, not when I was too cold to relax. "I'm not fucking you."

He dropped the blanket back down. "Then forget it."

"Fucking asshole…"

He propped himself up on one arm and looked at me, his chest bare. "You need to get over it. You're acting like I'm the villain here, when I'm just a realist. Maybe living in a castle taught you to believe in Prince Charming and fairy tales, but that's all a bunch of bullshit. Life is about survival. Nothing else."

"Life has to be about more. Otherwise, what's the point?"

He didn't have anything to say to that.

"There has to be more. There has to be some good in this world. If not…what are we fighting for?"

He gave a slight shake of his head. "To live. That's all."

"The cycle needs to be broken. The less fortunate shouldn't be damned down here."

"That's how the world is. You're either on top, or you're on the bottom—no pun intended."

It was discouraging, to think of the blessed at the top of the cliffs, while the less fortunate survived just to…survive.

"I'm not saying anything to you that someone else wouldn't say. So don't condemn me for being just like everyone else. Don't condemn me for my hatred. Don't condemn me for my need to survive."

I looked away, my stomach heavy and empty at the same time.

"Now get your ass over here so I can make it warm." He threw off the sheets again, his dick still hard as stone.

I wanted to stay put out of defiance, but my need for warmth and comfort was far greater than my need to be stubborn. With a dose of self-hatred, I left my bed and slid into his, ignoring that look of victory in his eyes.

My body had barely hit the mattress before I was

rolled onto my back, his fingers pulling my panties off my waist and down my legs. They got stuck on one of my ankles, but he left them there as he got on top of me, his thighs opening mine and his dick pressing against my glistening sex. It was hot, like a piece of firewood pulled out of the warm hearth.

He tilted his hips and slid inside me, giving a loud groan as he sank deeper. "Fuck, baby, I missed this pussy." With one hand fisted in my hair and his face above mine, he pumped into me hard, grunting and moaning as he pounded into me like a whore. He came seconds later, his length entirely sheathed inside me.

I took his load, my body on fire because he'd finished when I'd just begun. "Asshole…"

His dick didn't soften like it usually did. It stayed hard as steel, still stretching me and making me wince. "Just a warm-up." He started to thrust into me again, this time slow and steady, rocking my hips as he rolled his, our bodies moving in unison. His face lowered to mine, and he kissed me, his strong mouth taking the lead, giving me his tongue and accepting mine in return.

My arms hooked around his shoulders, and I kissed him as I felt my body rock back and forth, felt his dick push me into the mattress over and over, lighting my body on fire and making it permanently hum.

It was so fucking good.

He must have felt exactly what I felt, felt how much I enjoyed it, because he said, "I'll always be here for you, baby." He tilted his hips more, rubbing his body right against my clit, making me go hot and numb everywhere.

I held on to him tighter because I could feel it coming, feel the aftershocks before the earthquake. My nails started to dig deep, my thighs squeezed his hips, my sex squeezed his. My sighs and moans grew louder, filling the small cabin, echoing back at me. The window beside us began to fog because now it felt like an inferno below deck.

His hand clasped both of mine and pinned them above my head, keeping me flat against the mattress so he could watch the explosion in my eyes, watch my tears roll to the sheets, to reap the rewards of his hard work.

I felt it in my stomach before it hit farther south. My body squeezed his automatically, and my hips bucked on their own, getting more friction against my clit as I convulsed. My hands tried to break free. The tears bubbled in my eyes before they streaked like raindrops on a windowpane.

"Yes, baby." He pounded into me hard now, the sight of my climax the exact thing he wanted to come to. His hips worked hard to keep me in place, and his enormous dick slammed into me viciously as we came together, as he gave me another load of seed to accompany the first. "Fuck…"

We ground together as we finished, all the stress and exhaustion from the last few days gone. My entire body relaxed, and now I was so warm I didn't even want the sheets.

He pulled out of me and lay beside me, his big chest rising and falling with his deep breaths. He left the blankets aside like he was too hot for them too.

I lay there, the sweat from his hot body leaving a streak on my stomach. I could feel his weight inside me, feel its warmth, feel the way it made me his. My eyes closed, and I immediately felt my mind get swept away into the land of dreams.

Powerful arms encircled me and drew me close, right against heat that rivaled the sun.

I turned into him, finding his shoulder as a pillow, my leg tucking between his.

Hot and sweaty, we both went to sleep.

———

I WOKE up the next morning to the rocking waves. The boat swayed left and right, making my body shake slightly. My eyes opened to a squint, and I saw the early morning light through the porthole.

My hand automatically reached for him—but it found just cold sheets.

I continued to rock back and forth, my stomach tightening in discomfort. I hopped out of bed, got dressed, and went above deck to check out our situation.

The sky was dark with gray clouds, waves splashed over the sides of the ship onto the walkway, and it was windy.

This was just great.

Huntley was on the wheel, perfectly calm, his eyes focused on the horizon like this was just another regular day to him. "Morning."

"Anything I can do?"

"I got it." He turned the wheel to the left, getting away from a nasty wave. "There was a storm to the east. Looks like we're getting hit with the aftermath."

"Should I be worried?"

"No."

"Because I can swim."

"Doesn't matter if you can swim or not. Water is so cold, you'll be dead in two minutes."

"That's lovely…"

"Don't worry, baby." He gave me a half smile. "I won't let anything happen to you."

I walked to the line and tugged until the sail turned, catching the wind. "How much farther?"

"Two more days. I had to change direction to avoid the worst of it."

"Hope it won't be choppy the whole time… I feel sick."

"Just keep your eyes on the horizon."

"Not sure how to do that when I'm trying to sleep."

———

THE NEXT TWO days were rough, choppy waves and ruthless wind. Huntley didn't sleep much, even when it was pitch black, because he had to keep the boat on the right course. The waters pushed the boat on a different trajectory often, and if that wasn't corrected, it would take us even longer to arrive.

I slept intermittently down below, the waves waking me up constantly. I kept a pail beside the bed because the sickness would leave my stomach and empty out of my throat. I'd never been on a ship, so that was how I learned I was susceptible to seasickness.

When I woke up refreshed one morning, I knew the worst had passed.

Especially since Huntley was beside me.

My face was in the crook of his neck, and his hand was in my hair as we lay close together, a single entity under the blankets. My eyes opened, and I pulled away to see his hard face soft with sleep. His jaw was thick with hair because he hadn't shaved during our trip, but I liked the way it lightly scratched my skin when he was close, like when his face was pressed between my thighs.

I glanced out the window, seeing the morning light.

Hopefully, we were close. I cared more about getting off this damn boat than seeing dragons. I carefully moved out of the bed without waking him, donned my clothes, and headed to the deck to take a look.

The ocean was calm. Not calm like glass, but with gentle waves that didn't rock the boat from side to side. I tightened my coat under my crossed arms and looked at the horizon. I gave a loud gasp when I saw it.

Land.

Land was in sight.

It was far, probably another day's worth of sailing, but at least it was near.

And it wasn't as cold as it'd been either. The air had been frostbite on the lungs. Now, it was cool and pleasant, like the nighttime air on a summer evening. I moved to the front of the ship to get a better look, even though it wouldn't make a difference.

Almost there.

Now that the end was near, I remembered why we'd come here.

To heal a dragon.

Actually, dragons.

Something I'd never done before. How could I have done it before when I didn't even believe dragons were real? Dragons were mythical creatures, monsters in bedtime stories to get children to behave. They served kings in legends, torched kingdoms before they were conquered, ate humans in a single bite.

But they were real.

Footsteps sounded behind me, heavy boots on the wooden deck. Big hands moved to my arms, and a hard stomach pressed into my back. "There it is."

"What is it?"

"An island."

"But what's it called?"

"The true name? I don't know. But I call it Quartz."

"Why?"

"There's a lot of it there. In the rocks. In the sand."

"Isn't that valuable?"

"I'm sure it is. But what's it going to buy you? Money doesn't mean much at the bottom of the cliffs. It can buy you a whore for the night or an extra chicken for dinner, but that's it."

Thinking about all the sex he used to pay for had never bothered me, but now it got under my skin a little bit. I didn't voice that because the last thing I wanted him to think was that I cared. Or worse…that I was jealous.

"What is it?"

"What?"

"You got quiet."

He could read me that well? We'd become that close? "I've believed that dragons aren't real my entire life…"

"Another lie to throw on the pile."

"I don't know anything about their anatomy. I'm not sure how I can heal them."

"You'll figure it out."

"Healing a horse or a cow is different from a dragon. They're docile, can be tied to a post. Dragons can't be controlled. How am I even supposed to get close enough without getting bitten in half?"

"We'll figure it out."

"And even if I do heal them…what then?"

"They'll fly."

"So?"

"We'll have a very quick and effective way to get to the top of the cliffs. We'll burn anyone who opposes us, and they're not equipped to deal with an assault from the air."

Now my heart plummeted into my stomach because I

was handing Huntley the keys to the Kingdoms, to my father's coffin. It felt like a betrayal, even if I fully believed that my father was the barbarian he was accused of being. "Just because they're healed and can fly doesn't mean they're going to do your bidding. They aren't dogs. They don't need someone to take care of them like other animals do."

"We'll figure it out."

"Is that your answer for everything?"

"Yes." He released me and headed back to the hatch. "Come on."

"Come on what?" I turned around, seeing him in just his boots and breeches.

He gave a nod to the cabin and took the steps below. "Back to bed. We have a lot of time to kill."

———

THE CLOSER WE came to the island, the warmer it became.

It was humid, just like it was in the Capital in summer, with the heat pressing right against your skin and then dissolving into your bloodstream. It was a welcome change compared to the cold, the first time I'd actually felt warm since I'd left Delacroix. Layers of clothing came off until I was down to my breeches and a thin shirt.

Huntley changed too, but he was in his full black armor, with vambraces on his arms and a plate over his chest. His ax was hooked over his back, along with his sword and bow. He was back to his intimidating old self.

The gray color of the water changed to blue, glowing brighter and brighter the closer we came to shore. It was clear too, giving glimpses of the bottom. When I leaned over the side and stuck my hand in the water, it was refreshing to the touch.

Huntley raised the sail and brought the sloop to a gentle glide, slowing the momentum so we could approach the island at an easy pace. He dropped anchor, and then the boat came to a stop just feet from shore.

The land was lush, full of trees, vegetation, the sound of birds in the canopy. It was wild and vast, like the outskirts of the kingdom that hadn't fallen to deforestation. I couldn't see past the tree line or farther inland, so I had no idea what lay beyond.

Huntley turned to me. "I need you to do exactly as I tell you. Your smart mouth and stubbornness are normally a turn-on for me, but right now, I don't have time for that shit. Alright?"

He was more somber than when we'd sailed on a tiny-ass boat across the ocean, so this must be serious. "What's in there?"

"Outcasts."

"Outcasts?"

"The worst of the worst. People ejected from society. At least, that's what I've gathered in my visits."

"I'm not following…"

"Most crimes are punishable by death. That's merci-

ful. That's easy. But for the people who deserve worse…
they're exiled here. An island with limited resources,
where your neighbors are just as barbaric as you are. It's
the worst of the worst."

"Who's exiling these people?"

"I'm not sure. But it's a big world…and there're a lot
of people in it."

"You mean, there are kingdoms outside of ours?"

"It's not impossible, right?"

I'd never really thought about it.

"So, we stay low. We stay quiet."

I nodded.

"We do what we came here to do—and then leave. No
fires. No sex."

"Whoa…why not?"

He grinned. "Do you care about anything else?"

"I was referring to the fire—"

"Liar." His grin was arrogant now, but still so handsome. "I don't want someone to watch me fuck you.
They'll want to take you for themselves. And they know
this land better than I do, so…"

Now I felt sick, just the way I did during the biggest
waves.

"It'll be alright. Just do what I say."

"Okay."

His eyes took me in for a while. "Actually…it's a turn-
on when you listen, too."

I rolled my eyes and turned away.

His hand gripped mine hard and yanked me back,

right into his chest, right into his lips. His hungry mouth devoured mine like we hadn't just spent the day screwing below deck, enjoying every single position there was to experience. His hand squeezed my ass at the same time before he abruptly let me go. "Let's move."

––––––––

THE CAPITAL WAS WARM, but it wasn't humid like this. This place was tropical, with big green leaves that hung from branches, large flowers that were open along the forest floor and in the trees. It was so dense that all the whistles the birds made echoed in the canopy, so loud it was as if they called right in my ear. "This doesn't seem ideal for dragons."

He took the lead, chopping down vegetation in his way, inching deeper inland. "I don't think they had a choice."

"They're dragons. They always have a choice."

He lowered his sword to his side and immediately squatted, like he saw something.

I did the same and dropped down.

His eyes peered through the leaves, pulling them over slightly to reveal the distant light of torches.

We weren't alone.

I could make out the scene, a vine of ropes secured around a man's neck as he stood on the branch of a tree. Another man stood behind him, like he was about to push him off.

"Ready?" There was a man down below, a dagger carved out of stone in his hand, tied together with coconut husk. "And, go."

"Don't!" The bound man pleaded for his life, trying to break free of the restraints on his wrists and balance on the branch at the same time. He must have been kicked in the back because he toppled over, and just before he hit the ground, the vine bounced and yanked him back up.

I heard the crack of his neck.

The man with the dagger threw the blade at the moving target, hitting him in the stomach. "There's one." He withdrew another and did the same, but he missed his second shot. "Alright, one out of three."

The man was dead now, but he was still bouncing left and right from the springy vine.

The other man threw the third and impaled him in the shoulder. "Two outta three. That ain't bad."

I wanted to reach for my bucket and hurl.

Unfazed, Huntley just watched.

The place seemed warm and beautiful from the outside, but on the inside, it was a cage. A cage where evil fought evil to the death. "Let's hurry up and find those dragons…"

Huntley returned the leaves to their place and looked at me. "They're on the other side."

"Then why didn't we sail there?"

"Can't risk someone seeing the boat. They'd either steal it or sink it."

I didn't scare easily, but I was scared now, even with Huntley with me.

He watched me for a while, his eyes shifting back and forth as he took me in. "You want to leave?"

"Is that even an option?" We'd come here for a purpose, and that purpose hadn't been fulfilled.

"You're scared. And I've never seen you scared."

"Well…I've never been stuck on an island with the cruelest men alive."

"I don't think you're weak," he said. "I'll take you back to the boat if that's what you want."

"And then what?"

"I'll kill everyone on the island, then go back for you. I don't know how many there are, but there can't be more than a hundred."

"No…I'm fine."

"Are you sure?"

"Yes. I would die if something happened to you."

Now his eyes locked on me in a whole new way.

The words were already gone from my lips, and I couldn't take them back. When his stare became too much, I looked away, back to the big leaves that hid us from view of the maniacs. "You know…because I wouldn't survive out here on my own."

His stare continued. I couldn't see it, but I could definitely feel it.

Seconds became a minute. A minute became an eternity.

I finally found the courage to look at him again.

His stare was exactly the same—intense. "Let's keep moving."

———

THE INHABITANTS of the island lit torches at their dwellings, telling us exactly where they were.

At least, the ones who didn't care about giving away their positions.

Which meant they were probably the worst ones.

We stopped for the night in an area surrounded by dense trees, giving us adequate cover from the outcasts who lived in a never-ending war. We used one bedroll, didn't make conversation, hardly touched.

I couldn't sleep. My ears strained to hear every sound, to ignore the loud noises of the birds and focus on a breaking stick or shifting tree branches. My heart beat fast, too fast to close my eyes and go to sleep.

He must have felt it because he whispered, "Sleep."

"I can't."

"I'll keep watch."

"You're the one who deserves to sleep. Let me keep an eye out so you can get some rest. I can't sleep anyway, so…"

"How can you heal the dragons if you're exhausted?"

"Exhaustion doesn't interfere with my work. I've done it lots of times." Because I had been up late with a lover, not up late trying to survive on an infested island.

He stared at me for a while before he closed his eyes.

I felt him drift off right away. I could tell by the change in his breathing.

I stayed wide awake, listening to every sound, giving a slight jolt when I thought I felt something crawl up my arm. It was always nothing, but I was hyperaware of everything. At least in the cold, people were scarce. But here... Some of the most violent people were trapped on a small island...and there were only so many places to go.

TWENTY-TWO

Huntley

I LED THE WAY, KEEPING A CLOSE EYE ON HER WITH EYES IN the back of my head, getting through the lush vegetation with my ax chopping everything in our path. We did our best to cut through the center to save time, because going around the exterior would add more time than we were willing to spend.

There were no smartass exchanges on this journey, not like usual, and I actually missed that. Without it, it was just work, getting from one place to another. We circled around the mountain in the center, following the route I'd trod the last time I was here. Fortunately, we didn't cross paths with any of the inhabitants. I had before, and even though their tools were makeshift, they were still formidable foes. They took one look at all my gear, and greed glimmered in their eyes.

We finally made it to the other side of the mountain,

the land flattening out until it returned to the sea. Rocky outcroppings were near the shore, with enormous caves where the dragons could dwell. That was where I always found them. They had their side of the island—and the men had theirs.

"We should be in the clear now." I moved through the trees as I headed toward the caves in the black rocks up ahead.

"What do you mean?"

"This is dragon territory. The men don't come this far —not unless they want to be burned alive."

"That's a relief…I guess." She came to my side now, walking with me with less stress in her eyes.

"You didn't blink an eye when you met Klaus. Why is this any different?"

She turned to me, clearly provoked by the question. "Because most men are motivated by something. Money. Weapons. Women. But they don't have those things here, so…all they have is entertainment. It's creepy, I guess. They're slaughtering one another for sport. Disturbing."

"I guess there are worse places than the bottom of the cliffs."

"I'll say…"

We moved across the valley closer to the caves, taking a full day to tread miles to approach the area.

"This is no place for a dragon. With all the vegetation, they hardly have room to move around."

"The well-being of the dragons wasn't their concern."

"Assholes…"

When we reached the very edge of the tree line, we stopped because if we trod any farther, we would be visible to the entrance of the caves. I kneeled down and dropped my bag on the ground.

"You think they're in there?" she asked.

"Yes."

"Dragons like caves?"

"It's probably cool in there."

I opened my bag and pulled out the raw meat of a boar I had slaughtered. I'd wrapped it up and saved it to lure them out of the shadows. I prepared to throw it.

"Whoa…hold on." She steadied my hand. "What's our plan here?"

"I've got to get them out of the cave."

"And then what?"

"You do what we came here for."

She gave me that irritated stare, the one she always gave right before she ripped into me. "You think this takes two seconds? That I just run out there, do my thing, and take off before he notices? This is a really intimate process. I need to touch him. I need to feel his body. Depending on the severity of the injury, it could take hours."

Fuck, I'd been afraid of that.

"If that were the case, anyone could do it."

I grabbed the raw meat and chucked it far, making it land ten feet outside the cave. "We gotta start somewhere…"

"He's going to know someone threw that. He's not stupid."

"But he's also got nothing to be afraid of."

For a while, nothing happened.

It was quiet, the breeze moving through the trees, the birds singing in the canopy.

Then we heard it.

Thud.

Thud. Thud. Thud.

"Oh my fucking god, it's happening." She clutched her hands to her chest and moved behind one of the trees. "I can't feel my heart. I mean, I can, but it's beating so damn fast—"

"Shh."

"You *shh*. It's a fucking dragon."

His scales emerged in the sunlight, his feet covered in claws, his scales dark green like the leaves on the island. He was enormous, nearly as tall as the cave he'd just emerged from. Every step shook the earth, sent tiny vibrations like an earthquake was imminent. He approached the pile of raw meat on the ground and bent down to smell. His nostrils flared wide, and his breath was so strong that the meat tugged up slightly.

That was when he exposed his wings—or lack thereof.

Cut down to the bone, most of his flank was exposed, the glorious part of his physical being chopped away with a knife. It was hard to look at, like someone who'd lost an arm or a leg.

He sniffed the meat again before he closed his mouth over it.

And then I heard her cries.

Against the tree, she cupped her hand to her mouth, stifling her sobs. Tears glistened on her cheeks, but not the kind that I liked, not the kind that hit the sheets underneath her naked body.

He must have heard it too—because he raised his head and stopped chewing.

"Shh," I whispered to her.

She tightened her entire body and suppressed the sobs.

He stared into the tree line, intelligent eyes shifting back and forth as he searched for us in the shade.

Then he took a step forward.

Oh fuck.

Another.

And then another.

"Don't move," I whispered to her. If we ran, it would be much easier to spot us, like lizards that scurried across the path once they heard your footsteps.

Powerful eyes peered into the tree line, absolutely still, as if waiting for us to move.

We didn't even breathe.

Then he stepped closer—and closer.

I could take down a yeti if I had to, but a dragon…not gonna happen. All I could do was distract him long enough for Ivory to get away. I knew she could sail back on her own. She could figure it out.

His head moved into the tree line and gave a loud sniff, like he could smell us.

Ivory was motionless, her hand still clasped over her mouth, hot tears still on her cheeks.

He found her, his dark eyes just feet away from where she stood.

I could bring down my ax on his neck, but that wouldn't do much, not when his neck was the size of ten trunks combined.

The stare continued, the dragon focused on her as if he didn't realize I was there. Hot breaths left his nostrils and escaped as vapor, washing over her.

Her hand slowly dropped, her eyes still wet and glistening. "I'm sorry about what happened to you…"

I removed my ax from my back and gripped it tightly, ready to strike if this went south.

He came closer, his nose about to brush up against her skin, and inhaled a deep breath. It was like a horse that neighed, that breathed hot breaths on your hand after you fed them carrots.

His snout was directly in front of her, so she reached out her hand slowly and made contact with his scales.

Completely dumbfounded, I just stared.

She inhaled a shaky breath when she reached close enough to him to touch, when her fingers glided over the rough skin. "I'm going to try to fix you."

He withdrew his head from the trees then turned around to go back to the cave.

Thud. Thud. Thud.

He returned to the cave, the last part of his tail disappearing in the shadow.

For the first time in my life, I was speechless. Truly. All the way down to my spine. I stared at the side of her face, watched her wet eyes look at the entrance to the cave as if he might return. "What just happened?"

As if she didn't hear me, she held on to the tree, her eyes welling up all over again.

"Baby." I came to her side, my hand immediately diving into her hair while my arm wrapped around her waist.

Her chin dropped, and she looked at my chest, her fingers dabbing at the corners of her eyes to catch the tears before they had the chance to fall. "Whenever I heal, I feel the inside of the body, feel the strain to isolate the injury. But with him…he had so much pain everywhere…and that only happens with a broken heart."

My fingers ran through her hair, comforting her in the only way I knew how. Her tears were like drops of acid—and I had to drink them.

"Without his wings…he's nothing."

"Can you heal him?"

She shook her head, the words too difficult to say.

"You just told him you would try."

"And I will. But I don't have the resources. I can heal broken bones and internal bleeding, but this is…a complete regrowth. I've never done anything like that before. I need to go back to the library. I wish you had told me the situation before we came here…would have saved us a lot of time."

"The library? In Delacroix?"

"Yes." She finished dabbing her eyes, finally back to calm.

Now my heart sank like an anchor from our ship. "You know I can't take you back there."

"We have to. It's the only way."

Now I stepped back, a heavy dose of unease in my heart. "How do you know you'll find what you need?"

"I don't. But there're a lot of books—you've seen that library."

"Been a long time," I said, full of bitterness.

"Huntley, we have to."

"I'm not stupid, Ivory."

She stilled when I used her actual name, something I hardly did anymore.

"This was probably your plan all along."

"All along?" she asked incredulously. "I had no idea that their wings had been sawed off by fucking maniacs until just now. No, I didn't plan this."

"You probably had this idea before you even saw them."

Now her eyes flashed with a new level of animosity. "You really think I'd see something this heartbreaking and use it to my advantage? You really think I would leave this island, knowing I could have fixed them and simply chose not to? If you really think that…then you don't know me at all." She grabbed her bag from the ground and marched off, even though she had no idea where she was going.

―――――

WE WERE SO FAR AWAY from the main part of the island that we could make a fire, roast some fresh meat, and have a real dinner for the first time since we'd set sail. She sat on one side of the fire and I on the other.

We hadn't spoken since she'd marched off. She wouldn't even look at me now.

I couldn't stop looking at her.

"I'm going to fix their wings whether you help me or not." Her eyes stayed on the fire. "I'm not going to abandon them here, forsaken, not when they aren't even real dragons anymore. They're fucking mutilated. Who the fuck would do such a thing?" Angry tears burned in her eyes.

If she was lying, it was some of the best lying I'd ever seen. "Is there another way to get the information you need?"

"Not unless you know a healer. And I imagine you don't—because you wouldn't need me."

She was right.

"Maybe this information exists elsewhere, perhaps in the Grand Library at the Capital, but Delacroix is a lot closer."

"And how would this work? I return you to the castle, you slip inside and get what you need, and you just leave?"

I asked incredulously. "Your father must have men searching for you everywhere, night and day."

"I've been gone a long time, so he probably assumes I'm dead at this point." Her eyes dropped.

"It's too risky."

"Ryker." Her eyes lifted again.

"What about him?"

"He can smuggle out what I need."

I gave her a stare of pure incredulity. "You really think your brother would cooperate when you're my prisoner?"

"Wouldn't Ian?"

I stared.

"You have a brother," she said quietly. "You know they'll do anything for you."

"But this is different."

"I'll tell him I'll return later. But I just can't right now."

"Who said anything about you returning later?"

Her stare turned cold. "You're just going to keep me forever?"

"Yes."

"I don't believe you."

"I don't care."

"After everything we've been through together—"

"That's exactly why."

Now she tensed, her eyes turning still.

"I know you feel the same way. Don't pretend otherwise." Her words made me snap. When I imagined returning her to Delacroix and leaving her there…it drove me insane. She'd been a thorn in my side, a weed in my garden, but that weed had turned into the most beautiful flower I'd ever seen.

There was a long pause, as if she didn't know what to say. "My family deserves to know that I'm okay."

"Then tell them before you go."

TWENTY-THREE

Ivory
_____

WE RETURNED TO THE OTHER SIDE OF THE ISLAND, AND IT was such a relief to see that our boat was still there, bobbing in the water on the small waves that rolled to shore. We strode through the water, climbed aboard, and then set the sails to return the way we'd come.

I watched the island slowly disappear behind us, growing smaller and smaller until it started to fade in the sunset. There should be a large dragon in the sky above, powerful wings beating the wind to carry its heavy mass to the clouds.

The image of those clipped wings would haunt me for the rest of my life.

I felt pain for every creature that I tried to save, and it always hurt when I didn't get there in time. But this was different. It was barbaric mutilation, something so vile that evil wasn't a strong enough word to describe it.

Huntley was on the wheel, guiding us in the right

direction to return to our cold world. I could already feel the change in temperature, feel the humidity dissipate the farther we traveled.

The sun officially set, and we went below deck into the cabin to sleep.

Huntley stripped down to just his breeches before he lit the lantern that kept the cabin aglow. But instead of getting into bed, he sat in one of the armchairs, his elbow resting on the table beside him. His eyes were empty and glazed over, as if his thoughts were somewhere else.

"What is it?"

His eyes flicked to me.

I'd changed into one of his long-sleeved shirts but left my bottoms off since he would remove them once we went to bed.

His stare was still blank, as if days of abstinence weren't enough to surge his libido like it did for me.

I continued my stare.

His only response was a slight shake of his head.

"I wouldn't lie to you, Huntley. Returning to Delacroix is the only way I can help them. I'm not happy that you want to use them to further your own gains, but I have to help them, regardless of what comes next. That sorrow I felt…I've never felt anything like it."

"That's not what's on my mind."

"Then what is?"

His eyes flicked away once again, severing the conversation.

———

EVERY SINGLE DAY on the seas was spent in silence.

Huntley was quiet, closed off.

The sex was hot like it always was, but that was the only way we connected. The rest of the time, it was like he didn't want anything to do with me. Every time I asked him about it, he never had a reply.

I wasn't sure if he would ever tell me.

When it got really cold, I knew we were close.

Land appeared in the distance, hardly visible through the thick fog bank that obscured everything from sight. I kept my clothes bundled around my body and missed the humid heat of Quartz. Sweat had dripped down my back and I was always hot, but it was preferable to this bone-chilling frost.

Huntley turned the wheel a bit, as if he knew where the outpost was without any landmarks or direction from the stars. I had no idea how he'd become such a skilled sailor, considering he was on land most of the time, but this man seemed capable of anything. He raised the sail to half-mast, and we glided to the coast.

There was nothing else to do but wait.

I came to his side at the wheel, feeling the contact of the fog against my cheeks the second it hit. I could feel the cold moisture on my skin, like drops of rain from the sky. "Huntley."

He resisted my command for a while, his eyes still on the fog.

I waited, knowing he would meet my gaze eventually.

After a while, he did. His blue eyes were empty, their vibrant light blocked by storm clouds.

"Tell me."

It was quiet, the fog swallowing the sounds of the waves, of the breeze. The boat creaked from time to time, but the rest of the time, it was just pure silence. "I have a dilemma on my hands. I've been trying to solve it."

"What dilemma?"

"I've found a solution, but I'm not sure if you'll accept it."

My arms crossed over my chest.

"Queen Rolfe expects an attack on HeartHolme. The Teeth will come—which is something that hasn't happened in a very long time. It's something we can't afford, not if Necrosis strikes, which can happen at any moment. For the safety of her people, it's best to give them what they want to deter their bloodshed."

My heart pounded because I knew what they wanted.

"After you give us the dragons, she plans to hand you over."

It was such a betrayal—from him. "And you gave no objection?"

"I did. Didn't change anything."

"Well, I couldn't save the dragons…so I guess I'm safe for now."

"But after we get what you need from Delacroix, you won't be."

My arms tightened over my chest. I'd always felt safe with him, but now I didn't. "What's your solution?"

He looked straight ahead for a while, staring at the solid wall of fog all around us. "Marry me."

The breath that I sucked between my teeth was loud, even with the fog muffling everything. My hands tucked into the crooks of my arms, looking for warmth as a different kind of cold spread through my limbs.

He turned back to me. "She's not going to hand my wife over to anyone."

All I did was breathe.

"You would be a Rolfe, so I'd trust you not to betray me in Delacroix. Our souls would be bound forever."

"Huntley…you could never get married again."

"I know."

"And that means…I can't marry someone else…someday."

He stared.

"It's…it's a big deal."

"That's why it would protect us both."

"But can you really do that?" I asked. "Share your soul with someone…for convenience?"

His stare continued. "All I know is, I have to protect you, and I have to protect myself too."

"To sleep with you is one thing…but to marry you… That makes things so complicated. You want to overthrow my father and kill him. You want to remove Rutherford from his throne and take his place, just to forsake everyone down here all over again. I don't support your politics, and I never will."

"You could always object—since you'd be my queen."

My eyes hardened at the realization. "Then I object."

"What are your terms?"

This had quickly turned into a negotiation rather than a marriage proposal. "We defeat Necrosis."

He gave a loud sigh.

"The problem will persist until they're defeated."

"Or everyone dies in the attempt."

"Do you want to be a king for the sake of being a king? Because you're power hungry and egotistical like everyone else? Or do you actually want to make this world a better place? What kind of man do you want to be?"

He gave me his hard stare.

"Because if we're husband and wife, we have to be in agreement—about *everything*. If I'm going to help you remove my father from power, it has to be for a good reason. It has to be worth the betrayal. It has to benefit everyone in this fucked-up world."

He considered my words for a long time before he gave a nod. "Alright."

All my muscles tightened in disbelief. "Really?"

"I wouldn't lie to you."

"Then I have another condition."

His stare remained.

"You can't kill my father."

A bolt of lightning streaked across his face, the anger exploding in a rush.

"You can imprison him. You can punish him. But… you can't kill him."

"No."

"Huntley—"

"I said no."

"He's my father—"

"He raped my mother and murdered my father. I will not spare him."

"Then I won't marry you." I stepped back, my arms tightening over my chest.

He could barely speak, he was so angry. "After everything he did…you defend him."

"I'm not defending him. He deserves punishment. He deserves imprisonment. But he's my father…and it's complicated. It's just the way you felt for your mother when she was on her crazy tirade against me. It doesn't matter what she does—she will always have your loyalty."

"Unable to control her need for revenge is not the same thing as raping an innocent woman and making her son watch. How dare you compare the two—"

"I'm not comparing, okay? I'm just saying he's my father. It's one thing if you and your family tracked him down and killed him on your own, but if I'm going to help you make this happen…I can't have his blood on my hands. You must understand that."

"I wouldn't do it in front of you—"

"But I will be instrumental in your success. Without me, it wouldn't happen, and I can't live with that guilt."

His eyes shifted back and forth, livid.

"Take it or leave it."

The breaths he took deepened, like his anger couldn't be resolved by sheer will alone.

I held my ground.

He clenched his jaw before he gave a loud growl. "Fine."

"Promise me."

His eyes were so callous. He'd never looked at me like that before.

"I want your word—"

"I promise."

A weight was lifted off my shoulders, my guilt assuaged. "Then…I'll marry you."

———

WE RETURNED the boat to the outpost then continued on our way through the wilderness. Our horses were where we'd left them, fully fed and rested while we'd sailed across the sea, and we rode them back through the cold.

Huntley dismounted and walked his horse in hot spots, places where we had an increased chance of crossing paths with Plunderers. But the rest of the time, we rode hard, desperate to get back to HeartHolme after our long journey.

We slept together every night, but that was all we did, sleep.

And we didn't talk about the marriage.

How would that even go?

On the third day, we approached HeartHolme, the enormous stone gates opening once they recognized our dots on the plains. The horses trampled the wild flowers and weeds along the way, avoiding small rocks that could break their legs and jumping over larger rocks entirely.

I hadn't been an experienced long-distance horse rider before this, but now I certainly was.

We made it through the gates to the stables, and the men moved to retrieve the horses and remove their saddles. It was a little warmer surrounded by the walls and the rock than out in the open, and I envisioned that soft bed waiting for me, right in front of the warm fireplace.

Huntley spoke to his men before he came to me. "Come on."

I matched his stride and moved farther into the city, up the slight incline toward the castle at the top. "Now what?"

"I'll drop you off at the house. My mother will want to speak with me once she knows I've arrived—which will be shortly."

"Will you tell her about us?"

His breath escaped as vapor because it was a cold morning, colder than it had been when we left. "No."

"Why?"

"Because she'll probably kill you to stop it."

"I'm so excited for her to be my mother-in-law…"

He ignored my jab.

We made it through the city and to the two-story home behind the iron gate. I'd only spent a short amount of time there, but the sight of it tugged at my heart because it already felt like home. That first cabin we'd had felt like home too. I guess anywhere with Huntley felt that way…

We made it inside and up the stairs, and I dropped all the weapons he'd given me, the weapons I didn't have to use. I instantly felt twenty pounds lighter, and my spine straightened without the weight.

"I don't know if I want to sleep or bathe first. They both sound amazing."

Huntley dropped his heavy jacket and the rest of his gear, getting down to his naked skin.

"Or we can do that too…"

He cracked a slight smile as he opened his closet and pulled out his black garb, the royal clothing that indicated his status to the queen.

"You're leaving?"

"She'll want to speak with me immediately."

I was already half naked, so I dropped the rest of my clothing and sat on the bed. "Can you go afterward?"

He faced me, his fingers buttoning the front of his shirt, that smile gone and the intensity back. The last button was secured, but he continued his deep stare, seriously tempted. "We have the rest of the day when I return."

"Well…it's been three days."

Now he grinned, a full smile that was handsome and flirtatious. "It's been three days for me too, baby."

TWENTY-FOUR

Huntley

I ENTERED THE CASTLE GROUNDS, WATCHED THE GUARDS part to make way for my progress, and took the grand staircase to the next floor, where I would wait for my mother to join me. Asher, Servant to the Queen, was there, sitting at the table with a pile of scrolls in front of him.

He looked up slightly at my entry. "How were your travels, Huntley?"

"Shitty, like always."

"Hope something good came from it."

"Yes."

He left the table and departed the room, in a black outfit similar to mine, and disappeared from view.

I took a seat and waited.

When he returned, she joined him, but she wasn't in her royal garb. She was in a long-sleeved dress, comfortable as if she expected no visitors that day. She came straight to me, embracing me as a mother instead of a queen. Her arms wrapped around me, and she held me close, making me feel loved without saying a single word.

It made me feel like shit for what I was about to do.

She pulled away and squeezed my arms. "You're unhurt."

"Always."

"Good." She withdrew, and within a second, her eyes changed, turning cold and hard. "Have you secured the dragons?"

"No."

Asher stood behind her, his arms at his back. "You said you had good news."

"I do." I kept my eyes on my mother. "I can get the dragons. But Ivory needs information from Delacroix first."

Queen Rolfe could express so much with so little, just by the subtle change of her eyes. She went from calm to furious in a single blink. "She needs information? She's a healer. She needs nothing but her skills."

"She said she can heal injuries and broken bones, but she can't regrow tissue. It's something she's never done, and she needs access to the library to figure out how to do that."

"She insults me, thinking I'm that stupid."

"I thought the same."

"Now that she's officially useless, we should hand her over to the Teeth. She can be their dinner."

My stomach tightened at the thought. "I rejected the idea immediately, but after seeing her reaction to the dragons, I know she genuinely wants to help. Her tears were real. Her heartbreak was too moving to be false."

Her eyes narrowed. "Don't fall for her ploy, Huntley."

"It's not a ploy. This is what she does—heals animals. Obviously, she's passionate about it. She thought dragons were a myth, monsters in stories, and to see them inches from her face was an incredible experience."

I could tell that didn't mean a damn thing to her. "I'm not letting her return to Delacroix. The decision is final."

"She won't betray us—at least until after the dragons are healed."

"No." She turned away. "The discussion is over."

Asher barred my way so I couldn't get to her.

Mother moved to the table and took a seat, at her usual place at the head of the table. "The effort will take a day or so to organize. You can enjoy your whore in the meantime."

———

THE SECOND I walked through the bedroom door, she took all my stress away. The fire was strong in the hearth, and she was naked in my bed, her brown hair across the pillow, the sheets pulled to her chest so her arms and shoulders were visible. Her hair was washed and clean, and her eyes were soft because she was comfortable in my home.

She didn't ask about the conversation with the queen, like that was the last thing on her mind.

It was certainly the last thing on mine.

I unclasped my cloak, unbuttoned my tunic, and at the foot of the bed, I undressed until a pile of clothes was on the hardwood floor.

Her eyes looked me over—hungry.

My knees hit the mattress and made her body turn slightly in my direction. Farther I went until I held myself over her, my head dipping to hers for a kiss. The landing was soft, our lips coming together like white clouds against a blue sky. My eyes opened and looked at her underneath me, her eyes on my lips, wanting more.

I tugged the sheets from her body and hooked her leg over my hip as I pressed into her, our warm bodies coming together like two logs in a fire. My mouth sealed over hers again in a passionate kiss with hungry moves, a little bit of tongue, and lots of heavy breaths. I ground our bodies together at the same time, my shaft growing wet just from pressing against her entrance.

I hadn't showered in three days, but she didn't give a damn.

Her nails dug into my back as she dragged her hands down, slicing into my skin like I was fully inside her and making the bed shake. One hand went to my ass, and she tugged on me, too anxious to continue this unnecessary foreplay.

I directed myself inside her and felt her gasp against my mouth.

A moan came next, a quiet and drawn-out one.

With slow and steady thrusts, I rocked into her, my eyes on hers. "Welcome home, baby."

TWENTY-FIVE

Ivory

AS IF WE'D NEVER LEFT, HE WOKE ME UP THE NEXT morning just the way I liked, his lips on my neck, his hips between my thighs. It was all business, getting right to the point so he could start his day.

I loved morning sex.

I'd never had it before because my lovers had to sneak out in the middle of the night.

He bathed then left, and I went right back to sleep the second the door shut.

When I woke up hours later, I bathed even though I had bathed last night, because it was a pleasure I would never take for granted again. I took the money from his nightstand and bought myself a big lunch then returned to the house to sit in front of the fireplace in the bedroom and read one of the books I'd found on the sloop. I felt like a wife waiting for my husband to come home from his long day at work.

The door opened and closed downstairs, and I knew I was no longer alone.

I closed my book and listened to his heavy footsteps on the stairs. I'd heard them enough times to recognize them, for it to become habitual.

He entered the room in his royal garments, broad shoulders, muscular arms, with the height of a tree. His bright eyes locked on me, but his hands didn't reach for his clothes to undo them and leave them on the floor.

He approached my armchair then took a knee, making himself eye level with me, his hand moving to my bare thigh then underneath the bottom of my sweater, which covered me to my thighs. I wore his socks too, which came up to my knees. His fingers reached until he found the fabric of my underwear and lightly played with it.

My eyes savored his strong jawline, the shadow it produced underneath his chin, the way his eyes were so pretty but also so hard at the same time. This wasn't what I'd imagined for a husband, but it could be worse, far worse.

"You still want to do this?" His deep voice came out quiet, barely louder than the fire that burned behind him.

My eyes searched his face for an explanation.

"Because we need to do it now."

The realization came a moment later. "What's happened?"

His eyes remained steady, and his fingertips continued to play with my underwear beneath my sweater. "She intends to deliver you to Klaus tomorrow. Doesn't trust you enough to let you return to Delacroix—which is what I expected."

I guess that wasn't surprising.

"This is our only option."

"You really think our marriage will be enough to protect me?"

"You'd be family—so, yes."

A long stare ensued, and my heart beat so hard that tiny vibrations rushed to my extremities. I only had one soul to give, and this was the man I would give it to. There would never be anyone else. Forever. "Do you still want to do this…?"

His hand went to my neck, his thumb brushing over my bottom lip. "You're my baby, right?"

And just like that, all the fear disappeared. I realized I didn't want to do this just to save myself—but because he would be mine forever.

"We're loyal to each other first. Everyone else —second."

I nodded in his hand, feeling his thumb continue to trace my bottom lip.

"We will take the Kingdoms—and then we will destroy Necrosis. As husband and wife. As king and queen."

————

IT WAS the first time we'd held hands.

He grabbed mine as we walked down the cobblestone

path, the sun almost gone from the horizon, the sky blue and purple, little silhouettes of birds that hadn't found their refuge for the night.

He took the lead, guiding me into a building with a domed ceiling, the windows made of colored glass. The double doors were each twenty feet tall, but Huntley had no problem opening one with a single hand and pulling me inside.

The room was lit with white candles, wax dripping down the pillars to the golden plates they stood upon. An enormous sculpture was in the center, an armed soldier with a beautiful woman in flowing gowns. Candles were everywhere, and the place smelled like old books and stale air.

Huntley took me past the shelves of books in the center and the desks where the monks worked throughout the day. Farther he went, until he found the place of worship, at the feet of one of the gods.

Adeodatus.

A monk emerged, in an unremarkable brown robe, his head shaved because he wasn't allowed vanity whatsoever. "Huntley, I have come as you asked. But now, you must tell me the subject of this clandestine meeting." His eyes flicked to me, taking me in before he turned his attention back on Huntley.

"We wish to be married." His hand remained in mine, strong and warm.

The monk was quiet, unable to process the request. "Queen Rolfe isn't present."

"I want you to marry us anyway."

"I cannot. Queen Rolfe will have me ejected from the clergy."

"I won't let that happen."

"With all due respect, Huntley. You're not the King of HeartHolme."

"But I'm her son, and she will listen to me."

He turned quiet.

"I'll tell her I threatened your life."

"That would be a lie, and I will not tell lies."

He released me, withdrew his sword, and held it at the monk's throat. "How's this, then?"

The monk raised both arms and turned absolutely still.

"Marry us—or I'll slit your throat."

He didn't even take a breath, he was so scared.

"You think I won't do it?" Huntley pressed the knife right against his skin, drawing a thin line of blood.

The monk grimaced when he felt it. "Yes…I'll marry you."

Huntley sheathed his sword and returned to me.

The monk clamped his hand against the superficial wound.

"You won't have a scar," Huntley said.

The monk wiped the blood on his cloak then retrieved his books.

I stared at Huntley. "Was that really necessary?"

He dropped his chin to look down at me. "I did it for his own protection."

The monk returned and set up his supplies on the podium. Two books and a gold plate with a dagger. He opened the first book, flipped to the right page, and in the language of the gods, he spoke.

Huntley and I stood there, listening to words we didn't understand, looking at each other while our hearts beat erratically. His hand moved to mine again, and he held it, his eyes confident, his exterior calm.

When the monk read the final passage, the vibrations in the air were palpable. I could feel it in every breath I took. Feel it pressing all around me. It was an energy channeled down from the heavens, an energy that had the power to bind two souls together.

The monk addressed us. "Two souls. Two bodies. But they will merge and become one. If there are objections, now is the time."

Huntley looked at me.

I stared back, just as confident.

He gave me another moment to change my mind, to call the whole thing off.

But I didn't.

Huntley faced the monk again.

The monk grabbed the dagger, the hilt made of solid gold, and extended it to Huntley.

He took it and sliced it across his open palm, the drops of blood immediately hitting the floor at his feet. Then he extended the dagger to me.

I took it and did the same, wounding myself. The bloody knife was placed on the gold plate on the podium.

"Together," the monk instructed.

Huntley grabbed my bloody hand with his and held it against his chest, the red color dripping down both of our arms. The cut either didn't hurt or I didn't notice with all the adrenaline. He didn't seem to notice either.

With our eyes locked on each other, the monk continued.

"By the power of Adeodatus, your souls are forever bound. Death will part you in this life, but not in the next. You'll walk through this world as husband and wife, and you will enter the afterlife as souls forever intertwined."

———

THE HOUSE WAS EXACTLY as we'd left it.

The fire burned in the hearth, and the sheets were still rumpled from the morning.

But now, everything was different.

I could feel the change in my lungs every time I breathed. Could taste it on my tongue. Could feel it in my fingertips even though they were numb. My hand had stopped bleeding, but the old blood had stained the skin of my palm.

Huntley came up behind me and grabbed the bottom of my shirt. Slowly, he pulled it up, waiting for my arms to rise.

I lifted them above my head and felt the material fall away.

His mouth closed on my neck as he removed my shift.

I felt it then, a powerful sensation all over my body, a constant hum in my ear.

His arm wrapped around me as he kissed me, as he undid my trousers and got them loose.

My heart pounded in a different way, raced with a speed it never had before, but the vibrations were absent. I didn't feel it rattle in my rib cage like it did when I was afraid. It was powerful but also still, quiet.

I turned around and pulled his shirt over his head. A muscular torso met my gaze, powerful pecs and abs that were harder than his shield. I kissed him everywhere, right on the skin over his heart, and undid his pants at the same time. I could feel his heart beat against my kiss with the same enthusiasm as mine.

Naked, we got onto the bed, his narrow hips moving between my thighs as he pinned me against the sheets. The world around us felt blurry, while we were in clear focus. It was like being drunk but still having full control of your faculties.

My palms slid up his chest as I looked him in the eye, never seeing eyes so blue until now. "Can you feel that…?"

His mouth closed over mine for a deep kiss, his aggressive mouth taking mine like it'd been days rather than hours since he'd last had me. His moan answered my question. His hand dug into my hair and fisted it as he tilted his hips.

When I felt him slide inside me, I felt it then, even stronger. "Fuck."

He gave a kind of moan he'd never had before,

guttural and deep, with lips that paused against my mouth as he released it.

I felt the ache in my chest as if a boulder was on top of me. It was painful, but only in its intensity, like it was too much for my body to handle. It was powerful. It was beautiful. I gripped him to hold on as I breathed against his mouth, knowing he could feel it too.

He started to rock into me, our eyes locked on each other, our bodies on fire. "Yes, baby. I feel it…"

TWENTY-SIX

Huntley

IT WAS UNLIKE ANYTHING I'D EVER FELT IN MY LIFE.

It surpassed the adrenaline I felt in battle. Surpassed the greatest lust I'd ever felt with my favorite whore. It surpassed the pain in my chest whenever I saw my brother for the first time after a long estrangement. It surpassed everything I'd ever felt.

The sex was already great. Never thought it could be greater.

And I never thought the best sex of my life would be with my wife.

Wife.

Fuck, I was married.

Eternally bound to a woman in life and in death.

I looked at her beside me, her hair a mess, her lips swollen from our hungry kisses. She was all over me like usual. My arm was circled around her waist, and I cinched her closer to press a kiss to her brow.

She didn't stir.

It was the morning of her departure, the departure that I had prevented.

Now, I had to face the queen. Face her wrath. Face her disappointment.

And worse, her heartbreak.

I'd never really considered the consequences until I was forced to confront them. Keeping Ivory alive had been my priority, to the exclusion of all else. If only my mother were rational enough to listen, this could have been avoided, but I suspected she wouldn't think of it that way.

The high from last night disappeared once I realized what I had to do. And do now.

I left the bed, and she still didn't stir. Her hand automatically reached out for me like I was still there beside her.

I got dressed and left for the castle—ready for my fate. My heart had never felt so heavy, and my body had never carried so much dread. With every step, I came closer, and even though I moved at a slow pace, everything was happening so fast. Before I knew it, I was face-to-face with Asher.

"I will retrieve Her Highness." He disappeared, leaving me there to look out the windows to the valley in the distance. Last night was a series of flashbacks, of our sweaty bodies writhing together in the most intense passion either of us had ever felt. Was it that way for all married couples? Or was it just us?

I didn't hear her approach. She appeared before me, feathers in her hair, in a long-sleeved dress with the white feather stitched into the fabric over her chest. She had the same presence that my father had possessed—full of regal poise. "If you've come to change my mind, your endeavor will fail."

I knew exactly what to say, but I couldn't bring myself to say it.

Her shrewd gaze studied me, and the tightness of her eyes and mouth faded. "What is it, my son?"

"She is not going to Klaus. She is coming with me to Delacroix. That's final."

Asher's eyes narrowed to slits. "How dare you—"

"Get the fuck out, or I'll throw you through the goddamn window." I pivoted toward him, ready to make good on my threat because he'd been the ultimate kiss-ass since I could remember.

Asher looked to my mother for instruction.

Her eyes remained on me. "Excuse us, Asher."

It was the first time he'd hesitated before obeying a command.

I turned back to her. "She will get us what we need. We will secure the dragons and take back Delacroix and the Kingdoms."

"She can't be trusted. The second you turn away, there will be a knife in your back."

"She would never hurt me." Unless she was insanely jealous of another woman.

"You're a fool—"

"Because she's my wife."

The reaction was subtle, but it was deep. Like drops that spread into a puddle, her reaction grew bigger and bigger, turning her face pale, her eyes dark.

It was painful to watch.

Her jaw tightened, and she was rendered speechless.

"We married last night. It was the only way I could protect her from the Teeth. And it was the only way I could protect myself when I escort her to Delacroix. We're family now—and she will not betray me. She has pledged her loyalty to me. We will take back the Kingdoms, and she will help us accomplish that."

Her jaw was still tight, her eyes still empty.

I expected her to scream. Slap me so hard I hit the floor. But there was nothing.

I'd prefer her hatred to her silence any day. This was unbearable. "Mother—"

"Get. Out." Her voice was so calm it was eerie.

"This is the only way—"

"I said, get out." She turned her back on me and walked away.

I stood there, feeling shittier than I ever had.

Her bedroom door slammed a moment later.

I stayed there because I couldn't move, couldn't do anything else but think about the pain I had just caused.

She was a woman who never cried—but I heard her sob.

Sob her heart out.

———

WHEN I RETURNED, Ivory was awake, sitting by the fire with a bowl of oatmeal in her hands. The pot was still over the fire, so she must have just made it. In my sweater and socks, she'd invaded my home and made it hers.

She took one look at me and stopped chewing.

I fell into the other armchair, my eyes on the fire, unable to get that sound out of my head.

My mother weeping.

She set the bowl on the stool beside her. "Huntley?"

"I don't want to discuss it." I could feel her stare on the side of my face, feel it burn into my cheek.

She scooted to the edge of her chair, her hands in her lap. "I'm sorry."

I watched the flames, my broken heart so full just hours ago.

"I'm always here…even if it's just to listen."

My head turned to look at her, to see the same concern in her eyes that she displayed with the dragons, like my heartbreak was hers to share. "I knew she'd be angry. I can handle that. I knew she'd be disappointed. I can handle that, too…because it's the first time I've ever been anything less than the son she wanted. But her heartbreak… I can't handle that." I closed my eyes. "I feel…so fucking shitty right now."

Her injured hand went to mine, squeezing it just the way I'd squeezed hers last night. "She'll forgive you."

"I'm not so sure about that…"

"I've seen the way she loves you, Huntley. She will."

My eyes dropped to our joined hands, and somehow, her touch did give me comfort. This connection between us…it had the power to heal all kinds of wounds.

"Give her time."

"She's had over twenty years to let the past go…and you've seen how that's gone."

"Not the same thing."

"In her eyes, it might be. I married the daughter of the man who raped her, slaughtered her husband, and took her home."

Her thumb brushed over the top of my hand, soft to the touch. "Give her some time. Then tell her that I'm your ally, not your enemy."

"I did, but I'm not sure if she really heard me."

"She'll understand when you tell her again."

I turned my gaze back to the fire.

"I know how disappointed my father would be if he knew…"

I turned my head back to her.

"When he knows everything that I've done…he'll never look at me the same. Ryker won't either. Everything that's happened has made me question my relationship with my father, made me reevaluate my memories, and I can't think of a single time when he looked at me the way your mother looks at you."

My broken heart broke into even more pieces. The feeling was senseless, because I already knew that and never cared. But now, I cared as if it had happened to me directly.

"That's how I know everything will be okay…in time."

—————

"SO…WHAT'S OUR PLAN?" The morning light came through the windows. She was beside me, her eyes still in slits because she hadn't fully woken up yet, not without her morning coffee and oatmeal.

"We'll leave in a few days. Need some time to recuperate."

"That's fine with me." She pressed a kiss to my shoulder. "I love your bed."

"*Our* bed."

"Yeah…our bed."

We lay there together, enjoying the sunshine shining into the room and making it warm enough that we didn't need a fire. There must have been a bird on the tree outside on the patio because I could hear it singing. We stayed that way for a long time, neither one of us saying anything, until a knock sounded on the door.

"Who is that?"

"Probably Elora." I got out of bed and dressed myself. "I haven't seen her since I returned. She's probably pissed. She's always pissed."

She chuckled as she got out of bed. "Are you going to tell her?"

"Yes." I pulled on my boots then took the stairs to the

front door. I opened it, coming face-to-face with Commander Dawson, dressed in his uniform and cloak. My eyes darted past him, seeing my mother standing there, her eyes absolutely hollow. "If Queen Rolfe requires my presence, all she needs to do is ask and I'll come. No need to send—"

He slammed his fist into my face.

I fell back onto the floor, because I wasn't expecting my mother's commander to come to my home and punch me in the fucking face. The world blurred for a second then I started to get to my feet.

My mother stood over me and slammed her boot down onto my chest. "Another should do it, Commander Dawson."

My eyes locked on to hers in disbelief.

The rage was unlike anything I'd ever seen. Vindictive. Volatile. Heartless.

If it were anyone else, I'd kick their feet out from under them or get back on my feet and destroy them.

But I was paralyzed by it all.

Commander Dawson kicked me in the head—and I was out.

———

WHEN MY EYES OPENED, it was dark.

Pitch black.

The thudding in my head wasn't nearly as bad as I'd thought it would be, which told me it'd been hours since the trauma occurred. A quick look around told me I was exactly where I'd last been—on the floor of my living room. "Ivory?" My voice came out weak, so I rolled over and pushed myself to my feet. "Ivory?"

Silence.

Once the situation became clear, the adrenaline kicked in.

I sprinted up the steps and stepped into our dark bedroom. Empty bed. No fire. Nothing. Even though I knew she wasn't there, I said her name anyway, out of some desperate hope that she'd hidden away somewhere. "Ivory!"

Nothing.

I opened the closet door and pulled out my weapons, my ax, my short blades, my dagger, and donned my armor because I was going to fucking war.

I ran through the dark to the castle, the torches illuminating the streets along the way. It came into view, light from the torches in the entryway. I sprinted, ignoring the guards that stood on either side.

The door was locked.

"Open this." I looked back and forth between them. "Now!"

They exchanged a look. "Queen Rolfe said you're banned from the castle until morning."

I pulled out my short blade and held it to the throat of the guard on the left. "I don't want to kill you, but I absolutely will. Open this fucking door or die."

He didn't put up a fight at all. His hand reached into his pocket and withdrew the key.

I got it unlocked and pushed inside. I sprinted through the castle and ignored the guards who tried to stop me. I might be forbidden from being on the grounds, but I was still the son of the queen, and none of them wanted to touch me.

I made it up the stairs into my mother's war room.

Commander Dawson was there, as if he'd known I would come. "Huntley—"

"Bring her to me now, or we'll fight to the death—and you'll lose."

He remained still.

I withdrew my ax and gripped it with both hands. "Don't fuck with me right now. I swear to the fucking gods…"

He held up both hands slightly before he moved down the hallway.

I had to wait there for minutes—long, agonizing minutes—until she emerged.

She was in her sleeping attire, a nightgown with a robe on top. Her face was just as hard as it'd been before, carved out of marble because she was a goddamn statue. It was the look she wore when faced with enemies, faced with the possibility of war, with justice served to those who broke the law. She put aside her personal feelings—and felt nothing.

"Where is she?"

Silence.

"*Where the fuck is she?*" I'd never been this deranged in my life. This maniacal. This fucking insane.

She didn't flinch. "I gave her to Klaus—like we planned."

My hands loosened on my ax, and I nearly dropped it. "You…did…what?"

"I have saved HeartHolme from a bloody war—"

"You fulfilled your own need for revenge because you're incapable of feeling anything else."

She remained stone-cold. "It's done, Huntley. Forget about her."

"Forget about her? She's my fucking wife."

Now her eyes narrowed. "She won't be your wife anymore when she's dead."

My hands shook. My entire body trembled. My hands wanted to grip the ax and start chopping, and my mind barely resisted the urge. I'd never felt this way in my life, so angry that I would ever hurt my own mother. But fuck, that was what I wanted.

"You think I give a damn that you married her? Changes nothing."

"She's family."

She sucked in a breath, and it sounded like a hiss. "She'll never be anything more than what she is—a fucking whore."

"She said she would help us—"

"And you're a fool for believing that. She's just like her father. Violent. Malicious. Dishonored—"

"She is *nothing* like her father." I'd had enough of this, so I turned around and stormed off.

"Where are you going?" she called after me.

I turned back, all the muscles in my face twitching because I was out of my mind with rage. "To get my wife back."

Her sculptured faced slackened, and her eyes widened in terror. "You will not—"

"I will kill every man who gets in my way. So, if you don't want your men to die tonight, I suggest you tell them to stand down, because nothing is going to stop me from riding through the night and getting to her before it's too late." I continued to the stairs.

She ran after me, her bare feet growing louder as she came close. "Huntley!"

I didn't stop.

She grabbed me by the arm and yanked me back. "They'll kill you—"

I pushed her off. "Then I'll die."

Her eyes shifted back and forth as she looked into mine, terrified.

"She's my wife—and I'll die for her."

Also by Penelope Barsetti

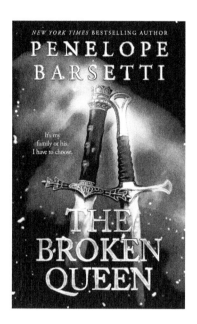

Queen Rolfe betrayed me.

My own mother.

The Teeth have my wife, and I can't allow myself to think about what they're doing to her. I need to raise an army to get her back, and if I can't, I'll march in there and do it myself.

Order Now

About Penelope

Penelope Barsetti is a New York Times, USA Today, and Wall Street Journal bestselling author. Her beloved novels have sold more than 5 Million copies, and her work has been translated into a dozen languages. Readers may know her by another name, Penelope Sky, where she writes contemporary dark romance.

An avid wine drinker, napper, and Netflix junkie, she lives in California with her family, but if she could live anywhere, it would be Florence, Italy. For those familiar with her work, you'll know exactly why that's the case.

Fantasy Romance is her favorite genre to read, and she's excited to release her own novels into the world.

———

Thanks so much for reading The Forsaken King! If you love my books and want to know about releases, give-aways, signed paperbacks, all kinds of good stuff, connect with me!

Sign up for my newsletter:
http://eepurl.com/hmfFgP

And be sure to visit www.penelopebarsetti.com

Text BARSETTI to 74121 to hear about new releases!

Special requests and fan mail can be sent to penelopebarsetti@gmail.com

facebook.com/Penelope-Barsetti-112214254634928
instagram.com/penelopebarsetti

Printed in Great Britain
by Amazon